BLESSED BE THE WICKED

BLESSED BE THE WICKED

An Abish Taylor Mystery

D. A. Bartley

CROOKED LANE

NEW YORK

This is a work of fiction. All of the names, characters, organizations, places and events portrayed in this novel are either products of the author's imagination or are used fictitiously. Any resemblance to real or actual events, locales, or persons, living or dead, is entirely coincidental.

Published in the United States by Crooked Lane Books, an imprint of The Quick Brown Fox & Company LLC.

Crooked Lane Books and its logo are trademarks of The Quick Brown Fox & Company LLC.

Library of Congress Catalog-in-Publication data available upon request.

ISBN (hardcover): 978-1-68331-720-3
ISBN (ePub): 978-1-68331-721-0
ISBN (ePDF): 978-1-68331-722-7

Cover design by Melanie Sun.
Book design by Jennifer Canzone.

Printed in the United States.

www.crookedlanebooks.com

Crooked Lane Books
34 West 27th St., 10th Floor
New York, NY 10001

First Edition: August 2018

10 9 8 7 6 5 4 3 2 1

In loving memory of Mom and Grandma,
who both enjoyed a good mystery.

All mankind love themselves, and let these principles be known by an individual, and he would be glad to have his blood shed. That would be loving themselves, even unto an eternal exaltation. Will you love your brothers or sisters likewise, when they have committed a sin that cannot be atoned for without the shedding of their blood? Will you love that man or woman well enough to shed their blood? That is what Jesus Christ meant.

—*A Discourse by President Brigham Young, Delivered in the Tabernacle, Great Salt Lake City, February 8, 1857*

ONE

The dead man in the closet was dressed almost entirely in white: shirt, trousers, shoes and socks, even the sash draped over one shoulder and the stiff, puffy cap on his head. The only exception was a dark-green apron embroidered with fig leaves around his waist. He was sitting upright in a heavy chair; his feet and knees had been bound with a thick white satin ribbon. An identical ribbon was wrapped tightly around the trunk of his body, fixing it in place. Both tied into meticulous bows.

The clothes were sacred, not meant to be worn outside the walls of the temple. This fact was making the Mormon police officers on the scene uncomfortable. Detective Abish Taylor, though, wasn't at all uncomfortable. The clothes intrigued her, almost as much as the apparent manner of death: there was a thick straight gash running from ear to ear under the dead man's chin. Blood had drained from that single wound onto his shirt and the ceremonial apron, finally pooling in a dark puddle on the floor.

Abbie knew this crime scene was tough on everyone. The younger officers were skittish because of how the body was dressed. They'd all been taught those all-white ensembles were an outward expression of secret covenants made with the Lord. Seeing this bloody body—dressed for the temple—in the basement of a McMansion was jarring. Abbie suspected this may have been the first time some of the young officers had ever thought about what it looked like to be dressed in those white clothes with a green apron wrapped around their waist. When you did it at the temple, you sort of were on autopilot. Everyone around you was dressed the same, you spoke in the same hushed tones, and you certainly didn't question anything you did. Abbie was sure most of the officers were struggling to suppress questions as they processed the scene. Hell, that's what they'd been taught to do since Sunday school—suppress questions—but she saw in the strained expressions on a few officers' faces that they were dealing with an internal barrage of doubts about a practice they had, until now, done without thinking. Of course, none of them would admit that, certainly not to her.

The older officers, though, Abbie felt for. These were men who had been going to the temple for decades, long enough that they had drawn their own thumbs across their neck dozens, maybe hundreds, of times in the macabre reenactments that had been removed from the temple ceremony a few decades ago. Abbie was sure Church leaders had hoped that changing the temple ritual would change history, would erase the Church's own sanctioning of deadly violence. The problem was, Abbie thought, you couldn't change history. You could talk about it; you could process it; you could expand your view about it; but you couldn't change it. Blood atonement was part of the history of the Church of Jesus Christ of Latter-day Saints. It always had been and always would be.

The LDS Church had disavowed it in the late 1970s and removed the penalty oaths from the temple ceremony in 1990, but anyone old enough to have been to the temple before then wouldn't be able to forget it. That's why the younger officers were merely uneasy while the older officers felt a sense of dread. Early Mormon leaders had taught that certain sins were so egregious that not even the blood of Christ was sufficient to wash away the stain of sin. Such sins required the sinner's throat to be slit from ear to ear and his blood to spill to the earth. Abbie had never been able to understand how this ritual was Christlike. No Sunday school teacher had ever been able to explain to her how the same divine source who taught complete forgiveness in the story of the prodigal son would centuries later make exceptions to his grace. The Heavenly Father Abbie had come to know as a child had high expectations of his children.

"I've got the knife." Officer Jim Clarke held up a standard bowie knife. It had been on the floor beneath the dead man's right hand. This was Clarke's first murder case, and the first time he and Abbie were working together. What Abbie knew about him was fairly innocuous: he was a local, a former high school basketball player, and a returned missionary. He was hardworking, meticulous, and, unlike Abbie, technologically savvy. Abbie wasn't sure why Chief Russell Henderson had chosen Clarke to be her number two, but she guessed it was because Clarke was the only guy at the Pleasant View City Police Department who didn't seem to have any trouble dealing with a woman as his superior officer. The rest of the small police force behaved exactly as she had expected them to when she'd taken the job a few months ago: white male with a strong undercurrent of chauvinism.

"Have you gone through those clothes yet?" Abbie asked.

"Nope," Clarke answered.

Abbie kneeled on the floor and looked through the neatly folded clothing behind the body. On the top of the stack was a cream Brioni shirt, a pair of camel Ralph Lauren Black Label trousers, a navy Armani sport jacket (size 48), and a pair of dark-blue socks with their tops carefully folded inside out. There was also a pair of barely worn, dark-brown Gucci loafers.

"No wallet or ID?" Abbie looked inside the back of the white shirt collar. Some Mormons embroidered their names in white thread on their temple clothes, but here there weren't any initials or insignia. The man wasn't wearing any jewelry, but the thick stripe of white skin on his left-hand ring finger indicated he'd probably worn a wedding band. In this part of the world, it would have been strange for a man of his age not to be married.

Clarke said, "No ID, but he looks—"

"There's no ID on the body," Chief Henderson cut in before Clarke could finish what he was saying. The interruption piqued Abbie's interest, but everyone in the basement was on edge. Being polite was hardly a priority. This death was not the sort of thing anyone in Pleasant View had ever encountered. Abbie had probably seen more dead bodies in New York in a single year than everyone else here had in their entire lives. Combined.

So far, Abbie's view of the chief was mildly favorable. He seemed to be honest. Undoubtedly, he would have preferred to have a man in her job, a man who was an active member of the Church, but he'd been decent to her since she'd started. Henderson lived by the rules. Those rules were usually pretty clear. He didn't miss a day of work. He went to church every Sunday. But Abbie had a queasy feeling in her stomach that something about this case was going to challenge her boss. The religious overtones of this death were going to test which rules mattered more to him: church or state.

"Okay, then, it's Mr. Doe." Abbie shrugged.

She took one last glance at the body sitting eerily upright in the large walk-in closet. The entire Pleasant View police force—four full-time officers, three part-time, and Chief Henderson—were all in the basement of this enormous house. The house was in one of the many wealthy new neighborhoods that crawled up the foothills of the Wasatch Mountains from Ogden to Provo. Where the mountains had just been mountains thirty years ago, now there were houses as far as the eye could see. The ones in this neighborhood, Ben Lomond Circle, ranged in size from huge to gigantic. This particular house was definitely in the latter category. Abbie wondered what the officers thought of the obvious display of wealth. This might have been the first time most of the guys had ever been inside a place this big.

"Detective Taylor," Clarke said, "the couple who found the body are upstairs in the kitchen. Do you want to speak to them?" Jim Clarke had never called Abbie by her first name. She wondered if he ever would. She reciprocated and called him by his last name, too.

"Yeah." Abbie had seen the husband and wife on her way to the basement. They had moved into the house that morning. The wife had been checking out the basement with her kids when she discovered the body. Abbie didn't expect to get any helpful information from them. She doubted they had anything to do with the dead man, but the possibility couldn't be ruled out.

Clarke followed Abbie up the plushly carpeted stairs leading to the main floor. "I heard they only paid six hundred thousand for it," Clarke whispered. That was definitely a post-real-estate-bubble price, Abbie thought. A few years earlier, this house would certainly have gone for well over a million.

Abbie walked into the kitchen. It looked like something out of a *Real Housewives* show. Everything was designed to impress. "Understatement" was not a word in the builder's vocabulary. Like the cameras people invited to follow them around in return for a check and notoriety, the purpose of this house was to hit you over the head with an obvious display of wealth that would appeal to those who couldn't distinguish between tasteful and expensive. Everything was over-the-top: there were the double-thick granite counter tops in the kitchen, twelve-foot ceilings, two sweeping staircases with custom ironwork in the marble entry hall, crown molding, and gleaming brass (yes, brass) fixtures.

The husband and wife sat in their brand-new, shiny kitchen. They both looked shaken and pale. Boxes were stacked everywhere, full of top-of-the line kitchen appliances, no doubt. On the counter between two boxes sat an orchid, still in its stiff plastic wrap with ribbons and a card attached that read "Welcome to Your New Home!" Abbie looked at the card and thought of the body in the basement. *What a housewarming gift.*

TWO

Having spent the entire day sifting through the very little evidence in the McMansion's basement, Abbie finally made it home and showered the day's crime scene off her body. She pulled her thick auburn hair into a messy bun and slipped on dark-gray sweatpants and a ribbed white tank top. In New York, her body was ideal for Herve Leger and Roland Mouret. There wasn't much use for body-con cocktail dresses in Pleasant View.

Abbie had once taken credit for her lean physique. She watched what she ate and was disciplined in her almost daily runs, but now that she was in her early thirties, she'd grown out of her youthful arrogance. Whatever she looked like was mostly the result of luck in the family gene department. Her mother had been stunning: beautiful skin, ideal bone structure, and a metabolism that required little effort to maintain a slender figure. Abbie now understood why her sisters teased her for being boyish. They both took after her dad's side of the family with ample thighs, short thick waists, and large breasts that didn't bounce back after childbirth and nursing.

Abbie walked into her kitchen. The inside of her cabin had been entirely renovated so that it felt more like an airy apartment in Stockholm than an old summer house on the side of a canyon in northern Utah. She opened the cabinet and took out a bottle of Montepulciano. She poured herself a generous tumbler. She needed it.

Today had been painfully slow because, with the exception of Chief Henderson, none of the officers had ever worked a suspicious death scene before and none of them wanted to ask Abbie how to do anything. Even though Abbie was technically running the investigation, Henderson had kept everyone on a tight leash. Even Clarke, who was supposed to be her partner, answered to Henderson first.

Abbie held her tumbler between both hands the way kids held hot chocolate when they came in from the cold. The act of cradling the wine was comforting. She was beginning to feel the cloud of depression threatening to settle in around her. She had been fighting it ever since Phillip's death. Sometimes she managed to go for weeks without its shadow, but it was always lurking.

She looked around her Scandinavian kitchen. It suited her. She had fallen in love with the place the moment she saw it. She loved how isolated and quiet it was. But right at that moment, she wondered if that isolation was such a good thing. She didn't have any close friends nearby. The job she'd thought would be an easy way to pass the time between hiking in the summer and skiing in the winter had just turned into something real.

What the hell had she been she thinking? Maybe her friends had been right. She was still grieving. She never should have made the rash decision to move back. She could have just stayed in New York, taken time off work, waited until she felt better. Phillip had left her plenty of money; she could've stopped working altogether. She could have moved anywhere if she really needed to leave New York. Utah had been her own crazy idea. At the time it had all made sense: she'd buy this quiet cabin in the mountains, find a job that kept her occupied—but wasn't too demanding—and then she would rebuild her relationship with her father, maybe even her brothers and sisters. That had seemed so important just a few months ago: to be part of a family. Damn it! Now she had a case that was certainly going to be demanding, and it was exactly the kind of case to destroy whatever chances she had of finding some kind of common ground between her—the black sheep of the family who'd left the Church—and her two sisters and three brothers who were all living as they'd been brought up to. Well, almost. Her oldest brother, John, had been open about his own doubts. He and Abbie had always shared a special bond. Now that she was back, he was the only person she really trusted. He was trying to smooth things over with the others, but so far he hadn't made much progress. Talking about acceptance and love was one thing; actually practicing it was another.

If this case became public, it would make everything harder. There was nothing like LDS history to stir the pot for the Taylors. Her father had spent his entire professional life being an LDS apologist. One could be forgiven for considering the term *apologist* an insult, but it wasn't for Mormons. It was used in the classic neutral sense to describe a person who spoke or wrote in defense of someone or something. That was Abbie's dad: one who spoke and wrote in defense of the Church of Jesus Christ of Latter-day Saints.

She took another long swallow of wine. She didn't want to make this call, but she knew it was the smartest thing she could do. If anyone in the world was an expert on blood atonement, it was her father, the respected Head of Church History and Doctrine at Brigham Young University. Most Mormons called BYU by its nickname, "the Y." Abbie tried not to call it that anymore because it was an insider term. Calling it the Y implied she was part of a community she had left, but every now and then LDS jargon would slip out of her mouth like a hiccup. She couldn't completely control it.

Abbie's father had a way of making everyone around him feel diminished. Abbie always felt worse about herself after they talked. He didn't say anything outright—anything she could point to—but somehow she ended up feeling like she wasn't smart enough, hardworking enough, virtuous enough, just plain good enough for her father. That was probably one of the reasons she'd been so eager to go out of state for college. All of her siblings had dutifully gone to the Y, even though her oldest brother had had the grades and scores to do better. BYU was more than just a university, though; it was a place where you met your spouse and transitioned from being an LDS child to an active LDS adult. For the Taylor children, BYU was also a place where they circled in the orbit of their illustrious father.

Professor Taylor was exacting. When Abbie was little, her mom had kept the house so spotless no one would have guessed six kids lived there. Even the refrigerator was devoid of kindergarten art projects or English tests marked with smiley faces that would be plastered on fridges in normal houses. The standards for Taylor family recognition required far more than a perfect score on a math test. And even then, such recognition would never show up on the refrigerator.

Her mom, in stark contrast to her father, had been fun and funny. Everyone who knew her loved her. She baked gooey brownies for breakfast when their father was away at academic conferences. ("So long as you drink your milk, it's the same as having pancakes.") In the summer, she'd run through the sprinkler with the kids and get just as soaked. In the winter, she could be counted on for a good snowball fight. And she laughed. Abbie's mom had the best laugh. It was a hearty chuckle from her belly. It was entirely unself-conscious and completely contagious. You couldn't hear Abbie's mom laugh and not smile. And her mom laughed a lot. There was very little that she thought was too serious or frustrating not to greet with laughter. When something went wrong, like the first time her brother tried to make borscht and the blender spewed hot, deep red beet juice everywhere, the first thing everyone in the house heard was her mom laughing.

But by six o'clock in the evening, everything in the Taylor household was orderly again. No smudges of leftover brownies, no remnants of borscht. Family dinners were in the dining room, with cloth napkins and classical music playing softly in the background. Professor Taylor controlled the conversation like a conductor. With the wave of his invisible baton, each child was called on to present informed and well-reasoned opinions. There had been no room for emotional conversations or silliness with Professor Taylor. There still wasn't.

Abbie took a long drink from her glass, then another. Then she dialed.

"Hello, Abish." No one but her father called her by her given name.

"Hi, Dad. I'm glad I caught you. I was hoping you could help me out with some historical research."

"Of course. I understand you're heading up an investigation into a death that is, well, curious in its appearance."

"Pleasant View news has made it down to Provo already?" Abbie asked.

"This is not the sort of thing anyone wants to become common knowledge. Surely you can understand that," her father said. "I'd like you to be careful with this investigation. Don't rush to judgment. It would not be advantageous for the details of the death to make it into any of the papers, particularly *The Salt Lake Tribune*." *The Trib*, as most people in Salt Lake called it, still maintained its reputation as a non-Church-run newspaper, even though its parent company was now the same as the *Deseret News*, which was proudly run by the LDS Church.

Abbie wasn't really surprised her father had already heard about the case. He was extraordinarily well connected. This death had all the hallmarks of the macabre ritual some argued Brigham Young and other leaders had supported during the early days of the Church. It was exactly the sort of thing an active member of the Church would think should be reported to the appropriate leader.

"What do you know about the case?" Abbie asked.

"I don't think we should discuss that. Suffice it to say I'm familiar with the religious significance of the details surrounding the death."

"Who told you about it? We haven't released any details," Abbie said.

"I'm not at liberty to discuss that," Abbie's father said. His tone indicated she was being impertinent by asking.

"Not at liberty to discuss that? Really?" Abbie could hear her voice getting loud. She was angry, and she knew her father would stoically tell her to calm down and then hang up the phone, feeling smugly superior because he kept his own temper on such a tight leash. She took another sip of her wine and a deep breath.

"Okay, then, can I ask you your opinion about the legacy of the blood oaths? I know it's been decades since they've been part of the temple ceremony, but there are a lot of people alive today who drew their thumbs across their necks or stomachs—"

"Let me interrupt you. I don't need to remind you what President Hinckley said before the changes were made, do I? He reminded us of our absolute obligation not to discuss that which occurs within the temple walls. All sacred matters deserve sacred consideration."

"I'm not asking about the temple ceremony itself. I'm interested in how members responded to the change. I'm not asking you to divulge anything sacred. I just want to know if there are active members in the Church who might miss the more orthodox ceremony."

Abbie knew her father was one of a few chosen men

who had been consulted when the presidency of the Church first began discussing the possibility of changing the temple ceremony. He had been included in meetings between Church leaders and several PR firms concerning the Church's "perception problem" among non-Mormons as well as new converts. The temple ceremony was particularly offensive to people who had not grown up in the Church and were not inured to its idiosyncrasies.

"Abish, you know I support the Prophet. When our leaders speak, the thinking has been done. When they propose a plan—it's God's plan. When they point the way, there is no other which is safe. When they give direction, it should mark the end of controversy."

Really? Abbie thought. Was her dad going to quote worn-out Church propaganda to her? She remembered this particular dictum about "all thinking being done" from Sunday school. She wasn't sure how long priesthood leaders had been trotting out this maxim to shut down dissent, but it didn't sound any less grating to her adult ears than it had to her ears as a child.

"I'm not asking you for an independent opinion on the changes to the temple ceremony," Abbie reiterated. She knew she was beginning to sound frustrated because, well, she was frustrated. Was her father capable of giving her a straight answer when it came to questions about Church doctrine? "I'm just asking if you think there might be people out there who believe the changes were wrong. You know this topic. If there's anyone who's an expert in this area, it's you. I'm just asking for your private academic opinion. No one from the SCMC will ever know."

There was silence on the other end of the line. Abbie knew she'd gone one step too far. The Strengthening Church Members Committee, the SCMC, was something Abbie and her father both abhorred—perhaps for different reasons, but abhorred nonetheless. The committee had been set up at some point in the mid-1980s to monitor speeches and writings—and later blogs and podcasts—of members of the Church, particularly anyone suspected of apostasy. Mormons could forward complaints about fellow members of the Church to the committee. The committee would then pass information on to relevant Church officials, who could begin disciplinary proceedings if they felt it was warranted. However much her father supported the Church, he harbored no illusions about the SCMC, an organization that one might argue resembled the old East German Stasi a little too closely for comfort.

Finally, Abbie's father spoke, slowly and deliberately. "Many members were unhappy about what they saw as watering down the gospel. They saw no need to make the temple ceremony more appealing to recent converts, or to a younger generation. I count myself among that more traditional group."

"Do you think it's more likely that, if there were somebody or a group of people who believed in blood atonement today, that person or persons went through the temple before the 1990 changes?" Abbie asked.

"Yes, I imagine that people old enough to remember the older temple ceremony constitute the most likely demographic of those who see the value of blood atonement. Barring the possibility of someone who has a keen interest in Church history. As far as I've been informed about the body you found, even the robe was draped across the proper shoulder. There is, of course, also the likely alternative that the act was self-inflicted. If you understand the need for blood atonement, you may also understand that in today's world it would be a lot to ask of someone else. It might be easier to do it yourself."

Abbie thought it was interesting her dad would bring up suicide, but said nothing about it. She wondered if he'd come up with the idea himself or had been instructed to pass on the theory to his daughter.

"When you were in graduate school, did you ever come across evidence that blood atonement was actually carried out? I know there are anti-Mormon stories about non-Mormons or apostates being found in ditches with their throats slit, but do you know of any reliable source that indicated blood atonement was really practiced?" Abbie's father had done his dissertation on the Church's Reformation period, a time in the 1850s when Brigham Young and other Church leaders had spoken frequently of the ritual.

Blood atonement was a touchy subject. After polygamy and anything to do with the temple, unvarnished LDS history was the least favorite topic of conversation for most active Mormons. Even her father, who had spent a good portion of his early academic career writing about the Reformation period, didn't like talking about the early days of the Church beyond the officially sanctioned version taught in Sunday school. But if primary source material on the subject of blood atonement was available, Professor Taylor had read it.

"Abish, I studied that a long time ago. I'm an old man and my memory isn't what it once was. Without going back and looking through my notes, the only thing I can tell you is that there were a number of leaders who spoke of sins that demanded blood atonement. Murder, of course, but there were rumors of anything from stealing cattle to breaking the Law of Chastity. I can't imagine it has any relevance today. I would suggest you not pursue this line of investigation any further."

"What the . . . ?" Abbie stopped herself before she said something she might regret, although at the moment she couldn't imagine regretting putting her father in his place. Abbie couldn't believe her dad was trying to tell her how to do her job. Did he think that now that she was in Utah, he had some sort of authority over her?

"Abish, that's enough. Good night."

Abbie stared at the phone in her hand. Had her father just hung up on her? She finished her wine and poured another glass. If her dad knew about the body, someone Abbie worked with had leaked very specific details of the crime scene. Even the wine couldn't numb the unsettling feeling spreading through her chest.

Abbie looked at her glass. She'd had too much wine on an empty stomach. She needed to eat something. She opened the fridge and stared inside. There was a single chicken breast along with some steamed green beans from a dinner she'd made two nights ago. If she toasted a few slices of almost-stale ciabatta, that would do for dinner. She picked at the leftover food and drank more wine. She couldn't stop thinking about blood atonement. She opened her laptop and Googled the term. The first page had links to either official LDS websites or avowedly anti-Mormon ones. Neither was helpful. She needed a reliable source. The conversation with her dad had been far from enlightening. Then she remembered the boxes. How could she have forgotten?

Abbie pulled down the stairs to her attic. There wasn't much room up there, but it was big enough to store Christmas decorations, high school yearbooks, and a few boxes filled with her father's old doctoral research. He had wanted her to follow in his footsteps when she was in college. For a while she'd thought she wanted to, too. She had even gone so far as to apply to graduate school in history—and she'd gotten into Yale just like her dad—before she dropped out in the first month. She'd been schlepping these boxes of her dad's books and notes with her ever since. Returning them would force a discussion about why she'd dropped out and throwing them away seemed disrespectful.

Her dad had sent them to her at the end of her junior year. They were precious. The books and copies were from a time before scanning and home printers. Abbie had decided to write her senior thesis on polygamy. Her dad's dissertation research covered much of the period Abbie was looking into. She'd started out believing what she'd been taught in Sunday school, but the more she researched, the less the stories she'd been told at church matched up with the primary source material. Still, she'd wanted to believe. She spent her senior year fasting and praying. She read the scriptures. She even spoke to her Bishop, who told her that she might want to find a research topic that was uplifting and in line with the teachings of the Church. Abbie wrestled with that piece of advice: if the Church was true, then how could it hurt to research its history?

Looking at the boxes now, she realized her father must have thought that supporting Abbie's academic interest would strengthen her testimony of the gospel. In the end, studying the history of the Church had led father and daughter to very different places.

Abbie carried the boxes down to the living room. They were heavy. The first box was full of Mormon hymnbooks and a few books in the phonetic English alphabet Brigham Young had created for the Saints living in the original State of Deseret. The alphabet had never really taken off, but Abbie still thought it was kind of cool that there had been an effort to help non-English-speaking converts integrate once they made it to Zion by adopting an almost entirely phonetic writing system.

The second box looked more promising. These were her father's actual notes. Abbie set a thick binder titled "Reformation" onto the coffee table. It was dusty and faded. Over the years, the light-blue front cover had become detached from the rest of the binder. She carefully turned to the first yellowed page, where her father had neatly printed "Table of Contents." The fifth tab was "Blood Atonement—History."

Abbie turned to the section, being careful not to damage the brittle paper. Her father's handwritten notes—dense sentences of small, tightly spaced words—were in the margins everywhere. Abbie's eyes darted up and down each page, searching for something that would help her understand what she'd seen in the McMansion's basement closet.

Finally, she found what she was looking for on a page

with the purplish type of a ditto machine. These notes were from another era. Despite how annoyed she was with the man at the moment, she couldn't help but smile at the thought of her father as a young graduate student making copies on some ancient duplicator. She was grateful he had. This was a copy of a page from *A Discourse by President Brigham Young, Delivered in the Tabernacle, Great Salt Lake City, February 8, 1857.*

> Now take a person in this congregation who has knowledge with regard to being saved in the kingdom of our God and our Father, and being exalted, one who knows and understands the principles of eternal life, and sees the beauty and excellency of the eternities before him compared with the vain and foolish things of the world, and suppose that he is overtaken in a gross fault, that he has committed a sin that he knows will deprive him of that exaltation which he desires, and that he cannot attain to it without the shedding of his blood, and also knows that by having his blood shed he will atone for that sin, and be saved and exalted with the Gods, is there a man or woman in this house but what would say, "Shed my blood that I may be saved and exalted with the Gods"?

Abbie's stared at the faded words. Beneath the quote, her father had written in his characteristically neat cursive:

> *Jedidiah Grant, JOD IV, 1856— I say that there are men and women that I would advise to go to the President*

immediately, and ask him to appoint a committee to attend to their case; and then let a place be selected, and let that committee shed their blood.

Abbie vaguely recalled hearing the name before, but couldn't for the life of her place him. He wasn't in the LDS canon. Another Google search later and Abbie discovered that Jedidiah Grant had served in the First Presidency of Brigham Young. He was a chief proponent of the Mormon Reformation and famous for his unforgiving fire-and-brimstone sermons.

The more Abbie thought about it, the more convinced she became that the body hadn't been staged. It wasn't window dressing; it was purposeful. The temple clothes, the bowie knife (a favorite of the Danites, a fraternal organization founded by the Church, later known for its vigilante efforts in the 1838 Mormon War), even the missing wedding band and wallet.

Elder Doe, as Abbie had taken to calling the unidentified man to herself because, well, he had to be a Mormon elder, had been given his final chance to be exalted with the Gods. Had he come willingly?

Abs, come on . . .

Abbie could see Phillip roll his eyes at the proposition that a man would voluntarily choose such a gruesome end, but Phillip had never understood the power of faith. He had been an atheist like both his parents before him. When he did the right thing, he did the right thing not out of fear of divine retribution or to gain favor in the afterlife. That was something Abbie loved about him. Phillip was a good and honest man because it was the right way to live, not because he wanted to be perfect or feared judgment.

Abbie had never been comfortable with the violent nature of the early Church. If she was being honest with herself, the ease with which everyone ignored this violence was one reason she had left. There had been so many instances of violence and so few honest explanations. Beyond the Danites, there was the Nauvoo Legion, the militia for the city of Nauvoo, Illinois, that had become a military force to be reckoned with until it had disbanded, not to mention the Mountain Meadows Massacre of a wagon train from Arkansas disguised to look like an attack by Southern Paiutes. From the very beginning, violence had been part of Church history.

Then there were the scriptures themselves. Killing glorified as an act of obedience to Heavenly Father. Before leaving Jerusalem for the New World, Nephi—one of the most virtuous characters in the Book of Mormon—was tasked with retrieving brass plates containing the history of his family and revelations of early prophets. After unsuccessful attempts to buy the plates from their wealthy owner, Laban, Nephi found the man in a state of drunken unconsciousness. Instead of simply stealing the plates, Nephi obeyed the command of the Holy Ghost to first kill Laban with the man's own sword, then take the plates. Why Nephi could not simply take the plates from drunken Laban, Abbie had never understood.

Just as she had never understood why Church members would reenact slitting their own throats in the temple. Symbolic or not, the ritual was disturbing. Abbie found it distinctly unsettling that LDS friends and neighbors had agreed, if only in theory, to willingly partake in such savagery in the name of protecting what was sacred.

Abbie's thoughts returned to the case. What had Elder Doe believed? What kind of man had he been? Had he thought he had committed a sin for which only this macabre ritual could make him worthy of exaltation? Or, had someone else thought he had?

THREE

"Henderson wants to see us." Clarke poked his head into Abbie's office. It was the morning after the biggest thing that had ever happened in the memory of anyone at the Pleasant View City Police Department. The moment she arrived at the station, Abbie felt a sense of purpose in the air.

Abbie had her own office, one of the perks of being the detective. It was clean and airy. She had furnished it herself with spare Danish furniture. There were neatly arranged books interspersed with a few well-tended plants on a bookshelf. Although Abbie had mixed feelings about displaying her professional awards and academic credentials, after some internal debate, she hung the framed degrees and awards that made her feel proud: her college diploma from Princeton, a Phi Beta Kappa certificate, and an FBI Medal for Meritorious Achievement. But what Abbie liked most about her office was her spectacular view of the Wasatch Mountains. She was lucky to have this space. The two offices on the other side of the building had views of the parking lot.

Abbie followed Clarke to Henderson's office.

"Please close the door." There was a sternness in the chief's tone Abbie hadn't heard before. Clarke did as instructed and sat down next to Abbie in front of the chief's desk.

"I'm pulling everyone off this Ben Lomond Circle case except the two of you." Henderson paused before he continued, "I don't think I need to explain that the way this man was dressed, well, it's not the sort of thing we want to get out."

"So, I'm not the only one who thought this death looked like blood atonement?" Abbie asked.

The moment the words left her mouth, she realized how incendiary they were. Abbie wished she could have swallowed them and said something a little less direct. Clarke looked at his shoes. Henderson blanched, but ignored the question. "The fewer people involved in this investigation, the better."

"Okay." Abbie thought there was a second reason Henderson wanted to limit the investigation. If anything went wrong with this case, she was going to take the blame. Henderson was letting her lead the case but not giving her backup.

"Have you heard anything from the Office of the Medical Examiner?" Abbie asked. "Do we have an ID yet?"

"Uh." Henderson looked down on the papers strewn across his very messy desk. "I don't think we've heard anything from the ME yet." He took a little too long to answer. Something was off, but Abbie wasn't sure what. It wasn't just the temple clothes and throat slitting. What was there about the body that was making both Henderson and Clarke nervous? Both were purposefully avoiding looking at her.

"That's it for now. Keep me up to date." Henderson's tone was sharp.

Abbie stood up. Clarke followed her. As soon as they had walked into the hallway, Henderson closed the door behind them. Abbie had never seen Henderson's door closed unless he was meeting with someone. She turned her head so that her ear was parallel to the shut door. She heard a muffled, "Hello? Yeah, I've got things under control, but . . ." Before she could hear the rest of Henderson's side of the conversation, a fellow officer walked by. She had to move away if she didn't want it to be obvious she was eavesdropping.

★ ★ ★

Abbie was well aware she didn't fit in Pleasant View for a lot of different reasons: she wasn't married, even though she still wore a plain gold band on her left ring finger; she didn't have any kids; and, probably more than anything else, she didn't go to church.

Clarke didn't seem to have quite the same disdain for a woman as the other guys did, but she wondered how he felt about the fact that she had left the Church. Clarke was an RM—a returned missionary. Everyone knew Abbie was a direct descendent of the prophet John Taylor, the third President of the Church who took over after Brigham Young. Most knew Abbie's dad, too, either from having taken his classes at the Y or from reading one of his books. It was pretty much impossible to miss Professor William Taylor's face on the back cover of some tome or other if you walked into Deseret Books. Abbie had walked into enough conversations that stopped abruptly to be fairly confident she was the topic of some discussion in her new job. It was hard for most Mormons to understand why someone would leave the Church, particularly if they came from a family as prominent as Abbie's. Clarke had never asked her about it, so Abbie had no idea what his feelings were on the subject.

Her status as an inactive Mormon notwithstanding, Abbie hadn't given anyone reason to complain about her. She made it into the station before anyone else in the morning, and she was usually the last to leave. She didn't grumble about paperwork. No one could say she didn't pull her weight. There had been a few times when she'd had to bite her tongue, but Abbie figured it was a small price to pay for a job that—until now—had given her plenty of time to enjoy the natural beauty of her home state. There was trail running, hiking, and mountain biking in the spring, summer, and fall; and then there was some of the best skiing on the planet in the winter. Her new colleagues found her choice of Pleasant View to be odd. Most LDS Utahns didn't consider leaving the state for anything other than college, graduate school, or a brief professional stint, because they liked living in a community where most people shared their values and lifestyle; the few who did leave usually did so because they didn't want that, and they rarely came back. Abbie's pat response was, "It's nice to have room to breathe and to do some good." If she made a negative comment about life in New York City, so much the better. The city on the East Coast was a symbol of liberal elitism.

Abbie didn't talk about her background, about why she'd moved away from New York. The rumor, as much as Abbie had overheard, was that her husband had died suddenly. Someone had found old pictures online from charity events in Manhattan, pictures of Abbie in form-fitting cocktail dresses and Phillip in black tie. Those pictures had inspired someone, probably not Clarke, to do a little more digging. Stories about the co-op on Park, the weekend place in Garrison, and the house on Nantucket certainly didn't help Abbie make friends in her new home.

Until yesterday, though, the whispers hadn't bothered her. She clocked in and clocked out. There had been some burglaries, drunk driving, and a few domestic violence incidents. Mostly, though, Abbie could come in, do her work, and leave without having to spend any emotional energy. She'd come back to Utah to escape the memories that ambushed her everywhere in New York. She'd come back to spend time outside. She'd come back to figure out how to be part of her family again. She hadn't come back to face real cases and real work.

That had all changed when they saw the body. Nobody had believed the call at first. Everyone had thought it was a prank. People died unexpectedly in Pleasant View from time to time. A few years ago, a teenage boy had flipped his Jeep Wrangler taking a turn too fast, and a year or so before that, two girls at Ben Lomond High had committed suicide. Then there were the normal deaths—old age and sickness. But not even Chief Henderson had been prepared for what they found in that closet.

★ ★ ★

Clarke followed Abbie back to her office after their meeting. He shut the door behind him. Abbie was grateful for the privacy, but she still didn't have a good read on her new partner. No time like the present to try to establish some kind of rapport.

"So, what do you make of that?" Abbie asked.

Clarke didn't answer at first. Abbie knew there was family history between Clarke and Henderson. That wasn't uncommon in Utah. Henderson had gone to high school with Clarke's dad and had spent summers working on the Clarke family dairy up in Logan.

"I, uh, I don't know," Clarke said finally. "This is a weird case. Everyone's on edge because of the temple clothes and, well, you know."

"The throat being slit?" Abbie knew she was talking about topics you weren't really supposed to talk about.

"Yeah, I guess," Clarke said. Both Abbie and Clarke were too young to have personal experience with penalty oaths.

"Do you know what blood atonement is?" Abbie asked.

Clarke shrugged and said, "Yeah."

Abbie didn't quite believe him. Clarke didn't strike her as a Mormon history buff. Even if he was, it wasn't likely he'd have found any books on blood atonement at Deseret Books, the LDS bookstore whose motto was "Bringing values home since 1866."

The Mormon Reformation period wasn't an era current Church leadership liked to dwell on. It was a time when some of the least Christlike practices had been adopted. Now excommunication was the most popular way of handling dissenters and troublemakers. No blood—or threat of blood—involved.

"We need to figure out who the dead man is." Abbie stated the obvious. They weren't going to get anywhere until they identified their body. The medical examiner seemed to be taking his time. Clarke didn't say anything.

"I've been thinking about how we can figure out who our Mr. Doe is." While Abbie liked her own joke of calling the dead man "Elder Doe," she didn't think her partner would share her sense of humor. "There just can't be that many people in Pleasant View who wear clothes like we found. They were high-end and the trousers and blazer had been altered. He must have had a dry cleaner and a tailor. I've got a list of local dry cleaners. If Doe is from Pleasant View, it's not at all unlikely that one of them will recognize these clothes."

Clarke mumbled, "You're probably right. Those clothes were expensive. The kind of stuff you'd definitely have to go to Salt Lake to buy, probably at one of the fancy stores at City Creek."

"I've already picked out a photo of our John Doe and cropped it so you can't see the neck, and I have the clothes from evidence. Do you want to come with me?"

Clarke looked hesitant. "I guess so, unless you think there's something else I could be doing that would be a more efficient use of my time here at the station." This was probably the most important case he'd ever encountered. Why would he offer to do desk work?

"Not that I can think of."

"Okay, in that case I'd love to come with you," Clarke said. Abbie didn't know exactly what was going on in Clarke's head, but she did know he wasn't a very good liar.

FOUR

Clarke followed Abbie to the parking lot. They climbed into her green Range Rover. It was an older model from a time when the only people who drove Range Rovers were people who actually needed them. The drive from the police station to thc first cleaner on the list was a short one, but it felt awkward. Every attempt Abbie made at small talk was greeted with a one-word response. She gave up and finished the drive in silence.

Since moving to Utah, Abbie herself hadn't needed a dry cleaner. Everything she wore now could be thrown in a washing machine. It was a big change from New York, where her housekeeper had done all the laundry and dropped off dry cleaning, which was delivered back to the apartment either that same evening or the next day. There were dry cleaners on nearly every block. In the area around Ben Lomond Circle, there were exactly three. Abbie had chosen the cleaner closest to the station as their first stop.

She pushed open a glass door with the words "Prestige Dry Cleaning" printed in large, blue letters. Somewhere inside the room, Abbie heard a bell jingle. An older woman sitting at a sewing machine in the front of the place looked up and asked, "Can I help you?"

"Hi." Abbie pulled out her badge. "I'm Detective Abbie Taylor, and this is Officer Jim Clarke, of the Pleasant View City Police Department. We're investigating a man's death. We think these clothes are his." Abbie showed the woman the blazer, trousers, and shirt inside plastic evidence bags. "Do you recognize any of them? I've also got a photo—"

The woman responded before Abbie could pull out the picture of Mr. Doe. "Size 48 Armani sports coat? Yes, I recognize it. We don't have many Armani blazers, let alone in a size 48." The woman smiled. "Unless I'm mistaken, it belongs to Stephen Smith. He and his wife are extremely good customers. They have expensive taste, and they need a lot of tailoring. Mostly letting things out. Mrs. Smith is the only woman I know who wears St. John suits to church."

While it certainly wasn't the case everywhere, Abbie remembered the irony of people showing off at church. Peter's admonition to be clothed with humility fell on deaf ears for a certain subset of Mormons who paraded in expensive new clothing and jewelry every Sunday.

"When is the last time you saw Mr. Smith, Mrs. . . . ? I didn't catch your name." Abbie said.

"My name's Edith Gundersen. I saw Brother Smith not too long ago. A few days, maybe? He'd spilled some gravy on a pair of taupe John Varvatos trousers. He was in a bit of a state, worried he'd ruined them. Let me check." Mrs. Gundersen stood up and went to the computer at the front counter. "Yeah, it looks like he dropped off the pants four days ago."

"Thanks," Abbie said. "Do you happen to have an address for the Smiths?"

The woman looked at her computer screen and printed an address on the back of a business card.

"Here you go," she said. "You said you're investigating a death. Nothing's happened? I mean, Mr. Smith is okay?"

"I'm sorry to have to tell you this, but we discovered his body yesterday." Abbie waited for a moment to let the other woman process the news.

Then she said, "Did you know him well?"

"Not really. Not to speak ill, but he was an arrogant son-of-a-gun when he came in here. He had a nice enough family, though. What happened?"

Abbie was a bit taken aback by Gundersen's candor, but concluded the woman was old enough to have seen a lot of death. She was of an age where she probably attended more funerals than weddings. Still, Abbie wondered what it said about the deceased that someone who knew him in passing felt comfortable offering up this character assessment.

"We're not really sure yet," Abbie answered.

"Well, it will be what everyone's talking about in Pleasant View."

"Why do you say that?" Abbie asked.

"You must not be from around here. Steve Smith is . . . was . . . a larger-than-life character. He and his wife were always donating money to the kind of causes that get you a picture in the paper. His construction company built a lot of the new houses around here. I think he was in the bishopric or stake presidency or something, too. I'm not exactly sure because my ward is up in Eden, but I'm sure anyone who lives in Pleasant View would know. You didn't?"

"I just moved here." In that moment, Abbie knew she'd been played. Like an idiot, she had walked into this dry cleaner's thinking she was doing real detective work when everyone in the Pleasant View Police Department already knew Elder Doe was Steve Smith. Abbie looked over at Clarke standing near the door. She saw regret—maybe guilt—on his face. Abbie was surprised Henderson had been so blatant. How could he explain that he hadn't recognized Steve Smith? He couldn't possibly argue that the blood and the position of the body had made it impossible to be certain, could he? Then there was Clarke. Abbie was livid. She felt betrayed. Not that she'd had any reason to trust Clarke, but she'd thought they were at least playing on the same team. Apparently, they weren't.

Abbie went through the motions of thanking Gundersen. She handed the woman her card. Without looking at Clarke, she walked out of the dry cleaner's. She climbed back into the Range Rover and slammed the door. Clarke quietly got in on the other side. Abbie was seething. She felt the knot of anger centered in her stomach spread through her chest and pound in her temples. If she opened her mouth, she would not be able to control what came out. She clenched her jaw and tried to focus on her breathing, counting her breaths backward from twenty-seven. Yelling at Henderson or Clarke, no matter how much they deserved it, was not going to get her anywhere. She went through all the possible reasons there were for nobody speaking up about who the dead man was yesterday: one—Henderson wanted to hamper the investigation because the death brought up uncomfortable questions about Mormon doctrine; two—Abbie's fellow police officers wanted to make her look incompetent; and three—there was no three. *Was this really how they were going to play it?*

Clarke didn't say anything the entire drive back to the station. He slumped in his seat. His body language seemed both apologetic and guilty. Abbie turned on music she thought Clarke wouldn't like as loudly as she could stand. By the time they got back to the station, Abbie was ready. She kept her expression neutral as she walked through the door.

"Chief, I've got a name and address for our Elder John Doe," Abbie announced loudly enough so everyone could hear. She surveyed the room. The two most junior guys had stopped filling out the forms they were working on, but they kept their heads down even as they exchanged obvious glances at each other. One of the most senior guys kept his back to her, but Abbie saw him turn his head slightly so he could see her and Henderson's reflection in a window. Clarke stared at his shoes as if he were willing himself to disappear beneath the floor. Henderson looked right at Abbie as the color drained from his face.

"Uh . . . yeah . . . Abbie, Detective Taylor, that's, uh, great. How did you . . . track that down?" Henderson stammered.

"It wasn't that hard." Abbie paused and watched Henderson struggle to recover his composure. He glared over her shoulder to the officers who were listening a little too intently. The men started shuffling papers and clicking on their keyboards.

"He's Mr. Stephen Smith of 54 West Lake Drive, Pleasant View." Abbie projected loudly over the sounds of the office. Her voice carried. She turned to Clarke. "Are you interested in heading over there with me?" she asked. Then added coolly, "Or would you rather stay here with the guys?"

FIVE

This was messed up. How the hell could anyone think it was okay to hide the identity of the dead man? What on earth could Henderson gain—besides making her look incompetent—by slowing down the investigation? He had to know Smith's identity was going to come out.

Abbie wasn't sure what made her angrier: that she'd let herself be played or that Henderson had been so brazen. There was nothing to be done now. If she reported any of this to people higher up the food chain, her fellow officers would all fall in line behind their leader and she would be the one looking crazy. Henderson had demonstrated that he controlled the police force in Pleasant View. On top of that, there was the matter of her partner. How was she going to keep working with him?

Abs, calm down. Let it go. You can't pretend you didn't expect an old boys' club to exist in a police department in a tiny town in the northern part of Utah.

Phillip was right. Okay, Abbie knew it wasn't really Phillip talking, but his voice sounded real in her head. After he first died, she'd heard him all the time. Well, not exactly heard him as much as engaged in full-on conversations with him. It happened most in their apartment in the morning when she read the paper. Phillip would comment on the news or the odd study on gun violence or pollution. Since she'd moved to Utah, she'd heard his voice less frequently, but she did still hear it from time to time.

Phillip was, as usual, right; this John Doe thing was exactly what she had expected when she took the job. So far, though, the old-boys behavior had been insignificant stuff, like not being invited to barbecues or being ignored in the break room. Nothing that could possibly affect work.

. . . and, Abs? Cut the kid some slack. He's the low guy on the totem pole. He was put in an impossible position: either respect his long-time boss or snitch to the new girl.

Abbie nodded to nobody. Phillip was being reasonable. She knew it and resented it, just as she had when they were together and he gave her sound and calm advice when she wanted to yell and break something.

Clarke joined Abbie in the parking lot.

"Hey." His voice was quiet and he said the word slowly. Abbie wondered if he was trying to both say hello and apologize at the same time. "I know how to get to the Smith house. Okay if I drive?"

"Sure." Abbie forced a smile. She was going to try to follow Phillip's advice.

It didn't take long to drive to Steve Smith's home. Clarke parked the squad car in the driveway, which immediately attracted the neighbors' attention—Abbie saw silhouettes in at least two houses discreetly peek out from behind sheer curtains—as soon as she and Clarke got out of the car.

"Wow, this must be at least eleven thousand square feet," Clarke whispered to Abbie. It was a big house. In the years since Abbie had left Utah for college, the rural landscape that had once been rolling foothills was now forested with houses: huge brick-and-stone structures with thin strips of grass separating one from the next. Abbie missed the sagebrush.

Clarke rang the doorbell. The front door was tall and made of some kind of shiny, dark wood with ornate bronze handles. Standing guard on either side of the door were two faux-stone lions, the sort of statues you'd see in catalogs catering to people who bought outdoor movie screens.

They stood listening to the doorbell play an electronic version of "Eine kleine Nachtmusik" for what seemed like an eternity. Abbie couldn't fathom what would possess people to install musical doorbells, but had the feeling that the person who chose this particular melody would describe it as "classy."

Finally, the door opened. A teenage boy looked at Abbie and Clarke. Without saying hello, he turned his head inside the house and yelled, "Mom, it's for you!" He walked away, leaving the door wide open.

Abbie saw a gleaming marble entryway with a star mosaic in the middle. Stairs swept up on the right to a landing on the next floor. To the left was a large sitting room filled with oversized furniture. It looked as if there was a dining room beyond that, but before Abbie could take in the rest of what she could see from the front door, a well-coiffed, plump, blonde woman appeared. Her nails were long and painted a deep shade of fuchsia. She wore pull-on lavender cashmere joggers with a matching top, the kind popular among a certain set of stay-at-home moms. Her feet were bare so you could see her toenails matched the color on her fingers. She was wearing an enormous, pear-shaped diamond ring on her left hand and diamond studs in her ears.

"Hello?" The woman's voice was high. She sounded more like a girl than a middle-aged woman.

"Mrs. Smith? Mrs. Stephen Smith?" Abbie asked.

"Yes," the woman responded, with a little upswing in her voice that made her affirmative statement sound more like a question.

"I'm Detective Abbie Taylor of the Pleasant View Police Department. This is Officer Jim Clarke. Is there a place where we can we sit down? We've got some difficult news."

Mrs. Smith looked a little worried, but if she had any particular concerns, she didn't voice them. She led Abbie and Clarke into the sitting room. The room was inelegant, even though it looked as if everything had been acquired specifically for the space. Like a woman whose shoes matched her handbag, it tried a little too hard. Mrs. Smith sat down on the yellow-and-pink floral love seat. Abbie and Clarke sat across from her in two overstuffed chairs that matched all the other upholstery in the room. Even the wallpaper matched. Abbie glanced at an oil painting above the sofa that had clearly been purchased because its colors coordinated with the furniture.

"Mrs. Smith, I'm sorry, but we have some very unfortunate news," Abbie said. "There's no way to soften this. We've found a body that we believe to be your husband."

Mrs. Smith responded without hesitating, "That can't be right. My husband's in Costa Rica on a business trip."

This woman hardly seemed capable of hurting anyone, but Abbie was well aware that when it came to suspicious death cases, it was often the person who shared your bed who helped you meet your maker. The professional in Abbie knew she had to consider the possibility that Mrs. Smith was complicit in her husband's death, but the human in her was struggling to deliver news no one was ever prepared to hear.

Abbie understood why Mrs. Smith would simply reject the possibility that her husband could be dead. That awful afternoon when Phillip died, Abbie had spent hours with her head drooped over the toilet, throwing up until there was nothing left but watery bile. It was her body's way of rejecting his death, as if by vomiting she could expel the unbearable loss and return to the world the way it was supposed to be, a world where Phillip was alive. Mrs. Smith might end up throwing up later, but right now she was going to deny the possibility out of hand.

"Mrs. Smith, I know this is hard." Abbie reached out and gently touched the woman's arm. "There's no easy way to do this. May I show you a picture?"

Mrs. Smith looked up at Abbie. For the first time since she and Clarke had arrived, her eyes reflected an understanding of the seriousness of their visit. Her face registered something—fear or dread—that she was about to see a picture of the man she married.

"Is this your husband?" Abbie asked.

Mrs. Smith closed her eyes slowly. Her eyelids couldn't

hold back the tears that first trickled and then streamed down her cheeks, mixing with eyeliner and mascara into black streaks. The blood drained completely from her heavily made-up face. Even the too-pink blush couldn't disguise the greenish pallor beneath.

"Yes," Mrs. Smith whispered almost inaudibly, "that's my husband."

Abbie looked at Mrs. Smith and then at Clarke. She saw the pain on his face and realized this was the first time he'd delivered such news. It hadn't occurred to Abbie that Clarke had never done this before. Now she regretted that she hadn't taken the time to prepare him for one of the hardest parts of the job. Abbie still struggled with it, even when she suspected the person receiving the news already knew what she was going to say.

"I'm so sorry for your loss, Mrs. Smith." Abbie paused. "Is there someone we can call?"

The widow nodded and pointed to the top drawer of a side table. Abbie opened it and took out the *Ben Lomond Circle 7th Ward Directory*. Printed on the inside cover were the names and telephone numbers for the Bishop, First Counselor, Second Counselor, and Relief Society President. The first three were the lay ministers for the area. Abbie noticed Stephen Smith was listed as the Second Counselor to the Bishop. The last name was a woman's. She was President of the Relief Society, the woman responsible for organizing the sisters in the ward to help with church members' needs during a crisis: everything from delivering food to making hospital visits. Abbie dialed the number for the Bishop, as was protocol. He'd call the Relief Society President himself.

"Hello. Bishop Norton? This is Detective Taylor of the Pleasant View Police Department. We've had to deliver some very difficult news to Sister Smith. Her husband's body has been found. I think she could use some company right now . . . Thank you. Of course, we'll wait until you get here. Bye."

In less than twenty minutes, Abbie heard a car pull up. She opened the door to see a man in a well-tailored suit emerge from a shiny black Lexus.

"Bishop Norton? I'm Detective Abish Taylor, and this is Officer Jim Clarke. Thank you for coming so quickly."

"Of course," the Bishop responded, then turned to Clarke. "Jim Clarke? Aren't you in the singles ward, oh, I mean the YSA?"

"YSA" stood for "Young Single Adults." The Church organized these wards exclusively for young unmarried people so that going to church every Sunday provided an opportunity to meet their future spouse.

"Yeah, I am." Clarke nodded.

Abbie watched the Bishop walk into the living room and sit down next to the widow. He was carrying the familiar leather-bound quadruple combination, or "quad," which was a single volume that included all the LDS scriptures: the Bible, the Book of Mormon, the Doctrine and Covenants, and the Pearl of Great Price. Abbie's parents had presented her with her own black leather set embossed with her name in gold after she'd been baptized and confirmed a few days after her eighth birthday.

"Melinda," Abbie heard the Bishop say softly. "Would you like us to give you a blessing?" Abbie saw the Bishop look over at Clarke.

In the months before Abbie's mom died, there'd been dozens of blessings. At first they had seemed like magic. Two authoritative men anointed her mom with a few drops of sacred oil and then laid their hands on her head. They spoke in deep hushed tones. Her mom described a feeling of calm afterward, but the miracle never came. As the end neared, Abbie grew to resent the blessings as arrogant and disingenuous claims. Her father, though, and everyone but her oldest brother took comfort in the ritual. At the end, Abbie couldn't believe anyone truly expected divine intervention could prevent the inevitable.

"Yes, I would. Thank you," Mrs. Smith answered.

The Bishop turned to Clarke. "Would you mind?"

"Of course not," Clarke said.

The Bishop pulled out a small metal vial attached to his key chain. He opened it and poured a few drops of oil onto Melinda's hair. He and Clarke then placed their hands gently on the widow's head.

"Dear Heavenly Father . . ." the Bishop began.

Abbie bowed her own head, not so much because she shared the faith of the three other people in the room but because she respected their right to believe what they chose. The two priesthood holders asked their Father in Heaven to give Sister Smith the strength she needed to get through this challenging time. Despite Abbie's own skepticism about the blessing itself, she hoped it would bring the widow some comfort, if that's what the woman deserved. For a moment, Abbie's thoughts strayed from the monotone recitation of the blessing to how the wife had responded to her husband's death. It was remarkable that Mrs. Smith hadn't asked any questions about her husband. Was she simply devoid of curiosity, or was she not surprised? Of course, it might have been that she was just in shock and questions would come later. Still, in all the times Abbie had delivered news like this, Mrs. Smith's reaction was unusual.

"I say these things in the name of thy son, Jesus Christ. Amen."

Abbie murmured "ay-men," pronouncing the word the way most Mormons in Utah did, with a long vowel sound for the letter *a*.

No peaceful calm had settled in the room. Things seemed exactly as they had before.

SIX

"I'll be right back, Melinda." Abbie watched the Bishop switch from comforter to crisis manager.

"Brother Clarke, would you mind staying here with Melinda while I make a few calls?" The Bishop was used to being in charge, but in this situation his authority was not absolute. Before Clarke could answer, Abbie said matter-of-factly, "We have a few questions for Mrs. Smith."

"Oh, of course. Please let me know if there is anything I can do to help." The Bishop walked into the hallway, presumably where he could make calls without being overheard. Abbie had excellent hearing.

"Jules? I'm here with Melinda Smith. Steve has passed away. Can you come over?" His tone was intimate. So he was calling his wife before anyone else in the bishopric or the Relief Society.

When he returned to the living room, the Bishop wrapped a soft throw blanket around Melinda's shoulders. In what seemed like no time at all, there was a soft tap on the front door. A lithe blonde with the body of a tennis player walked in. Her expression was the perfect combination of compassion and competence. She was carrying a plate of freshly baked snickerdoodles. The smell of cinnamon and sugar alone provided some kind of solace. Melinda dabbed at her eyes with the Kleenex the Bishop had handed her. She attempted a smile.

"It's good to see you."

"Oh, Melinda, I'm so sorry." The Bishop's wife sat down next to Melinda and placed the cookies on the coffee table. Melinda immediately reached for one.

The Bishop, who was still standing, said, "Jules, I'm going to call Sister Morris to—"

"Sweetheart, I already talked to her. She's coordinating everything right now. I told her we'd bring food tonight." The Bishop's wife turned to Melinda. "You won't have to worry about cooking. I know Sister Morris is making sure there's someone to help with the little ones, you know, getting to and from soccer practice and ballet. I also asked to have some help with the housekeeping, at least until after the funeral."

Abbie remembered well this Mormon efficiency in the face of crisis. Everyone did his or her part. Breakfast of easy-to-heat-up muffins or potatoes would be dropped on the doorstep every morning, followed by casseroles and pasta salads for lunch and dinner. Some of the moms would carpool and others would do laundry, vacuum, and wipe the surfaces in the kitchens and bathrooms. The Relief Society President knew exactly who could do what, and it didn't take long to make all the necessary calls. Of course, now there were also the handy online sign-up charts to help automate the process.

The widow took a bite into her third cookie.

"Mrs. Smith, I know this is hard, but we do need to ask you a few questions," Abbie said. "You mentioned that your husband was away on business. When did you last see him?"

"The day before yesterday," the widow said. "He had an early flight."

"Did you notice anything unusual before he left?"

"No. Steve was the same as always—happy, kind, fun. He was the most caring husband, the best father. He was a member of the bishopric! He always took care of us. I can't believe . . . I just can't believe he's gone."

Abbie had a natural talent for discernment. Even as a kid, she knew she was a good judge of character. That innate ability had been honed by years of working as a professional lie detector. Right now, there was a bell ringing in her head, telling her that the woman in front of her was not telling the truth. Something wasn't right.

"This business trip, where was he going?" Abbie asked.

"He was doing work for the Church," Mrs. Smith said. "Very important work, in Costa Rica. He had to take care of some financial details and construction plans."

"Was this trip a regular part of his business?"

The widow nodded.

"Do you happen to know any specifics about who he was working with? Any business partners?" Abbie asked.

"He was working for the Church. I don't know anything about the business. He dealt with the head of the bank, Zion Commerce, but I never had to help with any of that. Steve took care of everything."

Then the sobbing started. The widow buried her head in the shoulder of the Bishop's wife, who looked distinctly uncomfortable, but wrapped her arms around the crying woman anyway. Mrs. Smith's sobbing increased in intensity with each passing moment. There was nothing to be gained by extending the conversation.

Abbie stood up. Clarke followed her lead. Without saying anything, Abbie caught the Bishop's wife's eye and set her card on the coffee table. The other woman, still holding the whimpering Mrs. Smith, acknowledged the gesture with a slight tilt of her head. More questions would have to wait for another time.

SEVEN

Abbie sensed Clarke could use an emotional break after watching a wife find out her husband was dead. It wasn't that it ever got easy to break that kind of news, but one did get more used to it.

"Why don't we head back to the station? You can start looking into Smith's background. I'll drive over to Zion Commerce and see what I can find out."

"Sounds good." The relief in Clarke's voice was unmistakable. Abbie heard him exhale. It was clear he was trying to release the tension and grief he had internalized at the Smith house.

"Is that how it usually goes?" he asked.

"There really is no 'usually.' It's always hard. In cases like this, it's particularly difficult, because we may be telling someone who doesn't know what happened or we may be telling someone who knows exactly what happened."

"You don't really think Sister Smith could have anything to do with this?" Clarke asked.

"I have no idea," Abbie said.

"There's just no way, I mean, I just can't imagine,"

Clarke said. "Except, I don't know, was it weird that she didn't ask us any questions? I think I would've asked a lot of questions. I'd want to know exactly what happened."

They reached the parking lot at the station. Abbie climbed out of Clarke's squad car and into her Rover. She felt something she hadn't in a long time—the excitement of a real investigation. The unease she'd felt earlier because of the blood atonement connection was still there, but the part of her that loved the puzzle and the challenge of the hunt had joined the swirl of emotions.

Abbie drove to the bank and parked in front of a square brick building that had been a mediocre architect's idea of a modern financial institution in 1982. The glass doors seemed dated, and the utilitarian beige carpet needed to be replaced. The clock on the wall was slightly off-kilter. The entire effect was depressing.

Behind the tall reception desk sat a cheery-looking young woman with a plastic name plate declaring her to be "Tiffany."

"May I help you?" Tiffany asked in exactly the perky tone Abbie would have expected.

"Hello. I hope so. I'm Detective Abish Taylor of the Pleasant View City Police Department. We're investigating a suspicious death. Is your manager in?"

The young woman's smile disappeared from her lips, but her inherent happy disposition left the look on the rest of her face unchanged.

"Yes, just a moment please." Tiffany picked up the phone. "Mr. Browning? A detective is here to see you." She then looked back at Abbie. "The first door on the right."

The bank manager probably wasn't as overweight as he seemed, but something about his soft hands and puffy face gave the impression of immense roundness. He was wearing a cheap suit—the kind that had a sheen in the right light—and aftershave to match. His stomach strained at the buttons on his pale-yellow shirt (an unfortunate color choice, given his sallow complexion). The fabric was so thin Abbie could easily see the outline of his temple garments underneath. Garments were different from regular underwear that gentiles—aka non-LDS—wore. They had sacred markings embroidered on them: the mark of the square over the right breast, the mark of the compass over the left, along with a marking over the navel and the knee. After you'd been through the LDS temple, you were supposed to always wear them. Abbie had heard her fair share of stories about the protective powers of wearing these garments. There were tales of missionaries in terrorist bombings getting shrapnel everywhere but where the garments covered their bodies, of burn victims being spared where their bodies were covered by the sacred underclothes, of bullets not penetrating soldiers' special brown military-style garments; the stories of miracles went on and on. Beyond their supposed protective powers, the garments enforced a code of modesty on Mormons: no sleeveless dresses, no short-shorts or skirts, and nothing cut too low.

"Can Tiffany get you anything to drink? Water, Diet Coke . . . coffee?" the rotund manager asked.

"Nothing for me, thank you," Abbie answered.

Offering coffee was a quick way for a member of the Church to tell if you were LDS or not. Even though there had been some recent clarifications by the Church about the Word of Wisdom's position on caffeine in soda, the basics remained the same as always: no alcohol or "hot drinks," which officially meant no coffee or tea. Caffeinated sodas and hot cocoa lived in the realm of personal choice. Abbie remembered a neighbor who'd taken to peeling the Pepsi labels from her soda bottles so the trash collectors wouldn't know she drank it. In Abbie's own house, her mom had let them drink both cola and cocoa. Her dad had abstained from the cola but happily sipped hot cocoa with homemade whipped cream if it was on offer.

Abbie didn't want to draw attention to herself as being non-LDS. Since she'd started working in Pleasant View, Abbie had made it a policy not to accept an offer of coffee, tea, or even soda from someone she didn't know. She didn't wear anything that revealed she wasn't wearing garments. And she smiled . . . a lot, which was the Mormon way.

"Mr. Browning, thanks so much for making time in your busy schedule to see me on such short notice." It was obvious the banker didn't have much to do. The place was completely empty except for Mr. Browning and his friendly receptionist. You could actually hear the clock ticking above the banker's desk.

"Oh, but of course. We here at Zion Commerce Bank are happy to help the police department in any way we can. I must admit to you, though, I've never been involved in an investigation where there's been a death."

Abbie's comments about how busy the manager was—and consequently how important he was—had hit their mark. Some LDS men believed that the sheer fact that they held the priesthood endowed them with a sense of authority, warranted or not. Abbie had watched her mother and grandmothers err on the side of humility, even to the point of meekness, so as not to threaten. It made life easier. A lot of men, including the banker sitting in front of her, couldn't distinguish actual deference from a good imitation.

"So," he asked, "what can we at Zion Commerce do to help in your investigation?"

"I'd like to get your records for all of Stephen Smith's accounts, both personal and professional." Abbie held her breath. She wasn't sure whether the self-important banker was going to demand a warrant or not.

"That shouldn't be a problem. Let me see what I can pull up here." The banker looked at his screen as he typed. "I'll have Tiffany download everything to a thumb drive for you." The way he said "thumb drive" made it sound as though it were fancy newfangled technology of which he was rather proud. The man raised his voice so that the young woman at the reception desk could hear him. "Tiffany! Would you pull up Steve Smith's accounts?" The manager squinted at his screen. "They're all linked to the account number KT 0225-00-0511-03. Download them onto one of the complimentary Zion Commerce thumb drive key chains."

"On it, Mr. Browning," Tiffany said.

"Mr. Browning," Abbie continued, "how well did you know Steve Smith?"

"I knew him better than most of our clients. He was special, of course, not only because of the amount of money he entrusted with us, but also because of the number of accounts he had. He'd been through some bankruptcies in the last few years, but it seemed things were turning around for him financially. All on the up and up, of course." Abbie thought the last comment was strange.

"Do you happen to remember the last time you saw him?" Abbie asked.

"As a matter of fact, I do. It was about two weeks ago." The bank manager stopped himself for a moment. "I guess it's okay to discuss confidential things, because Mr. Smith has passed away. Of course, I would never be indiscrete." Abbie doubted the truth of this last statement but said nothing. The manager went on with his monologue. "Mr. Smith came to check on the money he'd wired to some of his accounts. He had one in the Cayman Islands, one in the Isle of Man, and two more in Costa Rica." The banker typed something on his keyboard and looked at the screen. "Yes, it was Costa Rica. Mr. Smith opened two accounts with the Banco de Costa Rica last year; one he said was for business, and the other was personal."

"You don't happen to know how much money he transferred into those accounts, do you?" Abbie asked.

"It was in the millions, that I know for sure." A few clicks on the keyboard later, he said, "Five-point-five million to the account in the Caymans, three million to the account on the Isle of Man, and ten-point-seven-five million to one account in Costa Rica."

"The ten-point-seven-five million in Costa Rica? Was that divided between the two accounts?"

"No. It looks like it all went to one account," the banker said.

"Can you tell whether it was the personal or the business account?" Abbie asked.

"I'd say it was the personal one—" the bank manager continued with a pompous tone in his voice, as though the fact that he knew a man who made multimillion-dollar bank deposits somehow made the manager himself a more significant human being. "As I said, Mr. Smith entrusted us with large sums of money. He certainly deposited more money than anyone else did at our Pleasant View branch. He preferred working with me."

"I can understand why," Abbie said. She hoped she sounded impressed. "How much did he keep here with you usually?"

"If I remember correctly, he usually kept around twenty thousand in his personal checking account. He had another account for his wife so she could take care of the family expenses. There was usually around ten thousand there for her every month. His business accounts were separate, of course," the banker answered. Again, he typed something and looked at his screen.

Abbie didn't want to interrupt this speech. Sometimes when you were a detective, you got lucky. Middle managers were particularly susceptible to the desire to appear knowledgeable, even if prudence—and in this case client confidentiality—should dictate silence. Some people liked to feel important in front of the police.

"Hmmm . . . it looks like there's about eight here right now," the banker said.

"Eight thousand?" Abbie asked.

"Eight hundred."

"Eight zero zero?" Abbie repeated to make sure she'd heard correctly.

"Yes. That's a bit strange. Mr. Smith's account requires him to maintain a balance of five thousand. I wonder if there's a mistake."

Abbie didn't think there'd been a mistake. After having been to Smith's over-the-top house, she knew his was a family who liked to spend money and spend it obviously. From what she had seen, there was a carelessness in their consumption: the widow in her cashmere and diamonds, designer kids' shoes and backpacks dropped on the floor, new cars parked in the driveway. Abbie had seen plenty of families who "only bought the best," as if the expense of their possessions reflected who they were as human beings. Abbie had known families in New York whose net worth threw off enough financial excess to ensure their capital was never threatened. These were people who could afford constant mindless consumption, but generally their consumption was discrete. They would never be seen with LVs printed on their luggage. Abbie was fairly sure the Smiths' net worth was nowhere near the number needed to support the material indulgences she'd seen at the house. Although, the numbers the bank manager was talking about were nothing to sneeze at, particularly in a place where the cost of living was a low as it was in Pleasant View, Utah.

"Mr. Browning, I'm curious to know what your opinion was of Mr. Smith. You seem to be a good judge of character. What kind of man was he?"

The banker inhaled dramatically; he did appreciate his ego being stroked. He leaned back in his chair and said, "Well, Mr. Smith was the kind of man . . ."

The banker's phone buzzed. He glanced at the number, and his facial expression shifted from self-satisfaction to anxiety in an instant. He looked at Abbie and then at the caller ID one more time.

"I need to take this call."

"Of course; I've taken too much of your valuable time already," Abbie said. She stood up, mouthed the words "Thank you," and closed the door quietly behind her.

"Here's the thumb drive, Detective Taylor," Tiffany chirped as she handed Abbie the bulky device. The words "ZION COMMERCE" were inscribed on the blue plastic in bright gold.

"Thank you so much." Abbie was walking toward the door when she heard the sound of Tiffany's voice shift to that of an apologetic child. "I'm so sorry, Mr. Browning, I already gave it to her. I can probably catch her in the parki—"

Abbie lengthened her stride. She let the front door of the bank shut behind her without looking back. She dashed to her car and drove away before Tiffany could possibly move from her perch behind the front counter of Zion Commerce.

EIGHT

"What did you find out at the bank?" Clarke asked when Abbie walked into the station.

"More than I expected to," Abbie said. "Smith had filed for a number of bankruptcies but recently came into some serious money. He had moved millions of dollars to offshore accounts in the Caymans, Isle of Man, and Costa Rica within the last few months. I don't have a full grasp of his finances, but at this first pass, they don't pass the smell test."

Much as she was still livid about the whole ID thing, Abbie knew nothing good would come of openly antagonizing Henderson after he'd warned Clarke and her to be discrete about this investigation. "Let's look at this in my office." Abbie showed Clarke the clunky thumb drive.

Clarke followed Abbie down the hall and shut the door behind him. Abbie opened the laptop on her desk and inserted the thumb drive. The screen opened up to a spreadsheet labeled "Celestial Time Shares" with columns identified only by letters. There were rows and rows of numbers, none of which made any sense to Abbie.

"Celestial Time Shares?" Clarke asked.

The reference to the Kingdoms of Glory—the LDS version of heaven—was impossible to miss. Joseph Smith had explained that there were three levels of heaven: the telestial, which was the lowest kingdom; the terrestrial, the middle one; and the celestial, where, according to 132:20 of the Doctrine and Covenants, those who made it in were Gods. If you were going to name a real-estate development after one of the Kingdoms of Glory, celestial would be the way to go.

Abbie heard Phillip say, with a twinkle in his eye, *I prefer to invest my money in Outer Darkness Time Shares.* Outer Darkness was the equivalent of Mormon hell. It was where Satan, his angels, and the sons of perdition would dwell eternally.

"Something funny?" Clarke asked.

"No." Abbie hadn't realized she was smiling. "Smith transferred millions to offshore accounts just in the past few weeks. He left less than a thousand dollars in his account here."

"Could there be a legitimate reason for Smith's offshore accounts? I mean, lots of people have them, right?"

"Sure, lots of people have them," Abbie answered with a deadpan face. She was far less sanguine than her partner about the possibility that these accounts had been set up for legitimate purposes. Anyone who'd lived among a certain socioeconomic class in Manhattan knew that when Americans sent their money abroad, it was rarely for reasons they'd want to discuss. Perhaps the reasons were legal, but they were rarely principled.

"I studied accounting in college," Clarke said. "Do you mind if I take a look?"

"I'd love that." Abbie was relieved. She was good with neither numbers nor Excel spreadsheets.

Clarke sat in front of Abbie's computer and stared intently at the screen. He scrolled between spreadsheets with columns of numbers that meant nothing to Abbie.

Clarke whistled. "Wow, Smith was some sort of magician."

"What do you mean?" Abbie asked.

"Well, it's amazing he managed to keep his businesses afloat at all, let alone for as long as he did."

"Does it look like Smith was doing anything illegal? Any sort of financial fraud?"

"Heck yeah." This was the closest Abbie had ever heard Clarke come to swearing. He recovered his composure quickly. "I'd like to take my time going through all this more carefully, but from what I can see so far, Smith was up to his eyeballs in, well, you know."

Abbie thought about what Clarke was saying. A certain subset of Utah businessmen had earned a reputation for being less than honest. To this day, she remembered a heated debate at the dinner table when her mom had brought up an article in *Sunstone* magazine with her father. Even as a child, Abbie had intuited that *Sunstone* was controversial. Now she knew that the periodical was independent of Church control but was devoted to LDS history, culture, and doctrine. Reading it indicated you could be someone who didn't always share the views of Church leaders. The article that started the debate was about the history of LDS fraudsters and con artists. Abbie remembered clearly that her mom had read a quote from an expert in fraud saying the Utah penny stock market was the slimiest financial market in the entire country at the time. Her dad couldn't disagree, but he wanted to shut down the conversation. From what Clarke was describing, Abbie wondered if there was something about the combination of wanting to appear successful—and therefore more perfect—within a community of people with a shared faith that made Utah particularly fertile ground for fraud.

"Take your time, then," Abbie said. "Use my office. It's probably better to be discrete about all this. Call me on my cell."

Abbie walked out into the parking lot. The sun was beginning its descent on the west side of the valley. Abbie climbed into her old green Rover and headed up the canyon, all the while wondering if swindling your investors was sin enough to warrant blood atonement.

Wouldn't it depend on who was swindled? Phillip's baritone voice asked.

Yes, Abbie thought, it just might.

NINE

Abbie felt relief as she drove the Rover past the rusty gate at the end of her long, gravel driveway. She always left it open. There was no sense in shutting it. If anyone wanted to cross onto her property, it wouldn't be hard. Most of the forty acres were wooded and steep. Unless someone knew there was a building up the winding road, almost anyone who drove past the entrance on the drive up Ogden Canyon would have assumed it was empty land used for deer hunting. Even in the winter when the aspen and cottonwoods had dropped their leaves, the house wasn't visible until you were nearly up the private drive.

Abbie called the place a cabin, but that wasn't accurate. Wealthy Swedish converts from Salt Lake had wanted a *sommarstuga* and built the place in the early 1900s. It had traditional white trim and red wood siding. At some point during the house's history, someone had winterized and expanded it. Now there were five bedrooms (all with en suite bathrooms), a sun-room, library, eat-in kitchen, dining room, living room, and a den. Abbie had fallen in love the moment she saw it. She had already sold the house on

Nantucket. She'd never really been a beach girl anyway. That was a remnant from Phillip's childhood. Abbie was happily willing and able to pay the full asking price for this private luxury. She had imagined she could have her entire family over for holidays and lazy Saturdays. Swimming, sitting around the fire pit, hiking. Since she'd moved in, though, only her older brother John had visited.

She curled up on a pale-gray velvet chair that faced the fireplace in the living room with a large glass of a Napa cabernet in her hand and thought about Steve Smith. Her stomach growled. She took the glass with her to the kitchen and opened the fridge. She stared at the bright white shelves. There were a few different types of cheeses in the cheese drawer and some leftover saucisson sec. She was pretty sure there was a jar of cornichons somewhere. That would be fine. She started slicing the sausage when she heard the door open. Abbie gripped the knife.

"Abs?"

"John! What the hell?"

Her older brother stepped through the door and gave his little sister a bear hug. "Mind putting the knife down? You look like you're ready to do battle."

"I was."

Then Abbie saw Flynn Paulsen. Flynn's family had lived next door to the Taylors in Provo. He and John had become best friends in Cub Scouts. They still were each other's closest friend. In high school, when John hadn't been around to look out for Abbie, Flynn had. They were both six years older than she was. Until she'd been a teenager, she'd thought of Flynn as a brother. Then, she distinctly had not thought of him that way.

Flynn flashed Abbie a dimpled grin and raised his eyebrow. He was as handsome as ever. He had cropped hair with a little salt and pepper, broad shoulders, and well-defined biceps that stretched, just a little, the short sleeves of his gray T-shirt. He was wearing dark jeans and dark-blue suede sneakers. He'd always been a good dresser.

"John thought you might need some food." Flynn raised his right hand, holding a white bag from the local barbacoa. The smell of spicy pulled pork wafted through the kitchen. Abbie looked at her slices of sausage and returned Flynn's smile.

"Yeah, still getting used to this whole can't-order-sushi-at-midnight lifestyle. What are you guys doing up here?"

"Flynn has a place in Riverdale," John said. Then Abbie remembered that Flynn's grandparents had had a house up here. John had mentioned that when they passed away, Flynn's parents and siblings had wanted to sell it and split the money. According to John, Flynn had had cash on hand to buy it at above-market value. He'd kept the house and everyone else had gotten the money. Apparently, everyone was happy.

John had pulled out plates and set the contents of the bag on the counter. "I got you the chicken with salsa verde and rice and beans." That's exactly what Abbie would have ordered.

"Nice little *sommarstuga* you have here." *Of course Flynn would know the Swedish word for summer cottage*, she thought. "Kind of tight, though. I guess you got used to living in small apartments in New York. It's lucky it's just you. However else could you fit all your things in a place with five bedrooms?" Abbie couldn't help but smile at Flynn's friendly sarcasm. He was right; the place was much too big for one person.

Abbie looked at her wine glass. "Can I get you anything to drink?"

"Water's fine for me," John said.

She looked at Flynn. "You wouldn't happen to have any Modelo or Tecate?"

She opened her fridge and peered inside, then held up a bottle and shrugged. "I have some Polygamy Porter."

"Polygamy Porter sounds great." Flynn took the bottle.

Abbie grabbed a second bottle for herself. Flynn was drinking beer? John didn't seem the least bit surprised. Abbie hoped she didn't look surprised either.

After they'd finished eating, John stood up and cleared the plates. He put his water glass and the plates in the dishwasher and crumpled the remnants from dinner into the plastic bag it had come in.

"You think you can find time in your busy detective schedule to make the drive down to Provo sometime soon? I can meet you at Dad's. It would be good. For both of you." John put his arms around his sister and gave her another hug. He understood that Abbie's feelings were still raw when it came to her dad.

"I'll think about it," Abbie said. She would. She did want things to improve, but she wasn't sure how to move forward. Doing nothing was not making things better.

John headed to the door.

"It's so good to see you again, Abs," Flynn said. "It's been too long."

"Yeah, it has been."

Flynn reached his arms around Abbie the way he had hundreds of times before. They hugged and Flynn closed the door behind him.

Abbie finished what was left of her beer and went upstairs. She washed her face and brushed her teeth. For the first time since she'd been back in Utah, she felt like she might be starting to belong. John was there for her, and maybe she did have at least one old friend. Sleep came quickly.

TEN

The next morning, Abbie sat at the sleek polished cement counter in her kitchen. She nursed her first cup of coffee as she scanned her computer screen, clicking on links to the Ogden *Standard-Examiner*, or what locals called *The Standard*; *The Trib*, as *The Salt Lake Tribune* was known; and the *Deseret News*, the official newspaper of the Church. She skimmed the headlines. No mention of Smith anywhere. There was bound to be an obituary soon. Obits weren't cheap, so most families in Utah ran them for only one or two days before the viewing when friends and family came to see the casket, usually at the funeral home the night before and at the church the morning of the funeral.

Abbie, skeptical of her own thinking, considered whether it was possible that the temple clothes and throat slitting were an elaborate misdirection, but she couldn't shake the sense it wasn't theater. It was odd, though. So far, it looked as if Smith had been just a good, old-fashioned greedy contractor who intended to leave the country with millions of dollars of other people's money. Abbie wondered about the blood atonement angle. Was her imaginary conversation with Phillip on to something? Did the question of sin depend on who was swindled?

The crime scene struck Abbie as earnest, not dramatic. Henderson didn't want to discuss it, but she couldn't entirely ignore it. Suicide would be a nice solution for Henderson. Even though he hadn't discussed the possibility with Abbie directly, she knew her boss wanted to close the case quickly and quietly. A suicide would let him do that without having to deal with the implications of the ritual, but they still hadn't heard from the ME.

Abbie poured a second cup of coffee, black with no sugar, and opened a small purple notebook. She'd kept a version of this notebook for as long as she could remember. Whenever she filled it with her indecipherable handwriting, she replaced it with another one—always purple. The one she was writing in now was about two years old. She opened it near the middle with a thin satin ribbon that served as a bookmark. On the top line of the page, she had already written the date they found Smith, a brief description of the body, and the question "Blood Atonement?" She looked at those words and underlined them with her black Waterman fountain pen.

She didn't know what to add to the blank page beneath the question she had posed herself. She just couldn't make a connection between the financial issues Clarke was looking into and blood atonement. Stealing was a sin. That was true. There was also something else. The Law of Consecration? Abbie had a distant memory of this law requiring members of the Church to dedicate time and material wealth to the establishment of the Kingdom of God. Would stealing constitute breaking this covenant?

Abbie looked back at the page. She had the Bishop's number. He was as good a place to start as any. She dialed.

"Hello?" A man's voice answered the phone.

"Hello, Bishop Norton? This is Detective Abbie Taylor of the Pleasant View City Police Department. I'd like to set up a time to speak with you about Brother Smith." Abbie surprised herself by how easily she fell into calling Steve Smith "Brother Smith." It had been over a decade since she'd lived in Utah—and she certainly hadn't been calling anyone "Bishop" or "Brother" in New York—but she found herself using these honorifics before her brain caught up with the words already spoken.

"Of course. Whatever I can do to help."

Abbie heard the smooth voice of an experienced salesman on the other end of the line. LDS leaders were generally not men lacking in self-confidence. Even when she was little, Abbie had chafed at the undoubting conviction that radiated from so many of the men who sat at her family's dining room table. Her dad enjoyed rubbing elbows with the higher echelons of the Church hierarchy. Her father was not only the direct descendent of the third President of the Church, but he was a respected LDS academic in his own right. Professor William Taylor nurtured friendships with many of the men who filled the ranks of General Authorities, Members of the First Quorum of the Seventy, and Apostles. He liked being close to the powerful men in the Church.

The Bishop offered a time to meet, and out of habit, Abbie arrived early. She parked behind the church and walked to a side door where she knew the Bishop's office would be. The glass door was open. Abbie hadn't been in a church for years. It felt both oddly familiar and foreign at the same time. She knew things had changed since she'd left. There was more diversity among the membership. More LDS live outside Utah than inside the state. Utah itself was more diverse, too. There were Thai restaurants in Provo and sushi restaurants in Bountiful. Even the Greenery Restaurant at Rainbow Gardens now served wine and Uinta beer alongside its famous Mormon muffins.

Abbie walked down the industrial gray carpeting in the hallway to a partly open door. She could hear both a man's and a woman's voice inside. She didn't want to eavesdrop on what could very well be a private conversation, so she knocked softly on the door.

"Oh hello, Detective Taylor," the Bishop said, "I'll only be a few minutes. Do you mind waiting?"

"Not at all," Abbie replied. A blonde woman, probably in her early forties, was sitting in the chair across from the Bishop. Just from her quick glance, Abbie sized up the woman as one of the fighters. In Utah, where most women in their forties had given birth to anywhere between four and six children, there were the moms who were acceptant of what multiple pregnancies and lack of time did to the female body. Their self-care was usually limited to ingesting carbohydrates, either sweet or savory, in less-than-virtuous forms and amounts. Then there were the moms who fought, and they fought hard. Diet and exercise were just the tip of the iceberg. For these moms, routines included maintaining long hair with regular highlights, manicures, pedicures, veneers, eyelash extensions and, not that it would ever be mentioned, plastic surgery. Utah women had plastic surgery at among the highest rates in the country. Mommy makeovers—breast augmentation, tummy tucking, and liposuction all done at the same time—were extraordinarily popular. Abbie couldn't guess about plastic surgery, but the woman talking to the Bishop was definitely a fighter.

Abbie shut the door, but she could still hear the voices on the other side. For a moment, she debated walking down the hallway to give the Bishop and the woman some privacy, but her curiosity won out. She stood where she was and listened. First, she heard the woman's voice.

"Thank you so much for seeing me on such short notice. I don't know how I wasn't on top of this. Normally I could live for a week without my temple recommend, but next week is my niece's wedding in the Bountiful temple and—"

"No need to apologize, Sister Morris. With all you've been doing with the Relief Society and Brother Smith's unexpected passing, well, I know you have your hands full." Abbie then heard the Bishop say, "This won't take too long."

So this was a temple recommend interview. Abbie remembered her first time. She was almost twenty-one and planning to go on a mission. Some of the questions had changed over time, but the purpose remained the same: to determine whether a member was worthy to enter the House of the Lord. Without a temple recommend, not only could you not go to the temple for yourself or do genealogical work like marriage or sealings for the dead, but you also couldn't attend a temple wedding, even for your own child.

Abbie listened as the Bishop went through the more

routine questions, such as whether the woman sustained the President of the Church as the only living prophet, seer, and revelator authorized to exercise all the keys of the priesthood—whatever that meant. Abbie's mom and grandma had often talked in hushed tones about their own struggles with sustaining the Prophet. Abbie hadn't been meant to hear, but she knew the quiet conversations had something to do with the man who had once been the Prophet of the Church. He was an outspoken proponent of the John Birch Society, a political group so reactionary even Ayn Rand and William F. Buckley Jr. had denounced it. Abbie's mother and grandmother were closet democrats.

After the question about sustaining the Prophet, Abbie heard the questions about chastity, paying tithing, following the Word of Wisdom, and wearing your garments. Then there was the inquiry about "supporting, affiliating with or agreeing with any person or group whose teachings or practices are contrary to the Church." This particular query infuriated Abbie. She knew it was meant, historically, to prevent polygamists from getting into the temple, but she had friends who were active members, friends who cared about going to the temple, who'd been denied recommends on the basis of this question because their political or social beliefs were at odds with their own bishop's or stake president's views. One of Abbie's closest friends from high school had been denied her recommend from the moment her son had come out and she had supported him without apology. That position made her *persona non grata* in her small ward in St. George.

A few more pleasantries were exchanged. Abbie

couldn't make out exactly what was being said, but it was clear the interview was coming to a close.

"So sorry you had to wait," the woman told Abbie when she exited the Bishop's office, shrugging her shoulders and smiling. "You know how it is. My niece is getting married next week, and I let my recommend expire."

"No problem," Abbie replied.

"Please come in," the Bishop called from inside his office.

Abbie hadn't noticed how athletic or handsome he was when they'd met at the Smith house. He had a strong jawline and the look of a man who in another life could have been a Ralph Lauren model. He was wearing tan corduroys and a trimly fit navy sweater with the collar of a green golf shirt peeking out. He was not dressed for official Church business, which would have required a suit, tie, and white shirt.

Bishop Norton motioned to one of two chairs set at an angle in front of his heavy wooden desk. Behind him were the standard framed pictures of Jesus, Joseph Smith, and the current Prophet. Abbie knew the present-day Prophet from dinners when she was a kid. The smile lines around his eyes belied his harsh nature. The current Prophet was a man who was certain of his own rightness; doubt was a moral failing. He and her father didn't agree on some of the more obscure points of doctrine. Her father was more willing to see nuances than was generally considered acceptable. Despite their differences, and there were many, Abbie had to give her dad some credit for his intellectual honesty.

"Hello, Abish." The Bishop smiled the perfect smile that came from veneers and spending two years on a mission having doors slammed in his face. Returned missionaries could smile through anything.

Bishop Norton leaned back in his chair and started reciting scripture. "'And it came to pass that they did call on the name of the Lord, in their might, even until they had all fallen to the earth, save it were one of the Lamanitish women, whose name was Abish, she having been converted unto the Lord for many years, on account of a remarkable vision of her father—' Alma 19:16, if I'm not mistaken."

The Bishop wasn't mistaken. Abbie was impressed both because he could quote the Book of Alma and because he remembered that she'd introduced herself as Abish when they first met. The tale of Abish was not the most common Book of Mormon story. It was the account of King Lamoni's servant girl, who believed in Jesus Christ and helped convert an entire kingdom to the "true gospel." Every Latter-day Saint was supposed to read the Book of Mormon regularly, preferably daily, but not too many people really did. Even fewer read the odd bits that were rarely talked about at church. Bishop Norton knew his scriptures better than most.

"Not many people recognize my name. I'm impressed," Abbie said.

The Bishop smiled.

"I noticed in the ward directory that Steve was your Second Counselor," Abbie said, quickly changing the subject. She didn't want the Bishop to control the conversation, which he was probably used to doing. "What can you tell me about him?"

Abbie was walking a thin line between pushing for

information and not being pushy. In Utah, politeness and friendliness were valued as much as competence and efficiency were in New York.

"Brother Smith was a good man. My understanding is he helped develop and build the entire Ben Lomond Circle neighborhood. His house was one of the first ones built. A number of members of the ward were involved in various aspects of constructing the houses, even this church."

Abbie felt her stomach tighten, which was the way her body signaled that the conversation had shifted into the realm of something less honest. When the Bishop said, "My understanding is," Abbie knew what he really meant was "I will technically cooperate with you, but I'm not really going to be helpful with your investigation."

"Can you tell me who in the ward worked with Mr. Smith?" Abbie asked.

The Bishop smiled again, showing off those perfect teeth. "Since my family just moved here a few years ago, I couldn't say for sure."

"Really?" Abbie let her incredulity linger in the air.

"Hmmm, let me think." The Bishop pretended to be racking his brain for details. Abbie knew he wasn't trying to remember anything.

"Brother Egan has a successful plumbing business. He may have worked with Brother Smith. Brother Zimmerman runs his family's cabinetry company. I don't know if he ever worked on any of Brother Smith's houses, but it wouldn't surprise me because they were friends. Brother Morris has his own masonry and ironwork business. I don't know if he ever worked with Brother Smith, but the Morris family has lived in the neighborhood for quite a while. I think they're family friends of the Smiths."

Abbie jotted down the names, then asked, "Do you know of anybody in the ward who didn't get along with Brother Smith?"

"No one I'm aware of. Brother Smith was very friendly. He was always there to lend a helping hand. During the winter, he and his sons shoveled driveways for the older members in the ward and mowed lawns in the summer. He was very generous in terms of making sure the storehouse was well stocked. Not that we have much need in this ward, but even here there are members who fall on hard times and need some help to become self-reliant again."

"How long have you known Brother Smith?" Abbie asked.

"We met in college at Weber State. We lost touch after graduation. My wife and I moved to Logan; Steve and Melinda moved here. Steve convinced me to buy our house here, and that's when we reconnected."

"How long had the two of you served in the bishopric together?" Abbie asked.

"Just over a year."

"He was paying his tithing in full?" Abbie knew this wasn't a subtle question. To be worthy of a temple recommend, Mormons had to tithe ten percent of their income. Some people tithed ten percent based on their pre-tax income. Abbie guessed Smith calculated his tithing on his post-tax income. There were very few circumstances under which an active LDS family would not tithe, and a non-tithing family would definitely be on the Bishop's radar.

Abbie had seen enough of Smith's financial accounts to suspect he had gone through a number of periods with "cash-flow" problems.

The Bishop said nothing, but nodded his head to indicate that he was affirming Smith paid his tithing.

"He hadn't spoken to you in confidence about any financial or business difficulties?" Abbie asked.

"No." The Bishop shifted in his seat.

"Nothing about filing for bankruptcy?"

"No." The Bishop had absolutely no intention of telling her anything important. Abbie was beginning to resent the arrogance of this man, who seemed to believe that by virtue of his gender and religious calling, he was entitled to tell Abbie only what he felt like telling her—which wasn't much. Abbie was about to let her frustration get the better of her when she realized she'd hit on something. There was something about discussing Smith's business and financial dealings that made the man sitting in front of a framed picture of Jesus Christ uncomfortable.

Abbie exhaled slowly. She wanted to savor this moment. In a low voice, she asked, "What about Celestial Time Shares?"

For the briefest moment, Abbie detected an element of unpleasant surprise—maybe even fear—on the Bishop's face, but he recovered quickly. He shook his head, shrugged his shoulders, and gave an apologetic smile.

"Sorry, doesn't ring a bell."

Abbie looked Norton straight in the eye and said calmly and very slowly, "This is a police investigation into the death of your Second Counselor. We know Smith filed for bankruptcy for most of his construction businesses in Utah. We also know he founded a new company called Celestial Time Shares."

The smile on Bishop Norton's lips didn't waver, but Abbie could see it was taking an enormous amount of energy for him to maintain his pleasant expression.

"Detective Taylor, I'm aware of the gravity of this situation, but as I understand it, Smith took his own life, for what reasons, I cannot guess. You're wasting your time and mine trying to understand his life." The Bishop looked down at his Tag Heuer watch and said disingenuously, "I'm so sorry, I have a meeting that can't be delayed. May I show you out?"

"No, that won't be necessary." Abbie stood up and walked out the door. She heard the Bishop's phone ring as she was just steps down the hall from his office. Abbie debated tying her shoe to give herself a reason for lingering, but Bishop Norton closed his door quietly and firmly before he answered the phone. The long hallway was dark and silent.

ELEVEN

"We need to figure out Celestial Time Shares. I don't know if it's the project itself or Smith's role in it, but Bishop Norton didn't want to talk about it."

"Huh?" Clarke looked up at Abbie, who was standing in front of his desk. He had been so engrossed in looking at spreadsheets that he hadn't noticed her. Clarke had convinced Abbie that no one in the office was going to have any idea what he was looking at. Henderson seemed preoccupied with something else. He'd ignored both Abbie and Clarke since he'd told them to be discrete.

"Let's go visit the widow again." Abbie said in a hushed tone. Henderson hadn't been giving her a hard time about keeping a low profile on the investigation, but she didn't want to tempt the fates.

"You don't think she knows about any of this?" He waved his hand at the screen, making it clear that he had very little confidence that Smith's wife had the intellectual capacity, let alone curiosity, to understand a spreadsheet.

"I doubt it," Abbie said. "Melinda Smith doesn't strike me as the kind of wife who takes an interest in finance. My guess is that so long as the money was coming in, she didn't much care how it got there. She pretty much said as much when we saw her last time."

"Then how is she going to help us figure out what happened with the bankruptcies or Celestial Times Shares?" Clarke asked.

"I have a feeling Smith had a home office," Abbie said. "His wife would know about that."

Less than a half an hour later, Abbie and Clarke were parking her Range Rover in the driveway at the Smith house. A few moments after they rang the doorbell, a slender woman in her mid-forties answered the door. She was the woman from the Bishop's office, the woman getting her temple recommend. Abbie's first impression of her had been accurate: she looked effortlessly chic in the way men mistook as natural but women knew was the result of hard work. Her sheer manicure was perfectly gleaming, her eyebrows were well arched without a stray hair to be tweezed, and she had the lean muscle tone that came from a clean diet and a disciplined regimen of Pilates and barre classes.

"Good morning. I'm Detective Taylor, and this is Officer Clarke. We're here to see Sister Smith."

"Good morning. I'm Sariah Morris, a family friend from the ward." The woman stopped speaking and smiled at Abbie. "You look so familiar. Do we know each other?"

"No, but we met briefly outside Bishop Norton's office."

Sariah would have no reason to remember Abbie's name, but Abbie knew she wouldn't forget Sariah's. Sariah, like Abish, was one of the few women referred to by name in the Book of Mormon. Plenty of LDS parents named their sons after men from the Book of Mormon. Women were not that central to the founding Mormon scripture, so there were far fewer names to choose from and, consequently, far fewer girls named after figures in the Book of Mormon. Sariah was a woman known for her role as matriarch. She was a mother who took care of her family, the wife of the prophet Lehi who led his family from Jerusalem to the "promised land" in the Americas.

"Ah, that's right," Sariah said. "So nice to see you again. We're in the kitchen."

Sariah led the way to the back of the house into an enormous kitchen with double-thick granite counters and gleaming cherry-wood cabinets. Melinda was sitting at the center island drinking a Diet Coke, the official drink of the LDS in Utah. Even the righteous could use a little oomph now and then, and, without coffee or tea, there were only so many options. In front of Melinda was a basket of homemade muffins. Judging from the crumbs, bits of chocolate, and pleated paper circles on the plate, she had already eaten two. Sariah didn't have a plate, but she did have a Diet Coke.

"Would either of you like a muffin?" Melinda asked.

"No thanks," Abbie said.

"They're the best on the planet. Sariah says the secret is breaking up both Cadbury and Hershey bars for the chocolate chunks."

"I'd love one," Clarke said enthusiastically. Sariah put her hand on Melinda's arm, signaling for her to stay seated. Sariah got up herself to get Clarke a plate. She placed an oversized muffin on it and handed it to him. He peeled back the ruffled paper and took a bite.

Melinda looked tired, but less shaken than she had the day they delivered the news. There was an awkward silence as Clarke chewed another bite of his muffin, which, apparently, was as good as advertised. This was probably as comfortable as it was going to get under the circumstances.

"Sister Smith, we're hoping you can tell us a little about what your husband was doing in the days before he went to Costa Rica. Are you up for that?" Abbie had thought long and hard about using the designations "Sister" and "Brother," since the words had just slipped out of her mouth the last time she was here. Since returning to Utah, she had assiduously avoided using terms that would indicate she was part of the community she'd consciously left. That was a personal decision. Now, though, it was professional. She knew she'd get further in this investigation by not drawing attention to the fact that she wasn't an active member of the dominant religion.

"Yeah, I think so." The widow looked at Sariah. "Can you stay, please? I really don't want to be alone." Sariah had already grabbed her tote bag from the chair where it was resting. The widow turned to Abbie. "Is it okay if she stays?" she asked, like a child asking permission from a teacher for a hall pass.

"Of course," Abbie said. Sariah put down the bag and sat back down next to Melinda.

"Can you tell us a little more about your husband's business in Central America?" Abbie asked.

"Sure. He was working on a big project to build a resort. The plan was to do this one and then more all around the world. He started last year. He had some pretty important investors from the Church. Last year, Steve had a meeting at the Joseph Smith Memorial Building with some General Authorities . . ." Melinda paused for a moment and then added, "Not to brag or anything." Which, Abbie noted, was exactly what Melinda was trying to do. For whose benefit? Abbie's or Sariah's?

"Do you remember anything unusual about the day he left?" Clarke asked. He had finished his muffin, although he was clearly eyeing another one.

"Not really. It was an early flight. I was still asleep. Well, not quite asleep, but I didn't get out of bed. Steve tiptoed around, getting ready, trying not to wake anyone up. It was dark, and he didn't turn the light on in the bedroom. He came over to my side of the bed and kissed me . . ."

Melinda stopped talking, as if she had just realized this was the last time her husband would kiss her. Abbie knew what it was liked to be ambushed by your own emotions. Out of nowhere, something that was otherwise innocuous would trigger a deluge of tears. For months after Phillip's death, Abbie had worn waterproof mascara because she never knew what would set her off. She'd bolted out of an elevator once just because a man was wearing the same aftershave Phillip had worn. She'd collapsed into a whimpering heap on the ground just as the doors closed, sparing her the embarrassment of showing such raw emotion to complete strangers in an office building in midtown Manhattan.

Melinda took a deep breath, dabbed her cheeks already smeared with black mascara, and went on. "He put his suitcases in the Hummer the night before so he wouldn't have to worry about them in the morning. He kept his computer and his temple clothes in his carry-on. Steve went to the temple every week, no matter where he was."

Again, Abbie wondered why Melinda was adding this information about Steve's religious devotion. Clearly, it was important to her that everyone in the kitchen believe her husband was thoughtful, successful, and—most important—a devout Latter-day Saint.

"Steve drove himself to the airport?" Abbie asked.

"Yeah," Melinda said.

"Do you remember what time he left?"

"I'm not exactly sure," Melinda answered. "I didn't look at the clock. I know he wanted to be at the airport by six or a little after that, so it had to have been around five, maybe. Steve usually drove a little faster than the speed limit."

The fact that Smith exceeded the speed limit wasn't surprising. Abbie was beginning to get a sense of the kind of man Steve Smith had been in life: a guy who didn't think the rules applied to him.

"I know this is hard for you to think about right now," Abbie said, "but do you remember anything unusual about your husband's behavior before he left?"

"No, I mean, Steve was himself. He was an optimist, always looking for the bright side of things. You know? Like, even though there was this downturn in construction in Utah, Steve had business contacts in Costa Rica. Next thing you know, he had this great opportunity to build a resort for people traveling to the temple there. At least that's how he explained it. I never really understood exactly how his businesses worked, but he was a genius. He really was. When he had to close down Smith Contractors or

Smith Construction, Steve still made sure we were taken care of. He made sure the businesses were separate from our finances so that even when he had to declare bankruptcy for the business, the family was protected. He was so smart."

Melinda started crying again. She grabbed another muffin from the basket. Sariah got some more tissues. Between sobs, Melinda took big bites. Abbie understood the desperate craving for anything that could dull the pain, even if only for a moment. When Abbie had gone through those first brutal weeks of grief after Phillip died, she'd sipped bottomless glasses of sauvignon blanc. She'd drunk to numb the pain. She'd drunk until she fell asleep and it left her fuzzy-headed in the morning. Melinda's drug of choice was rather innocuous by comparison. White flour, sugar, butter, and chocolate were probably healthier than wine.

"Thanks," Melinda mumbled to her friend. The widow's face was splotchy, with dark black streaks running down her cheeks. She blew her nose loudly and then took a sip of Diet Coke and another bite from the muffin.

"Was it hard having your husband gone? You had to take care of everything here by yourself?" No matter how broken this woman seemed and how much Abbie could sympathize with losing a husband, she still knew Melinda Smith was a person of interest, if only because she was married to the dead man.

Melinda shook her head. "Family was the most important thing to Steve. He always provided for us. Sometimes that meant he'd have to miss things at home because of work. That was okay. I can take care of things at home. I mean, that's how we do it . . . did it." Melinda started crying again, but took a deep breath and regained her composure reasonably quickly this time.

"You said Steve drove himself to the airport. Is his car still there?" Abbie asked.

"Oh, no. I picked it up. If his flights to Costa Rica didn't leave so early, we would've all driven to the airport as a family to say good-bye, but Steve liked getting an early start to his day, and he didn't want to wake us all up. He drove himself and left the car in short-term parking. It was pretty easy for Sophia, my oldest daughter, and me to pick up the car from the airport. She has her driver's license. I drive the Hummer back and she drives my car. Last year we made a shopping afternoon of it. Sariah and her oldest daughter came with us that time. It was a girls' day. We went to City Creek Center first, did some shopping, had lunch at that fun place in Nordstrom's. Then we picked up the car later. We had a blast, actually."

Melinda continued, "This time, Sophia and I went to the airport on our own and came right back. Steve's car is a bright-yellow Hummer, so it's hard to miss, even though he didn't park it where he said he would."

"Where was it supposed to be?" Abbie asked.

"It wasn't a big deal. Like I said, Steve parks in short-term. He always leaves the Hummer on the second level on the northeast side. For some reason, this time he parked it on the northwest side."

Abbie jotted a note in her purple notebook. Given how early Smith was supposed to have been at the airport, it was difficult to imagine that he wouldn't have had his choice of parking spaces.

"And you and your daughter drove back?" Abbie asked. Clarke had started on his second muffin.

"Yes. Sophia loves to drive my car. It's a white BMW convertible." *Of course it is*, Abbie thought, immediately chastising herself for her snarky thought. Abbie's eyes rested on the Louis Vuitton tote bag hanging from the back of the widow's kitchen stool. The dry cleaner had this couple pegged. The Smiths were not a family of understated taste. If they were going to spend money on something, they were going to make sure everyone knew about it.

"His bags weren't in the car?" Abbie asked.

"No."

Abbie watched carefully as Melinda answered her question. The widow was processing information and was evidently thinking very hard. Then she blurted out, "I don't know if it's my place to ask, but I don't understand what's going on. I know Steve was a little overweight and had high blood pressure. His doctor told him with all of his work stress and his eating—well, he warned him that unless he lost some weight and ate a little better, he was at risk of having a heart attack. Steve looked so healthy, though. We weren't really worried. Why are the police involved in that? Why didn't the airline call me right after it happened?"

Now the widow's reaction made sense. Melinda hadn't asked how her husband had died when she was first informed about it because she'd thought her husband had died of natural causes; she'd thought he had finally suffered the heart attack his doctor had warned about.

"Sister Smith, your husband didn't die of a heart attack, and he didn't die at the airport." Abbie paused, watching

Melinda digest this information. "We found your husband's body in an empty house not too far from here."

"It wasn't a heart attack? Are you sure?" Melinda asked.

"Yes, we're sure," Abbie said.

"What happened then? Robbery?"

"No, it doesn't look like it. We're in the early stages of this investigation. I'm really not at liberty to discuss the details right now." There was a missing wedding band and wallet—true—but Abbie was pretty confident stealing those was not the motive behind Smith's gruesome end.

"Sister Smith, do you know of anyone who would want to harm your husband?"

"What?" Melinda's voice went up an octave and increased at least a few decibels. "Not a soul. Not a soul! Everyone loved Steve. He was on the board of the Chamber of Commerce. He was in the bishopric. He coached the soccer team. Everyone who knew Steve loved him. Everyone."

Well, clearly not everyone, Phillip whispered.

"Sister Smith, did your husband seem down or depressed before his trip to Costa Rica?" Abbie asked.

"Are you asking if Steve could have killed himself? No! That's just insane. Steve would never ever do anything like that. He was tough. There wasn't anything he couldn't handle." Melinda's words flew from her mouth at a speed Abbie hadn't thought the woman was capable of. Melinda was incensed at the very thought that anyone could suspect her husband could commit suicide.

Clarke spoke up. "Sister Smith, we're not suggesting that your husband would do anything against the teachings of the Church, but we have to be thorough in our investigation. Do you understand?" Clarke's tone was exactly what the moment called for.

Melinda inhaled deeply and then exhaled. She nodded. "I guess I understand, but, you know, he would never, never do anything like that."

Abbie decided to change the subject to the real reason for their visit. "Did your husband have a home office?"

"Yes, he did," Melinda answered, visibly relieved to be talking about something other than the possibility that her husband could have killed himself. "It's upstairs. Steve didn't let any of us in there, but I snuck in to straighten up sometimes. It was always a bit of a disaster."

"May we see it?" Abbie asked.

"Sure. I have no idea what's up there, but if you don't mind the mess . . ."

Abbie and Clarke followed Melinda up the marble staircase to the second floor. At the top of the stairs, they walked down a long hallway until Melinda stopped in front of a closed door. She tried opening it, but it was locked.

"I'll get the key." Melinda seemed unsurprised that the door was locked. Abbie wasn't exactly astonished, either. Given that Abbie expected to find details of why Smith had moved millions of dollars to offshore accounts in that office, he'd have been an idiot not to keep the room locked. Melinda walked to the other end of the hall into the master bedroom. Abbie could see an elaborate bed with a mass of velvet and satin pillows in shades of gold and ivory. The kind of pillows with tassels and fringe some women believed made a bed more appealing. Abbie thought it was likely Steve appreciated the ornate style, too. There was a large framed picture of the Salt Lake Temple hanging above the carved headboard. Melinda returned with a key and opened the door.

The view from Smith's office was spectacular. You could see out over the valley and all the way to the Great Salt Lake. A heavy mahogany desk stacked with papers dominated the room. Dark wood filing cabinets flanked the left of the office. To the right, there was a built-in bookcase with a flat-screen TV.

"Do you need me to stay?" Melinda asked.

"No," Abbie said as she surveyed the room. "Do you know where the keys to the cabinets are?"

"Oh, here you go." Melinda handed a key ring to Abbie. "I think these open everything in here." Abbie wondered if Melinda had ever tried the keys herself to get a glimpse into what her husband kept locked up. Abbie doubted it.

"Thanks," Abbie responded. Clarke took out his camera and started taking pictures. Abbie spent a few moments taking in the room, imagining the person who had picked the furniture, filled it with papers and mementos, and was comfortable in its cluttered state. If the contents of the trash can near the desk were any indication, Smith's doctor had been right about his diet. It was full of empty cans of Dr. Pepper, crumpled bags of Doritos, and Snickers wrappers.

Abbie clicked the remote lying on top of a pile of papers on the desk. The television lit up to one of the ESPN channels. She sat in the leather chair and looked at the TV. You could comfortably watch from the desk. She imagined that Smith would come into his office sanctuary away from the chaos of his large Mormon family, lock the door, open a can of Dr. Pepper and a bag of chips, and watch the game. She wondered how much work had ever actually been done here.

"Let's start with the filing cabinets," Abbie instructed. There were three of them. Hanging on the wall above the middle cabinet was a framed football jersey with "Bonneville 37" emblazoned on it. Was it common for middle-aged men to display mementos of their teenage athletic victories? Abbie had no idea.

Clarke tried to open the top drawer of the cabinet near the door. It was locked. Abbie tossed him the key ring. After a few tries, the lock clicked open. Abbie looked over at him. His face was flushed.

"You okay?" Abbie asked.

"Uh-huh," Clarke answered, but it was clear he wasn't exactly okay.

"What's the matter?"

Still a deep shade of pink, Clarke held up a few magazines: *Hustler*, *Penthouse*, and *Barely Legal*.

Abbie smiled. It was rather sweet Clarke was blushing. It was also instructive to know what this father of five and member of the bishopric indulged in. It may not have been the most hard-core porn out there, but it was hardly at the least offensive end of the spectrum either.

"Anything interesting beyond the magazines?" Abbie asked. Clarke shook his head and quickly closed the drawer.

"Hey." Abbie didn't want Clarke to dwell on being embarrassed. "Would you mind giving the airport a call to get whatever security footage they have?" Abbie wanted to check out Melinda's story as quickly as possible. "Since the Olympics, I'm sure they have pretty decent camera coverage."

"Yeah, they do," Clarke said with some authority. He scrolled through his phone and then dialed a number. He stepped into the hallway once he reached a live human being and spoke softly.

Abbie looked through the next drawer. Her inhale was sharp. This was it. Here was the Celestial Times Shares information, neatly organized, with typewritten labels for each file: "Temples—Currently Operating," "Under Construction," and "Announced." Inside was a list of all the LDS temples around the world. At the time Smith had typed up his information, there had been 141 operating temples, thirteen under construction, and sixteen more planned. Somebody had underlined several of the temples in red pencil: Bern, Switzerland; Buenos Aires, Argentina; Fukuoka, Japan; Hong Kong, China; Kona, Hawaii; Nauvoo, Illinois; Palmyra, New York (the childhood home of Joseph Smith); San José, Costa Rica; and Winter Quarters, Nebraska, which was not a destination for anyone who wasn't LDS, but every Latter-day Saint knew the temporary settlement in Nebraska where Mormon pioneers had waited out the harsh winter of 1846–47 before heading to what would become their final destination in the Wasatch Mountains.

The Church had grown a lot since Joseph Smith translated his golden plates in upstate New York. There had been only six members—and no temple—in 1830. Now there were over fifteen million members of the Church around the world.

Abbie pulled out a glossy brochure. "Celestial Time Shares" was written in large gold letters over a closeup of the Angel Moroni perched on a spire. The cover was stiff, made of the heavy, shiny paper used by high-end real-estate brokers. The first page looked like a personal letter. It started out with "Dear Fellow Latter-day Saint"; then Smith explained to the potential investors how there would soon be over 150 temples around the world, but no place to accommodate the Saints who didn't live nearby but would like to visit those temples. Celestial Time Shares offered access to exclusive temple resorts. Each resort would be a gated community—or, in cities, a building with careful security access—near a temple. If the temple wasn't located within walking distance of the CTS property, CTS would provide regular, safe shuttle service to the temple. The resorts themselves promised traveling Saints all the comforts of a luxurious home away from home, with swimming pools, fitness centers, restaurants compliant with the Word of Wisdom, and media and game rooms, along with concierge and babysitting services. Local members of the Church would provide all the services on CTS properties so visiting members could relax among people who shared their faith and life choices.

The rest of the brochure was full of pictures of temples around the world and architectural renderings for the various resorts. Each resort was meant to reflect the "local culture." Abbie, true to her cynical form, thought the sketches looked more like what middle-class families from Utah would think was reflective of the country they were visiting than they actually were. The sketch for the Tokyo resort looked exactly like the one in Costa Rica, but the roofs in the Japanese resort were shaped like pagodas.

Abbie looked into the next file. If what she'd found so far was good, this was the jackpot. It was a typewritten sheet of CTS investors that had been updated the week before Smith died. There were asterisks next to several names and a handwritten question mark next to the name "George Boalt." In the footnote section on the second page, the asterisks were explained as "securities payment in lieu of cash." Steve Smith had been entrusted with a tidy sum by anyone's standards.

Abbie didn't recognize all the investors' names, but two did jump out: Bishop Greg Norton, who had said straight to Abbie's face that he didn't know anything about Celestial Time Shares, and Kevin Bowen. Abbie didn't know Bowen personally, but he was a General Authority who frequently served as a spokesman for the Church. Bowen was particularly interesting because Abbie guessed that someone of his stature in the Church would not be able to make investments without specific Church approval. Bowen was also interesting because he was the largest investor, with over ten million dollars in the project, giving him a majority stake in Celestial Times Shares.

Then there was this guy George Boalt with the question mark.

TWELVE

"Okay, so this is a list of all the people who gave money to Smith?" Clarke asked. Clarke was sitting in Abbie's office with the papers they had found at Smith's house. He was checking the list against the spreadsheets they had from Zion Commerce.

"It's a pretty good matchup, except for the names with asterisks next to them. I can't find any place where those sums were deposited," Clarke said. He squinted at the screen and scrolled between pages. "Did you notice how the asterisks are all locals?"

"No, I didn't. Are you sure?" Abbie asked.

"Well, I'm not completely sure, but I recognize a lot of these names," Clarke said. "Plus, it looks like the big numbers came from people where there are deposits. The smaller numbers look familiar, though. Like I think I've seen them somewhere."

Abbie was out of her depth. She wasn't sure she'd be able to distinguish any of the numbers she was looking at except for the over-ten-million investment. She certainly wouldn't remember having seen specific numbers before.

She didn't doubt Clarke, though. He was the kind of guy who remembered details like that.

"Any chance the numbers you remember came out of one of the bankruptcies?"

"Hmmm. That's a possibility. Do you want me to check that now?" Clarke asked.

"No, let's do it later if we need to. I'd rather check out this guy with a question mark next to his name: George Boalt."

Boalt's place wasn't far from the station. Clarke drove the police car and turned onto a dirt road off the main highway where he saw a sign for "Boalt Air." He parked the car between a beat-up Dodge truck and a shiny Chevy Silverado. The lights inside the small cinder-block building were on. Inside, the place was dusty and a little rundown, but there were a few new catalogs scattered on a small wooden table by the door. There was a big water cooler with paper cups stacked on top and a cracked leather sofa that had certainly seen better days. They walked up to the counter. Abbie hit the top of a small silver bell, the kind of bell you saw at motels in horror movies.

A thin man in his early sixties came out from a back room. He was wearing well-worn Wrangler jeans, a cowboy shirt, and an old leather belt with a large silver buckle. He looked as if he spent most of his time outside; his skin was tan and the wrinkles were deep. Abbie bet his family kept horses somewhere nearby.

"Hullo. Can I help you?" the man asked.

"Hi. I'm Detective Abbie Taylor of the Pleasant View City Police Department, and this is Officer Jim Clarke." They held up their badges. "We're looking for George Boalt."

"Well, you've found him." Boalt smiled easily.

"We're looking into the death of Stephen Smith." Abbie paused. "You worked with him?"

"Yup," Boalt said. The smile lines around his eyes were deeply etched, but his eyes weren't smiling anymore. "Why are you here? Did someone kill him?"

"Do you know anyone who might want him dead?" Abbie asked.

"Steve Smith?" Boalt shook his head. "Nope. There'd be a long line of people who'd want to throttle him, but kill him? Nah. Well, at least not till he paid everyone he owed money. I knew him a long time, since he was a kid working for my dad. When he was a kid, he was a hard worker. Something changed when he was the boss."

Clarke asked, "What do you mean?"

"Well, when Steve was a kid, you could trust him. He would say what he thought and do what he said. My dad would let him work on jobs in the evenings after everyone else had gone home 'cause you could trust the kid to work and not steal anything. When he started running his own show, though, he didn't treat most of us all that well. Then the bottom fell out of construction. Steve wasn't very good about making payroll or paying off his debts."

"Really?" Clarke asked.

"Yeah. First, he didn't pay the Mexicans what he promised. Those guys were off the books, so they couldn't do much about it, but, still, it just wasn't right. After that, he started paying all the subcontractors late. That happened to me a few times in the last couple years. I installed the central air in a four-thousand-square-foot place up near Riverdale.

It took almost six months before he paid me for it. Then there was that enormous place on Lake View Drive. That was a lot of work. I should've known better than to get involved with Steve again, but it was a big job, and I needed the work. The place was something like sixteen thousand square feet. Top-o'-the-line everything. Steve wanted everything done real quick because some big shot was going to have a Halloween party there or something. Anyway, some days we were working almost around the clock. Steve owed a bunch of us for that job. When we were done, he stopped answering his phone."

"What ended up happening with the money he owed you?"

"My daughter got me in touch with some lawyer. He told me if I wanted to see my money, I was going to have to file some kind of legal thing. The lawyer checks in with me on a regular basis, he says that stuff is happening in the bankruptcy, but it's real slow. I don't know the details, but I want my money."

"Have you ever heard of a company called Celestial Time Shares?" Abbie asked.

"Celestial? Like Mormon heaven? Sounds familiar, but I couldn't tell you why."

"What about shares in a real-estate development deal?" Abbie asked. "Did Smith offer you anything like that?"

"Ah. Yeah. He might have. I'm interested in cash, though, not investments. That's why my daughter got the lawyer."

"Could you give us your lawyer's contact info?" Abbie asked.

Boalt opened several drawers before he found what he was looking for: a ballpoint pen. He grabbed an old flier from a Days of '47 rodeo and scribbled with it to get the ink flowing.

"The lawyer's first name is . . . Dale . . . or maybe it's Wayne . . . I'm not sure. Actually, my daughter is taking care of it. She wants to be a lawyer. Helga'll know everything. I'll give you her info."

"Thanks," Abbie said as Boalt handed her the paper.

"Don't get me wrong, Steve started out a good kid. Somewhere along the way he got greedy and a little too big for his britches, if you know what I mean. All those fancy cars and fancy clothes . . ."

Abbie handed Boalt her card. "Call me if you think of anything."

"Sure, but I doubt I will." He was probably right.

After the door to Boalt's shop closed behind her, Abbie said, "Let's check in with the daughter now. She's in Logan."

Clarke started the drive back along the dirt road while Abbie called the daughter's number. She was home. She said she'd wait for them.

Logan, the Cache Valley county seat, was known for its historic temple, the campus of Utah State, and dairy farms. It was as quiet as it was beautiful. It wasn't a long drive, but it was long enough for Abbie to notice that Clarke didn't say anything. She might have been curious, but instead she was grateful for the silence; it gave her a chance to think. Boalt's description, like that of the woman at the dry cleaner's, didn't conform to the portrait of a loving father, husband, and upstanding member of the Church.

It was early afternoon when they arrived at Helga Boalt's apartment on Utah State's campus.

"My family's dairy is just north of here," Clarke said. This was the first time Clarke had ever spoken to Abbie about his family, even though she knew he came from a large one.

"It's beautiful." Abbie smiled. "Do you get up here very often?"

"Not as much as I'd like. It's so close, but somehow, you know, it's hard. My brothers are running things now that my parents are getting older. I miss seeing them every day. You know?"

"Yeah, I do." Abbie was surprised that she was telling the truth. Her dad drove her crazy, with good reason. Her sisters had never accepted her decision to leave the Church. Only her oldest brother, John, had embraced her. Still, Abbie wanted to get back to a place where she was part of the family—maybe not quite every day, but more often than she was now. She had nieces and nephews who were growing up, and her dad wasn't getting any younger.

Abbie and Clarke walked up the stairs to Helga Boalt's apartment. Clarke rang the doorbell and waited. A few moments later, a girl came to the door. She was wearing gray sweatpants and a light-pink tank top. It looked like she'd slept in them.

"Hello?" The girl looked Abbie and Clarke up and down. She spent more time looking at Clarke than she did at Abbie.

"Hello. I'm Detective Abbie Taylor of the Pleasant View City Police Department. This is Officer Jim Clarke. We're here to speak with Helga Boalt."

The girl turned her head back inside the apartment and yelled, "Hel–ga!"

A few minutes later, they were sitting in the living room on an orange hand-me-down sofa. The room was decorated in the classic college style of mismatched bits and pieces inherited whenever a family member redecorated. The sofa sat awkwardly across from a red-and-green-plaid chair with a brown stain that covered most of its back. The other chair in the small room was a black faux-leather recliner with a pink-and-yellow crocheted blanket draped across the armrest.

"Hello." Helga Boalt was plain and serious-looking. She was dressed carefully in ironed, pleated khaki pants and a boxy, button-down shirt in a shade of teal. Her brown belt accentuated a thick waist. It was evident that she had put both thought and care into her wardrobe choices, but her roommate in the slept-in sweats and tank top looked more stylish.

"Hello. This is Officer Clarke and I'm Detective Abbie Taylor of the Pleasant View City Police Department."

Helga asked to see both their IDs. She took her time examining them. Abbie doubted the girl could distinguish a real ID from a fake one, but that was not going to stop Helga from trying.

Finally, the girl nodded. "Why do you want to speak to me?"

"Ms. Boalt, we're investigating the death of Steve Smith and—"

Helga interrupted, "Steve Smith is dead?"

"Yes, he is. We spoke to your father. It sounds like you

know a lot about Mr. Smith. I'm hoping you can give us some of your insight into what he was like."

"Well," Helga said, "Steve Smith was an arrogant man who thought he could get away with things because of who he was at church. I doubt anyone in Pleasant View will tell you this, certainly not anyone who goes to church, but Steve used his position in the bishopric to bully people. You know, he and the Bishop, they're old friends. Since my dad doesn't go to church, he couldn't be threatened by suggestions it might be hard to get a temple recommend. Even if he did go to church, he doesn't care about living his life according to the rules of judgy Mormon moms and arrogant priesthood-y dads."

No one could accuse this girl of being diplomatic, but she wasn't entirely wrong about the judgmental nature that sometimes poisoned religious communities. Abbie had known a bishop or two who had used his church position in un-Christ-like ways.

"How well did you know Mr. Smith?" Abbie asked.

"Pretty well," Helga answered. "You probably don't know about this, but Steve was trying to sell this idea of a Mormon resort someplace in Central America—Belize or Costa Rica or something. I don't think for an instant he really had plans to do anything, but it was a great way for him to get money and pretend he was paying back debts he owed." Helga paused from her monologue for a moment. "I'm double-majoring in prelaw and accounting."

Abbie recognized the girl's desire to impress the police and gave her what she wanted. "Tough double major." Abbie had come across plenty of people like Helga in both her personal and professional life. The young woman was a know-it-all, the kind of person who would point out trivial details in a casual way, like, "Well, actually, you said a month, but it really was four weeks and two days." Helga Boalt probably didn't have many friends, because she was the kind of person who thought being right mattered more than being nice. Abbie had dangled a treat right in front of Helga's ego by asking her to share her "insight."

A self-satisfied smile flickered across Helga's face, and then she continued. "So, anyway, I never trusted Steve Smith, even if my dad claims he used to be a good guy. The guy was a snake, a jerk, and a bully. Whenever I went to see my dad on a job site and Steve was there, he would leer at my friends. It was creepy. I mean, he's old *and* married. So when Steve offered my dad shares in this sham resort company instead of money, I told my dad not to accept."

Abbie made a "hmmm" sound so as not to interrupt the flow of the girl's monologue.

"Another thing no one else will tell you is Steve was telling people he had major investors in his resort company. He bragged that important people like Apostles and General Authorities were on board. You know, the kind of LDS leaders people in Pleasant View would respect, so they wouldn't ask too many questions about the business plan."

Abbie was interested in the financial angle, but the comment about leering at young girls was interesting, too. Even if it was just gossip, and it probably was, Abbie couldn't pass up the chance to get another view on the dead man.

"You mentioned Mr. Smith made you uncomfortable

by how he looked at you. Can you tell me a little more about that?" Abbie asked.

"Oh, he never looked at me. Steve liked his girls to be—how shall I put it?—superficially pretty and academically challenged," Helga said. "Believe me, if he could do more than look, I think he would have. He was disgusting."

"Do you think he ever did more than just look?"

"I doubt it," Helga said. "I mean, who'd want an overweight, middle-aged married man? Even if it did seem like he had lots of money."

"Do you think anyone else noticed Mr. Smith's leering?" Clarke asked.

"Hmmm, I doubt it. People are pretty good at not seeing what they don't want to see." Helga's voice was firm.

"And what about the Church leaders who invested in this real-estate deal? Do you have any idea who they might have been?" Clarke asked.

"Nope. Steve always talked a big game but was vague on specifics. I doubt there were any investors at all, although he claimed he went to Central America looking for the right property. For all I know, he went to St. George for the spring."

Abbie waited for more, but Helga took a few breaths and said nothing more.

"Do you remember the last time you saw Steve Smith?" Abbie asked.

"It's been months, at least since before the beginning of school," Helga said.

"So you wouldn't know how he was behaving in the last week or so?"

Helga shrugged and shook her head.

"Thank you so much for your time, Ms. Boalt," Abbie said, "I really appreciate it. Here's my card. Please don't hesitate to call if you think of anything that might be useful in our investigation."

Helga took the card and put it in the pocket of her teal button-down. "Of course."

Once Clarke and Abbie were in the car, Clarke said, "I don't know how you managed to be so, well, nice. Helga Boalt has to be one of the most irritating, self-satisfied people I've ever met."

"Self-awareness and humility may not be among Ms. Boalt's most dominant personality characteristics, but she was helpful. Not only do we now know that Smith probably convinced the people he owed money into taking CTS shares instead—I bet those are the numbers that didn't match up—but we know he was telling people there were major Church authorities investing in the project.

"Maybe you're right," Clarke said. He couldn't quite hide that he begrudged saying Helga might have been helpful. "I wonder if there was anything to her comment about Smith paying too much attention to attractive young women."

Abbie didn't say anything, but she felt pretty sure that was one observation Helga Boalt had gotten entirely right.

THIRTEEN

After talking to George Boalt and his daughter, it was time to interview the largest investor in Celestial Time Shares. It hadn't been easy to get half an hour of Elder Kevin Bowen's time. Abbie had been on the phone ever since she and Clarke had gotten back to the station from Logan.

Elder Bowen was one of the youngest—and busiest—members of the First Quorum of the Seventy. Most non-Mormons didn't understand how hierarchical the LDS Church was, thinking it was structured more like most Protestant churches. They would have been wrong. The First Presidency, which consisted of the Prophet and two Counselors, was at the top of a clearly defined pyramid of divine authority. Beneath the First Presidency was the Quorum of the Twelve Apostles, and then, beneath the Apostles, was the First Quorum of the Seventy. These men exercised global leadership of the Church. Their words held both temporal and spiritual weight for millions of Latter-day Saints around the world.

"You know the chief wants us to keep him informed about what we're doing. Plus, he wants us to be discrete.

I'm not sure talking to a General Authority is discrete. Does he know you're going to see Elder Bowen?" Clarke asked as Abbie passed his desk.

"Yes," Abbie lied. She expected Henderson to be angry if she spoke to a General Authority without asking his permission beforehand, but she calculated that the cost of dealing with Henderson after the fact was better than risking the possibility that Henderson wouldn't authorize the interview at all. Abbie was beginning to like Clarke, and she wanted to spare him any potential fallout. Antagonizing the powers-that-be was not Clarke's strong suit. Abbie was used to it.

She turned back to Clarke. "Any word from the airport?"

Clarke shook his head. "The guy who heads up security was out when I followed up. The guy I talked to just now said there was some problem with the date we want. You want me to call again?"

"Yes. Please."

The drive to Bountiful where Bowen lived was quick. Traffic was light. There'd been a storm the night before, so the thick polluted air that sometimes sat in the valley like pea soup had been washed away. Instead of greenish haze, the sky was clear and blue. Abbie listened to KUER for the day's news, but the radio voices just served as background noise for the thoughts circling in her head about the man she was about to meet: Elder Kevin Bowen, the telegenic face of the Church of Jesus Christ of Latter-day Saints.

Bowen's house was an elegant stone structure with a backyard abutting a golf course. Evidently, he'd been well compensated in his business career before accepting his calling to the Seventies, the shorthand term used to describe the Quorum of the Seventy. The landscaping was meticulous. No detail had been overlooked. The Bowen house had a three-car garage to the left of the entrance. A white S-class Mercedes was parked in the driveway. This house was the home of a man confident of his superior taste. Abbie assumed there was designer luggage in the closets and photos in tasteful silver frames documenting expensive family trips abroad. She pictured a mother and father who were fit and—if not actually good-looking—expensively dressed and well-groomed. This was probably a family who felt they were entitled to the better things in life and couldn't imagine anyone not wanting to live life the way they did. Abbie didn't expect to like Bowen very much.

She rang the doorbell.

"Hello! You must be Detective Abish Taylor. Please, come in. Such a loss for our community, but our Heavenly Father works on his own timeline. I'm not sure I'll be able to help you, but I'll do whatever I can."

If you'd ever looked at the leaders of the LDS Church on the official website, and Abbie had, you'd know there was column after column of smiling male faces with neatly cut hair in dark suits with red or blue ties. The men ranged in age from their mid-forties to almost ninety. All but a handful were white. Most of them had the plain good looks of salesmen.

Bowen, though, was anything but plain. He was tan and athletic with a bright smile full of perfect teeth. He had thick blond hair and intense green eyes. And he was tall. Really tall. At least six foot four. Abbie remembered hearing he had played basketball for the Y when he was in college. She believed it.

Bowen led Abbie into a beautifully appointed sitting room with a view of the Bountiful temple. They sat down.

Abbie knew her way around the friendly surface talk most Mormons learned at an early age. As young as five or six, children stood up in church meetings to bear their testimony that they "know the Church is true." By adulthood, most Latter-day Saints were able to engage in conversation using key phrases, smiles, and well-timed tears to convey religious conviction (even when there was none, Abbie thought cynically). Bowen's phrase "but I'll do whatever I can" was code for "I won't help you very much."

"This conversation is routine," Abbie said, "We're speaking with everyone who invested in Celestial Time Shares. According to our records, Mr. Bowen, you were the largest investor in the company. Ten million, eight hundred seventy-five thousand dollars? Is that right?"

By calling a member of the First Quorum of the Seventy "Mister" instead of "Brother or Elder," Abbie had made it clear that this was an official police investigation and that, no matter how high-ranking Bowen was within the Church, she was not going to treat him differently from anyone else. Bowen's upturned lips remained frozen in a smile on his confident face, but he shifted his weight in his seat. The message had been received.

"That sounds about right," Bowen replied casually, as though investing nearly eleven million dollars was something he did so frequently he didn't bother to keep track. "You know, Abish—may I call you that? I took several classes with your father at the Y. He's an inspiring man. How's he doing?"

"He's very well. Thank you for asking."

Abbie waited a moment. She wanted the basketball player to understand she was not going to let him control the conversation.

"Mr. Bowen," Abbie asked, "what did Steve Smith tell you about your investment?"

"Well, property development is an enterprise with a certain degree of risk. Steve didn't pretend otherwise. The plan to build gated communities near temple sites so members can combine temple duties with wholesome family vacations is a brilliant one. If the project in Costa Rica goes well, and I expect it will, there are dozens of other potential sites. Those of us who invested knew we wouldn't see returns for a few years, but we're all happy to wait."

"Did you know Mr. Smith transferred most of the money he received from investors to personal accounts?" Abbie asked.

"No, I didn't know that."

Bowen paused. Abbie wasn't sure if that was because he already knew about Smith's transferring funds and was trying to give the impression he didn't, or because he was surprised but didn't want her to know. Either way, it was interesting.

He continued, "It doesn't surprise me. Steve mentioned that setting up corporations was extraordinarily complicated in Costa Rica. He knew the area, and I trusted him."

"Did you ever see the property where the resort was going to be built?" Abbie asked.

"No. I've never been to Costa Rica, but my understanding is Steve went scouting last year and found the site he wanted to develop. I think he'd already bought the property and was in the process of lining up contractors, getting the necessary building permits, that sort of thing. When I last spoke with him, he'd already finished the initial architectural plans."

Abbie nodded to indicate she was listening, but she didn't say anything because she hoped Bowen would keep talking long enough to share something useful.

"It's so inspiring to see the Church growing so quickly in Latin America." Bowen had now shifted to LDS propaganda mode—smooth lines he'd rehearsed in some variation hundreds of times before. "The Saints there have such strong testimonies. This project is not only going to benefit the members who travel there, but it's also going to provide jobs for Costa Rican Saints who work at the Celestial Time Shares property. Steve told me that the Relief Society President has a long list of sisters eager to provide childcare for visitors and to take care of housekeeping and cooking at the resort. There is plenty of landscaping and yard work for our Costa Rican brothers. All of us involved in Celestial Time Shares want local members to work at the properties."

Abbie let silence hang in the air for a moment longer than was comfortable. She needed to steer the conversation away from Church marketing. She asked, "Do you know Steve Smith's wife?"

"You know, I can't say that I do. I know he was married and I'd heard his wife went with him to Costa Rica last year. I don't know much more than that. In truth, I haven't known Steve for that long. I met him through a dear friend—why, you actually know him." Bowen paused for a moment. Then he said in a tone that was supposed to indicate some new piece of information had just occurred to him, but his delivery was too well rehearsed. "Russell Henderson, the chief of the Pleasant View Police Department. Your boss, I believe."

Was Bowen trying to intimidate her?

He continued. "Russ and I served our missions together. Russ knew Steve, which was a key reason I was so comfortable making the investment." Not only had Henderson called Bowen, but he had introduced Smith to him as well? Did Henderson know about Celestial Time Shares from the get-go, too?

If Bowen had hoped to scare Abbie by letting her know he was a friend of Henderson's, he was going to be disappointed. If there was one thing Abbie detested more than an old boys' network, it was being bullied by an old boys' network. Now she had an idea about how her father had found out about Smith's death so quickly. If Henderson was Bowen's friend, then it wouldn't be at all surprising that he'd let the Church PR man know about the discovery of a body that could, at the very least, be embarrassing to Church leaders. Especially if that body was of a man who was building LDS resorts. The line from Bowen to one of her dad's highly placed friends was short.

"Did you have any sense that Mr. Smith was using the funds invested in Celestial Time Shares for his own personal interests?" Abbie watched Bowen carefully. For a fleeting moment she saw something change in his demeanor, but the man hadn't climbed the LDS leadership ladder for nothing. As soon as Abbie thought she saw something register on his face, the expression was gone, replaced with the hint of an enigmatic smile.

"No. I trusted Steve Smith completely. He was a good man."

"Do you know anyone who may have wanted to harm Mr. Smith?" Abbie pressed. She wasn't expecting an answer, but she might as well try.

"I would have no idea about that. As far as I was aware, he had a stellar reputation for hard work, business acumen, and getting the job done. I was singularly impressed with him when we met to discuss the details of the project."

Abbie didn't think she was going to get any more information from Bowen at that point. The trip to Bountiful had been worth it though, if only because now she had some idea of the network that was making her job more difficult. She also wondered why Bowen had mentioned that Smith's wife had accompanied him to Costa Rica last year. Was Melinda Smith telling the truth about that trip or was Bowen?

"Thank you for your time. That's it for now." Abbie stood up. "Here's my card. Should you think of anything that may be helpful to our investigation, please don't hesitate to contact me."

"I'll certainly give Russ a call if I think of anything," Bowen responded.

Abbie ignored his insult to her authority. "I can show myself out."

Bowen didn't bother to stand, but she could feel him watching her as she walked past the entry table with its tasteful arrangement of cream roses in a tall crystal vase.

On the way to her car, Abbie felt her phone vibrate. It was Henderson. She let it go to voicemail.

FOURTEEN

"What part of 'Keep me up to date' did you not understand?" Abbie played the message from Henderson only once while she was stopped at a red light leaving Bountiful, but she could recite his angry words verbatim. Henderson was not a man to swear, so the two-minute-and-thirty-seven-second voicemail was peppered with "heck" and "dang." If there had been any doubt in Abbie's mind that this investigation was being monitored, it was gone now. Henderson didn't just sound like a furious boss; he sounded like someone who'd been on the receiving end of his own talking down. Henderson wasn't the puppet master. There was someone else, and that person was very unhappy. She would have to talk to the chief first thing in the morning, but it was better to let her feelings settle. Right now, she was mad as hell. Henderson hadn't mentioned his connection to Bowen. He had tried to hamper the identification of Smith. He was probably the guy divulging information about the case. It wasn't a stretch to describe his actions as obstruction of justice. That was a non-starter though, and Abbie knew it. The men would close ranks. If she made accusations about the well-respected chief of police and a beloved General Authority, she'd be out of a job before you could say amen.

★ ★ ★

The early morning sun lit up the mountaintops on either side of the canyon. Abbie could hear birds outside her open window. She laced up her running shoes, double knotted them, and headed downstairs. The temperature was perfect for a run. It was a little cool right now, but after a few minutes of running it would be exactly right. She needed to clear her mind and get into the right headspace to deal with Henderson.

As she rounded the second bend in the trail, she was already lost in the strong beat of her "running" playlist—a long list of songs with the shared characteristic of having a strong and constant bass line. It made it easy to run.

Buzzing interrupted the beat. Abbie looked at her phone. It was Henderson. It wasn't even six thirty, but her boss knew she was an early riser. Abbie briefly entertained the idea of letting the call go to voicemail again, but knew it was better to answer.

"Am I interrupting your morning run?" Henderson asked. He sounded much calmer than he had last night. Maybe a night's rest had quieted both of their tempers.

"Yeah, do I sound out of breath?" Abbie responded.

"A bit," Henderson said. "You know why I'm calling?"

"My conversation with Bowen."

"You shouldn't have ambushed him at his home. He wasn't happy about that. I'm not happy about that. I thought

I was clear about being kept in the loop on this case. You and Clarke need to keep this discrete, but you also need to keep me informed. Do you understand?"

"Yes." Abbie did understand. "It won't happen again."

"It had better not. In case there is any doubt in your mind, if you want to speak with any Church authorities, you need to come to me first. I don't care if it's a Sunday school teacher or the Prophet himself. You come to me first. This can't happen again. Understood?"

"Understood." Abbie exhaled. That wasn't as bad as it could have been. The music started again and Abbie picked up her pace.

Come on, Abs, you know how to play this game. Abbie heard Phillip's gentle scolding over the music. He was right. If Abbie wanted to stay here in Utah, she needed to adapt to its peculiar rules. It didn't matter how Abbie felt about the Church; it was a force to be reckoned with. Sure, she needed to hold her ground, but she needed to be reasonable, too. There was no professional advantage to being perceived as a loose cannon. If making Henderson more comfortable was part of the strategy for solving this case, so be it.

Abbie veered up a steep trail to the left that ended with an unobstructed overlook of Pineview Reservoir. She gazed over the water and mountaintops as the sunlight filtered into the valley. Once Abbie stopped moving, she could feel the dry air was still crisp. She stretched her calves and quads for a few minutes, enjoying the view, then started to run back home. *Home.* Abbie caught herself thinking this word. She wasn't sure if she felt *at home*, but she was beginning to feel more comfortable. Maybe her instincts, the ones that had seemed so rash when she left New York, were on to something. Maybe her solitary cabin in the canyon was home.

The run back always seemed shorter than the run to Pineview. Abbie was on autopilot until she spotted an SUV she didn't recognize parked next to her old Rover.

She stopped. She wasn't so much nervous as curious. Two visitors in two days would be a record. There was also the question of who knew where to find her: her dad, brothers, and sisters, even though only John had ever made the trip. Now Flynn knew, too. Otherwise, no one Abbie could think of had her address. Abbie wasn't listed in the phone book, and she'd done her best to keep her Internet footprint light: no Facebook, no Instagram, and no Twitter. She was a hard woman to find.

"Hello?" Abbie called out from the path behind her patio. The man sitting in an Adirondack chair facing the fire pit turned to face her.

"Good morning," Bishop Norton said.

He looked a little tired, but he was the same man who had so adeptly consoled Melinda Smith that first day they met. He was the same man who had blatantly lied to Abbie about his knowledge of Celestial Time Shares.

Abbie wasn't entirely sure what she was feeling. She was curious why he was here, but she was irritated that he had invaded her privacy and was livid he had lied to her about his investment in CTS.

"Why don't we go inside?" Abbie asked. Her voice was neutral.

The Bishop stood up and followed Abbie into her

kitchen. She poured herself a cup of coffee. "Can I get you some orange juice?" She motioned for him to have a seat on one of the counter stools neatly arranged around the center island in the kitchen.

"Thank you," the Bishop said. "Orange juice would be nice."

Abbie opened a cabinet door and took out a tall glass. She poured some juice from a bottle marked "fresh-squeezed organic" and handed the glass to the Bishop. He immediately took a big gulp. He seemed nervous, an emotion he probably rarely felt. Abbie didn't want to rush him, so she slowly poured more coffee into her cup and took a sip.

"Beautiful morning. This is my favorite time of year, when the leaves are out and the mountains are still green," she said. If a little small talk would smooth the way for the Bishop to explain why he was sitting here in her kitchen, Abbie would make small talk.

"I agree, but I have a soft spot in my heart for the winters here." The Bishop took another swallow of juice, then began, "I guess I should tell you why I came to see you so early in the morning. I pegged you for an early riser. Guess my judgment on human nature is reliable . . . sometimes, anyway." He smiled, revealing a sense of self-deprecation Abbie hadn't thought he had in him.

"I'm not really sure where to start," he said. "In fact, I'm not really sure if I have anything to tell you, but there are a few things that have been bothering me since we spoke. I thought it might be better to talk unofficially. Not at the station . . ."

Abbie waited.

"I know Steve was having cash-flow problems. I don't think it was a big deal, but he asked if he could borrow a hundred and fifty thousand."

Abbie thought that to most people, $150K *was* a big deal. She wondered if the Bishop really thought it wasn't.

"This was just before he started work on the Celestial Time Shares project, so I thought things turned around for him. I did—"

"Speaking of Celestial Time Shares, the last time we spoke, you told me the name didn't ring a bell. Not only do you know about the company, but you're a major investor." Abbie's voice still sounded neutral, but she was aware that her words had an edge to them.

The Bishop stared into his orange juice. He was probably not accustomed to being called out on anything, let alone his own lies. Abbie reminded herself he had come on his own and maybe, just maybe, she should give him the benefit of the doubt right now.

"You're right. I wasn't straight with you about Celestial Time Shares. It didn't seem relevant . . ."

She raised her eyebrow.

"Okay, I didn't want to be connected with Steve's death. I don't have any excuse. I see that now. The fact that I wasn't straight with you has been gnawing at me ever since you were in my office. It was wrong of me."

Abbie was momentarily disarmed by the *mea culpa*. This was an apology. Maybe the Bishop wasn't such a bad guy after all.

"I didn't lend Steve the money when he asked. My wife didn't feel comfortable with it. Steve seemed fine. He never brought it up again. I assumed that was the end of it, but I found out later he'd borrowed money from another ward member and hadn't paid him back. I don't know exactly how much money he borrowed, but I think it was at least as much as he'd asked to borrow from me."

"Was it odd for someone in your bishopric to ask to borrow that amount of cash?"

"Well, yeah, but Steve was the kind of guy who—I don't know how to put it—things sort of always worked out for him even when it seemed like they shouldn't."

"What do you mean?" Abbie asked.

"I've known Steve since high school. His dad was one of the wealthiest guys around. Steve was that guy every other guy wanted to be and every girl wanted to be with. Life just went his way. We went to Weber together for college. I studied hard just to make it by. Steve coasted and barely graduated, but he had this background in construction and his dad lent him money to start his first company. The timing was perfect. The Olympics meant everyone wanted something built. A guy with Steve's gift for sales and talent for building—well, Steve made a bundle. I got to tell you, this plan for Celestial Time Shares sounded like another one of Steve's magic ideas. The guy built Ben Lomond Circle from the ground up with somebody else's money. Look at the neighborhood now. It's one of the nicest in northern Utah. The guy could find a great business opportunity blindfolded and with his hands tied behind his back. Not because of his hard work or intelligence; he just had some kind of instinct."

For the first time in her encounters with him, Abbie felt the Bishop was being completely honest.

"Okay, so that explains why you'd invest with a guy who seems to turn everything to gold, but now this same guy is asking for a fairly sizable personal loan. What am I missing?"

"You're not missing anything. It was strange from beginning to end."

"First, tell me who lent Steve the money and what happened," Abbie said.

"Brian Anderson. He's a lawyer. He came to me because I'm the bishop. Steve hadn't paid him back. I was going to speak with Steve about it when he got back from Costa Rica. I thought the whole thing was probably a misunderstanding. Steve is not good with details, and Brian is all about the details. Anyway, I never got the chance to talk to Steve."

"Was the lawyer angry?" Abbie asked.

"I wouldn't say angry exactly, but I do think Brian felt Steve had cheated him. I think he was worried Steve would never pay him back."

"Do you think Steve would do that?" Abbie asked. "You think Steve wouldn't repay a friend?"

"I'd like to say no, but I'm not sure," the Bishop said.

"Do you think you would have seen money from the Celestial Time Shares project?"

"Definitely." The Bishop sounded sure about this answer.

The coffee in Abbie's mug was lukewarm. She was

beginning to feel the discomfort of wearing clothes that had been sweaty and were now drying on her skin. She wanted to shower.

"I should go. I've taken up too much of your time."

"Thank you for stopping by. You've saved me a trip to talk to you about Celestial Time Shares."

The Bishop looked regretful again. "Sorry about that."

"If you think of anything else, however irrelevant it may seem, please don't hesitate to give me a call."

"Sure." The Bishop walked toward the door. "Oh, there's one other thing. I mean, there might be. It's hard for me to say because I don't know anything really, but I started noticing last year that every time we visited the singles ward that, well, Steve seemed to be a little overly familiar with a few of the young women there. I never spoke to anyone about it. I probably would have completely forgotten about it if it hadn't been for this past Wednesday night. I was at the singles ward for an evening discussion about chastity and morality for adults preparing for temple marriage. I saw a few of the young women there and something just struck me. I don't know what and I can't articulate it any more clearly; it's just a feeling I have that Steve might have been paying too much attention to some of the young women there."

"Are we talking harmless flirtation or something more?" Abbie asked.

"I don't know," the Bishop said. "There was definitely flirting going on. It might have been innocent, but even that is inappropriate."

"Do you know the names of any of these young women?" Abbie asked.

"There were at least three or four I noticed: Lindsey Thompson, I think. Meghan Silver, Madison Hansen . . . and Jessica Grant."

Abbie grabbed her purple notebook from the counter and jotted down the names next to the name of the lawyer. "Do you think anyone else noticed the flirting?"

"I wouldn't be surprised. I don't think it was subtle, but if anyone did notice, they haven't said anything to me about it." Norton opened the door and stepped outside.

"I'm glad you stopped by," Abbie said. "By the way, how did you know where I live?"

"You know how good Church records are," Norton said. Abbie didn't, but she did remember getting emails and Christmas cards in college and when she moved to New York. She had never given it much thought, but clearly the Church managed to keep track of the whereabouts of members, even those who had gone astray.

As Abbie walked upstairs to shower, she tapped into her phone, CHECK OUT ATTORNEY BRIAN ANDERSON PLS.

She hit send. Clarke would have an address by the time Abbie made it to the station.

FIFTEEN

When Abbie walked in, Clarke was sitting at his desk, which was a study in chaos: two wrappers with the remnants of some kind of breakfast sandwiches clung to wrinkled waxed paper, a large Coke, and an empty hash brown container competed for space with precariously stacked notebooks and file folders. Looking at Clarke's lanky frame, you'd never have guessed how much food the man could eat.

"I've got the address for the lawyer. He's got an office in Ogden. Do you want to drive?" Just then, Henderson's clipped voice cut through the background noise in the station. "Abbie. Jim."

Clarke followed Abbie into Henderson's office and shut the door behind him without being asked.

"I got the report from the ME this morning. It's officially a homicide. Time of death was Sunday morning like we thought, the body was not moved, and other than a healthy dose of Xanax and chocolate-chip cookies, there wasn't much in his system."

"Xanax?" Clarke asked. "Isn't that more of a woman's drug?"

Clarke must have realized a moment too late that what he had just said might have come across as sexist. He looked at Abbie and added, "Uh, I didn't mean—"

"Don't worry," Abbie said. "I'm well aware that Utah tops the leader boards for prescribing anti-depression drugs, particularly for women, although I couldn't give you a statistical breakdown along gender lines." Abbie gave Clarke a lopsided smile so he knew she was joking. Sarcasm, the humor of choice for New Yorkers, was less well received in this part of the intermountain West.

"I've emailed a copy of the report to both of you. I told you both to be discrete until we could rule out suicide. I still am ordering you to be discrete. Unless I see a need for more manpower, I'm keeping this investigation limited to the two of you. If anything, the fact that this isn't suicide makes it even more important to keep this case quiet."

"There's no question, then?" Clarke asked. "I know we all kind of figured . . . well, it's just such a strange way to kill a person."

Henderson shrugged. "There's no doubt. Believe me, I don't like the idea that there's someone out there who could do this to another human being. We need to get this person locked up, which means focusing on the investigation and not letting any of this get out to the press."

"It won't," Abbie said.

"Oh, one more thing. Smith had been hit in the face pretty badly, the right jaw. None of us picked up on it at the scene because Smith had covered it up with makeup, the kind of stuff people use to hide tattoos. According to the ME, the injury happened about a week before he died. It was pretty bad, but things were healing. It had nothing to do with the cause of death."

Abbie was relieved that the report had finally come back from the ME. She certainly had never thought Smith's death had been a suicide, but she was well aware that the chief and the rest of the Pleasant View PD had hoped it was. A suicide made it much easier to sweep under the rug. Now that she knew about Henderson's friendship with PR man Bowen, she understood the obsession with keeping the investigation out of the papers. "Dead Guy Found in Temple Clothes With Throat Slit" would not be a headline Church leaders in Salt Lake would like to wake up to.

"And where are we on the airport?" Abbie asked. Clarke explained that he'd been trying to get through to the head of security but had been completely unsuccessful in his efforts so far. Maybe Henderson would have some pull.

Abbie turned to Henderson. "We're following up on what Melinda Smith told us about Smith's movements the morning he was killed. We can't seem to get the security footage from the airport."

"So strange that we still call it 'footage,' given that everything's digital now, don't you think?" Henderson mused.

"Yes, it is," Abbie said. "Still, whatever we call it, we need to know whether Smith's car was at the airport."

"I'm sure they're doing everything they can. They're extremely busy and understaffed, you know. Do your best. Talk to me before any important interviews. I don't want to slow down this investigation, but it's important that we maintain good relationships with members of the community. You never know when we may need to work with someone on the next case. You both understand, I'm sure."

"Yes, sir." Abbie heard the message: the chief wanted Abbie and Clarke to investigate, but he didn't necessarily want them to solve the case. *And they were supposed to play nicely with others.*

SIXTEEN

"I want to print out the ME's report before we see the attorney. Can you get started on tracking down whether Smith had his own prescription for Xanax?" Abbie asked.

"On it," Clarke said. He sat down at his desk. Tracking down prescriptions could be very straightforward or impossible. She was going to let Clarke take a crack at it, and she'd step in if she needed to. It would be helpful to know if Smith was on an antidepressant, even if suicide had been ruled out.

Abbie went back to her office and started reading as the report came off the printer. It was as Henderson had described: the contents of Smith's stomach included milk and chocolate-chip cookies. The ME had also made a note about the bruise. It was on the lower right part of his cheek and jaw. The ME said the hit had come from below and was probably a direct hit with a fist, although he couldn't be sure.

Clarke tapped on Abbie's door and then came in. "Finally, a break. I called over to Mountain View Health. The pharmacist there is a friend of my mom's. The Smiths filled all their prescriptions there. Steve wasn't taking anything regularly, but Melinda has been taking Xanax for years."

Abbie knew a prosecuting attorney was not going to like hearing that a family friend had divulged confidential information, but Clarke had shown initiative and gotten the information they wanted.

Clarke said, "I guess Smith could've gone someplace else to fill a prescription or gotten it illegally."

"True," Abbie said. "You ready to check out the lawyer?"

★ ★ ★

The lawyer's office was near the old Union Station in Ogden. A shiny brass plaque engraved with "McConkie, Hughes and Anderson" affixed to a polished door led to an upscale waiting area. A well-groomed receptionist in her early twenties sat behind a tall desk with fresh flowers. Abbie introduced herself and Clarke and then gave the young woman her card. The receptionist picked up the phone and, in a hushed tone, informed Brian Anderson that the police were there. She directed Abbie and Clarke to his office.

"Hello, Detective Taylor, Officer Clarke. Please have a seat." The lawyer was a small man. Maybe five foot five, but probably not. Abbie looked at his shoes and suspected he was wearing lifts, or what were now called "height-increasing insoles." He looked as if he could have been a wrestler. He was broad and strong, even with the softness that came from too much food and too much time spent at a desk.

"Thank you for making time to see us," Abbie said.

"Of course. Now, how can I help you?"

"We're investigating a homicide," Abbie said, "Steve Smith was killed."

"I'd heard he had passed away. I thought it was a heart attack or maybe . . . well, I didn't know it was a homicide. That's terrible." The lawyer looked genuinely surprised, but Abbie sensed there were other well-concealed responses to the news of Smith's homicide. Attorneys were trained to maintain confidentiality. Over the years, Abbie had come to know that interviews with lawyers were challenging because it was hard to distinguish between actual dissembling and professional discretion.

"How would you describe your relationship with Steve Smith?" Abbie asked.

"That's quite a broad question. We knew each other from church. We were friendly, I'd say."

"You must have been, to lend him a hundred and seventy-five thousand last year," Abbie said without missing a beat.

"Not really." The lawyer returned Abbie's volley with similar speed.

"What were the terms of the loan?"

"Twenty-two-point-five-percent interest." The lawyer had a clear memory of the details without being prompted. "Repayment in full one year after the date of the loan."

"A pretty good deal for you," Abbie said.

"A pretty good deal for both of us. Steve needed the money and he couldn't ask anyone else for it."

"You thought he was a good risk?" Abbie asked.

"I did," the lawyer replied.

"Why? He had filed for bankruptcy with Smith Construction, and couldn't get a bank loan. Why did you think he was a good risk?"

This question caused the lawyer to pause. Abbie wondered if he was trying to decide how much information to share or if he just didn't have a good answer to the question.

"At the time Steve came to me, he was getting this project in Costa Rica off the ground."

"You thought the project was promising?" Abbie asked.

"As a matter of fact, I did. That's why I was confident Steve would be able to pay me back. I knew he was in talks with at least one rather substantial investor."

"Someone from the Church?" Abbie asked.

"I believe so." This time it was clear to Abbie that professional discretion was not the source of her gut response to the lawyer's answer. This time, the lawyer was lying. Looking around the office, it was evident that Brian Anderson had done well for himself. Abbie glanced at his diplomas hanging on the wall behind him: undergrad at BYU and law school at Harvard. Anderson was not an idiot. He was not likely to make a loan for nearly two hundred thousand dollars without being rather certain that this real-estate project in Central America was likely to be successful. A ten-million-dollar investment from a General Authority would provide that assurance. There was little doubt in Abbie's mind that Smith would have been able to convince his "friend" to lend him money only if he had told him about Bowen's investment.

"Do you have a name for this substantial investor?" Abbie asked.

"I don't," the lawyer said. Abbie was certain he was lying to her, but she wasn't sure why.

"So now, you're out one seventy-five K?"

"It looks like it, and, worse, I had to admit to my wife I made a mistake. She wasn't happy about the loan in the first place. I'm going to be hearing about it for a long time." This time, the attorney was telling the truth. He was not going to relish living with his wife saying "I told you so" for the foreseeable future.

"Did anyone besides your wife know about your loan?"

"Not from me."

Lie number three—or is it four? Abbie was beginning not to like the short, smart attorney sitting across from her.

Attorney Anderson continued, "I don't think Steve wanted anyone to know, not even his wife. I got the distinct impression Melinda didn't know anything about their current dismal financial situation."

"Why did you think that?" Apparently, Abbie wasn't the only person who didn't think Melinda Smith was the kind of woman who had a clue about where the money she spent came from.

"That's a good question. I'm not sure why I thought that. It might have been something Steve said about needing money in the joint checking account. I don't like to make assumptions, but I think Steve was trying to keep up appearances. If he had to come to me for money, things must have gotten pretty bad for him financially. If he didn't have that Costa Rican project, I'm not sure what he was planning to do." Anderson picked up his pen and started tapping it on a yellow legal pad.

"You're left-handed?" Abbie asked.

"Uh, yeah." This was the first time the well-spoken man had used a filler word.

"Did you attack Steve Smith about a week before he died?"

The lawyer sighed loudly. He leaned back in his chair. He did not seem ready to do battle.

"I wouldn't use the word 'attack,' but, yeah, I hit him. I'm sorry I did. I shocked myself as much as I shocked Steve. It was one swift punch. I was just so darn mad. As soon as I did it, I apologized. Steve understood. He understood why I was angry. We were fine after that. It sort of cleared the air. He told me not to worry about getting my money back. He said he'd get it to me before he headed to Costa Rica."

"Did you know the date Smith was leaving for Costa Rica?" Abbie asked.

"The exact date? No. I knew he was going a week or two after we talked. Steve didn't tell me the exact day I'd get my money. He just said he'd get it to me before he left."

"When was the last time you saw Smith?" Abbie asked.

"The day I hit him."

"Do you know of anyone who might have wanted to kill Smith?"

"Not specifically. Steve and I live in entirely different professional worlds. I didn't know the people Steve worked with any more than he knew the people I work with. Having said that, and I say this reluctantly because I don't wish to speak ill of him, I wasn't oblivious to the rumors that

Steve left a lot of unhappy creditors when he filed for bankruptcy. There were plenty of angry people in Pleasant View who weren't paid for their hard work. It had to rankle when they'd see Steve and Melinda show up at church every Sunday driving expensive cars and wearing designer clothes. I don't think Steve Smith had much of a fan club."

SEVENTEEN

Abbie and Clarke headed back to the station after the conversation with the lawyer. Abbie had gone to her office to process the ME's report and what they'd learned from the attorney when her phone buzzed. It was a text from John. He was inviting her to dinner at his house, an impromptu thing. John had always been a pretty social guy and his wife was extremely laid-back. They were the kind of people to have a group of friends over at a moment's notice, pick up a stack of pizzas, toss a few big salads in large wooden bowls, and everyone would have a great time. No fuss, just fun.

John lived in Salt Lake, which was pretty much the halfway point between Abbie's place and her dad's. Her brother had made it clear that their dad would be there along with a few other friends but no other family. John knew things were still tense among his sisters and brothers when it came to Abbie. Apparently, he had decided to build one bridge at a time. Their dad was first. Abbie was tempted to claim she couldn't make it because of work, but the fact was she could make it. Smith's funeral was tomorrow morning. Henderson certainly wasn't breathing down her neck to solve a case she suspected he wanted to die a slow death anyway. There wasn't any need to burn the midnight oil going through the Zion Commerce documents or the contents of Smith's home office for the umpteenth time.

OKAY, I'LL BE THERE. Abbie hit send and the text swooshed through the air until it magically appeared on John's phone.

GREAT! John used exclamation points in his texts.

Abbie couldn't understand how John himself had managed to forgive their dad after their mom died. She had thought about it a lot and had come up with two theories. The first was that John really did believe the entire Mormon eschatology. If he believed that the family would be together in the Celestial Kingdom for eternity, forgiving their dad for disappearing in the days leading up to their mom's death wouldn't be so hard because a couple of days was nothing in the scheme of forever. The second theory was that John was naturally not judgmental. Actually, that wasn't so much a theory. John was one of the least judgmental people Abbie knew. It wasn't that he wasn't perceptive, but rather that he didn't feel it was his place to evaluate other people's beliefs and actions. If anything, Abbie begrudgingly admitted to herself, John not being judgmental made him more discerning, not less.

Clarke stuck his head through the open door of Abbie's office. "There's a basketball game at my ward tonight, if it's okay . . ."

"Go," Abbie said. "I'm heading out soon, too."

"See you tomorrow at the funeral, then." Clarke smiled

and walked down the hallway to his evening of church-sponsored fun.

Abbie looked at the time in the upper right corner of her computer screen. If she left now, she'd be able to pick up something sweet at the cupcake place on Kiesel Avenue in Ogden to bring as a hostess gift. There would undoubtedly be a huge number of kids at John's. Most Mormon families in Utah had at least four, which meant that even a dinner party with just three couples could easily add a dozen kids to the mix, usually more. Picking up two dozen cupcakes wouldn't be overkill.

Abbie checked her reflection in the rearview mirror of her Rover. She didn't look as bad as she had expected. She pulled out her sheer raspberry lipstick and dabbed a tiny amount on each cheek for color, then applied some to her lips and rubbed them together. Her hair was hanging in a tousled mess past her shoulders. There was nothing to be done about that.

The drive wasn't bad, considering the traffic on I-15. John's house was in the Avenues, one of the original nice neighborhoods in Salt Lake. The houses were older, more elegant, and much smaller than their McMansion cousins crawling up the foothills. It was almost like stepping into another era. By the time Abbie arrived, there were two large SUVs parked in the narrow two-car driveway. Abbie pulled behind a third SUV at the curb in front of the house. As soon as she opened her door, she breathed in the pleasant scent of charcoal and beef coming from the backyard.

The front door was open. Three teenage boys sat on the porch eating burgers and chips. They smiled at Abbie as she walked in carrying two large white boxes filled with cupcakes. A few teenage girls were huddled at one end of the long dining room table picking at hot dogs and baby carrots. The heart of the party was clearly in the backyard.

"Abs! I'm so glad you could make it. I told John this was ridiculously last minute, but you know him." Abbie's sister-in-law grinned at her husband's little sister. Abbie handed her the pastry boxes before they hugged.

" 'The Olde Cupcake Shoppe.' " She read the dark purple cursive on the lavender label affixed to the boxes. "You completely shouldn't have, but I'm very glad you did." Abbie's sister-in-law had a notorious sweet tooth, although you wouldn't know it to look at her.

The French doors that led to the backyard were open. John was at the grill with his oldest son, who was holding a large tray of toasted hamburger buns as his father slipped burgers onto them. A long picnic table was bustling with kids and their moms. In the center were all the fixings for burgers and hot dogs, including a big bowl of their mom's homemade hot dog relish, which was nothing more than diced dill pickles and white onion mixed with ketchup and yellow mustard, but somehow it was divine.

There was a small round table at the far end of the yard beneath an old apple tree. Her father was sitting there with two other men.

"Aunt Abbie, a burger or a hot dog?" Abbie's nephew hollered.

"A burger would be great." Abbie walked to the grill.

"I'm so glad you made it. Dad is, too." John handed Abbie her burger. It had a crispy brown shell encasing what Abbie knew was the perfect medium-rare meat inside. John was particular about his grilling. He would have made the patties several hours ago so that they could rest after he'd coated them with just a hint of vegetable oil and seasoned them with salt and pepper. Her brother had raised backyard grilling to a high art form.

"I'll join you over with Dad as soon as I get this batch done," John said. Abbie walked to the picnic table, where she squirted ketchup and mustard on the open bun and then layered pickles, red onion, and lettuce on the patty. She grabbed a handful of waffle-cut potato chips and a few carrots and cherry tomatoes.

Her dad looked older than she remembered, but still distinguished. If he had not actually become a professor, he could have played one on TV. It was as if old tweed jackets and corduroy trousers slightly beyond their donate-to-Goodwill date had been made for him. He could happily talk for days about his area of expertise. Luckily for him, in the state of Utah there was an endless supply of eager listeners.

"Abish. John told me you might be able to make it. It's nice to see you." Professor Taylor's stilted conversational style was not solely the result of the iciness in his relationship with his daughter. Decades of lecturing seemed to have atrophied his non-monologue conversation muscles. He always seemed to be holding court.

One of the two men sitting at the table introduced himself to Abbie; the other man was Flynn.

"Nice to see you, Abs." He stood up and gave her the kind of quick hug close friends and family members gave each other when they greeted.

Abbie took a chair across from Flynn and next to her dad.

"As I was saying, the idea of the preexistence . . ."

Abbie concentrated on the result of her brother's grilling genius, letting her dad's words blend into white noise. She just didn't have the energy for a serious academic discussion. Flynn was making all the polite sounds of following along, but it was clear this religious conversation was no more interesting to him than it was to Abbie. The other man, however, was enthralled. He kept asking questions and Professor Taylor kept answering them.

Finally, John made it over. The moment he sat down, the entire table lightened up.

"Done! The grill is officially closed. If any of those teenage boys are still hungry, they'll have to eat cupcakes." John winked at his sister.

The wife of the man who was eating up every word that dropped from Professor's Taylor's lips came over to inform her husband that one of their daughters had an early morning dance-team practice, so they needed to get everyone home. The man seemed loathe to leave, but said his good-byes as instructed. The moment provided John and Flynn an excuse to disappear, too.

"So, I'm told this case of yours has turned out to be a homicide." Abbie's dad had barely touched his burger. He had nibbled at a few potato chips and drunk most of what looked like lemon-lime soda in his clear plastic cup.

"You've been correctly informed," Abbie said.

"No leads though?" Abbie's dad asked. Abbie couldn't help but wonder if she heard a hint of relief in his usually stern tone.

"No. I can't really discuss this. You know that," Abbie said.

"Yes, yes, of course. I just wondered if you'd found any links to the Church, you know. No tenuous connection to Church business interests or anything . . ."

Abbie waited for her dad to finish his thought. He didn't. It was, for Professor Taylor, a rather clumsy attempt to fish for information. Abbie wondered if he'd realized he'd tipped his hand by mentioning a business connection. Was Bowen's investment that important? Or was keeping Bowen's connection to Smith's business from becoming public that important?

Apparently, from across the yard, Abbie's conversation with her dad looked friendly enough. John kept glancing her way, trying not to look as if he was keeping an eye on them. She wondered how long he was going to leave them there sitting under the tree. The sky was turning lavender with streaks of pink. Abbie had Smith's funeral in the morning and it would take well over an hour to make it home.

"Dad, it's been good to see you," Abbie said finally. She had given up on John coming back to check on them and rescue her.

"You, too," her dad said.

Abbie wasn't sure that she meant the statement any more than he did. They had been civil, though, and that was a start.

"I've got an early morning, so I need to get going." Abbie bent down to give her father a rather awkward hug. She walked across the yard. The other families had successfully harangued kids into SUVs. Both boxes of the cupcakes were empty. Flynn was standing alone with John. They were laughing about something. Abbie walked over to say goodbye to her sister-in-law, who was busily tossing paper plates and plastic cups into an oversized black garbage bag. "Thanks so much." Abbie tossed some napkins and a few plastic cups into the bag. Her sister-in-law set the bag down and gave Abbie a hug.

"You know how much you mean to us. We're always here for you. I'm always here for you." Her sister-in-law stressed the word "I," then continued, "That husband of mine can be a pain. I'm just a phone call away."

Abbie knew her sister-in-law meant every word. The two of them had always gotten along. She knew her other sisters weren't so keen on John's wife. That might have had something to do with why she and Abbie got along so well.

"Thanks," Abbie said. "I know."

"You leaving?" John and Flynn had come over, hands full of the remaining detritus from the dinner. They each deposited their collection into the trash bag. John gave his little sister a big bear hug.

Abbie stood facing Flynn. The sky was dark now and the backyard was completely abandoned. The light from the kitchen spilled onto the patio. Abbie could hear the pleasant banter of a happily married couple inside as they finished with the cleanup. Her dad must have gone inside as well.

Flynn hugged Abbie. "Let's see each other again soon." Abbie hugged him back. She didn't look on purpose, but she couldn't help but notice he wasn't wearing a wedding band. She made her way to her Rover, which was now parked alone in front of the house. As she climbed into her old car, she felt the flutter of butterflies in her stomach. She pulled away from the curb and started the drive home.

You know, it's getting to be time. Abbie heard Phillip's words whisper in her ear. She wasn't sure how she felt about that.

EIGHTEEN

Organ music floated from the chapel into the lobby. Abbie had expected to have some kind of emotional response when she arrived at Smith's funeral. The last funeral she'd been to had been Phillip's, and before that it had been her mom's. Still, despite her best efforts to prepare, she felt a despair that nearly suffocated her when she walked into the church. The viewing had started about an hour ago and was ending now. The mortician had done a masterful job. The gash in Steve Smith's neck was completely hidden beneath his white button-down shirt and tie. Endowed members of the Church were buried in their temple clothes, so Melinda Smith had had to find a second white suit for her husband. The white clothes Steve had been wearing when his body was discovered were still in the police evidence closet. Abbie doubted they'd be able to get the bloodstains out anyway, even if the suit was mostly made of a polyester blend.

People began taking their seats in the chapel. Abbie took the program a young man handed her and then sat next to Clarke at the back of the chapel. While friends were shuffling into the chapel, the family was ensconced in a private room with the casket for the last viewing of the body. Bishop Norton would be making some soothing comments to them about salvation. Then a family member would give the family prayer before they joined the rest of the people gathered in the chapel.

The men were dressed in suits and ties. The women wore either blouses and knee-length skirts or loose-flowing dresses, mostly in floral prints of all sizes and colors. Abbie knew the lack of dark colors could strike non-Mormons as strange, but LDS funerals were not focused on grief because death was just part of the eternal plan of salvation.

Abbie glanced at the program. Exactly on cue, at the scheduled start time, Bishop Norton stood at the podium.

"Brothers and Sisters, on behalf of the Smith family, I welcome you all on this solemn occasion. I say solemn and not sad, because even though Brother Smith was called back to our Father in Heaven at a time few of us expected, we can all take comfort in knowing that his passing is part of our Heavenly Father's plan. Steve and Melinda Smith were married in the temple, and they, like all of us, have the opportunity to live eternally with their family in the presence of our Heavenly Father as long as they follow the principles of His restored gospel."

Abbie had always found LDS funerals strange because they focused so much on Church doctrine and so little on the person who died. Bishop Norton said a few more words about God's plan for salvation and resurrection. After that, Steve's younger brother spoke, providing a résumé of the Church leadership positions Steve had held during his life.

Then he made a point of mentioning how he never swore, always paid his tithing—even when it was difficult—and followed the Word of Wisdom. He proclaimed his brother to be a model of Christlike behavior. Abbie felt discomfort settle in her stomach. She knew the religion of her birth was not unique in its focus on perfection, but Abbie felt there was a shallowness in suggesting that the absence of sin made a person perfect. This kind of perfection—flawlessness—felt cold. Abbie believed spiritual teaching should help people become more compassionate of shared human shortcomings, not less forgiving of them. Jesus probably swore from time to time; he got angry enough to turn over tables and he certainly drank wine. Abbie wondered if Christ himself—with his distinctly antimaterialistic ways, his motley crew of friends, and his long, straggly hair and a beard—would be considered Christlike in this crowd.

"Amen." Abbie was brought back from her daydreaming as everyone murmured their shared agreement at the end of the prayer.

The family was getting ready to head to the cemetery. Others were milling around the lobby waiting to line up at the buffet tables in the multipurpose room next door, where the Relief Society was preparing the post-funeral luncheon. Abbie glanced around the lobby. She saw Melinda with a girl who looked as if she must be her oldest daughter, probably the girl Melinda had told them liked to drive her BMW convertible. They were standing with the Bishop. The attorney was talking to a beautiful blonde who looked familiar to Abbie, but she wasn't sure why. She scanned the room for other familiar faces. The woman from the dry cleaner's was there, but she didn't see anyone else she knew.

"Taylor!"

Abbie turned around to see Clarke whispering as loudly as he could. She knew he was trying to be discrete. He was failing.

"Is everything okay?" Abbie could see Clarke was agitated or excited or both, maybe.

"I just got an email from a secretary who works at the airport. I think she's the assistant to the head of security. She has transferred all the footage we need to a thumb drive. She asked if we wanted her to mail it to us or if we wanted to pick it up," Clarke said.

"You told her we'd pick it up," The words came out of her mouth with more enthusiasm than she intended.

"Of course!"

"Let's go,"

They both knew that whatever information they got from the airport, it would move the case forward. If the Hummer had never been in short-term parking, Melinda Smith was going to have some explaining to do. If the Hummer had made it to the airport, how had it gotten there?

Clarke was speeding, but Abbie didn't mind. Before she knew it, they were walking into the office of airport security.

"Hello," Clarke said to a young man sitting behind a desk, "I'm Officer Jim Clarke. Mrs. Sullivan said she would leave an envelope for me."

"Oh, yeah." The young man handed Clarke a padded

manila envelope with "Officer Jim Clarke" neatly printed on it. "Here you go."

"Thank you!" Clarke exclaimed.

The drive from the airport didn't take any longer than the drive to the airport did, but somehow it seemed to last an eternity. Abbie couldn't wait to see the footage. As soon as they got to the station, they both sprinted to Abbie's office.

She motioned for Clarke to sit down at her computer. He inserted the thumb drive. Clarke peeled off a Post-it with "Short-term parking" written in tiny letters on it. The time stamp said 12:01. It was dark, and until 4:30 there were only a few cars that came through. After 4:30, though, there was a pretty steady stream of cars and trucks. Abbie was standing behind Clarke as they both stared at the screen. It was extraordinarily boring . . . until it wasn't.

At 8:36 AM, there it was: the yellow Hummer. The camera was angled to give a pretty clear view of the plates; it was Smith's license number, all right. The angle of the recording was not so great for identifying the driver, though.

"Is there anything we can do?" Abbie asked. She knew the tech guys could sometimes perform miracles. Her eyes were blurry and her head hurt from staring at the screen so long.

Clarke shook his head. "I don't think so. The problem is the angle of the camera in the parking lot. No matter how much we clean up the picture—and I don't think there's much room for improvement—it's not going to change the perspective. I'll double-check that with IT though—the angle of the camera is what the angle of the camera is. I doubt we're going to get anything clear enough to identify who was driving that Hummer."

"Okay, let's just look at it again," Abbie instructed.

Clarke sighed. He was getting frustrated, too. "Dang it! I can't even tell if it's a man or a woman driving." The driver was wearing a dark hoodie and was definitely smaller and shorter than Steve Smith.

"You're right. We're not going to be able to tell who the driver is," Abbie said, "but someone took the trouble to drive that yellow Hummer to the airport, and that someone knew when Smith was leaving for Costa Rica. Even if we can't identify the driver, we know a lot more than we did yesterday."

NINETEEN

Abbie had suggested they get something to eat after spending the better part of the day at Smith's funeral and then staring at the computer screen. Getting away from the station would do both of them some good.

The restaurant was dark, even though there was a wall of windows at the back. It was one of those Mexican barbecues where you pointed at the meat, vegetables, and sauces you wanted and the person behind the counter assembled your taco, burrito, or bowl. You took your food on a large orange tray along with pale-brown recycled paper napkins to an open table of your choice. The chairs matched the trays.

Clarke got a Sprite, an oversized beef burrito, and two pork tacos. Abbie opted for two chicken tacos with extra-hot tomatillo salsa. She filled her pebbled red plastic cup with lemonade and a lot of ice.

"Something's been bothering me about what happened with the airport. I'm not sure it's anything, but I think you should know." Clarke had already finished off one of his tacos and was starting on the second. "I've never been involved in a murder investigation. You know that, but I have worked with security at the airport before. A few years ago, there was a big Ponzi scheme run by a bishop up in Huntsville. The guy ended up getting caught on the tarmac at the airport down in St. George. He was on his way to some non-extraditable place in Latin America. Anyway, that's not the point I'm trying to make . . . the point I want to make is . . . I worked with security at the airport then. They're efficient and quick. It took hours, not days, to get the footage we needed."

"I'm not sure I'm following," Abbie said.

"The secretary who called, well, she said something odd. She apologized that it had taken so long. She told me she hadn't checked the logbook, but she saw my original request. She said it had been flagged and, even though she wasn't usually the person who took care of this kind of thing, she was in early and had time to review all requests to make sure they were up to date."

"Okay . . ." Abbie took another bite of her taco.

"Well, she's the secretary for the head of security, the guy who was supposed to be traveling, the guy I was told was traveling. I was just making conversation, you know, being nice, and said something about it being hard to keep track of things for your boss when he's out of the office. She said her boss wasn't out of the office, that he never misses work and hasn't traveled for over a year."

"Any chance you could've misunderstood?"

"No," Clarke said. "I've been on the phone with the people at the airport more times than I can count since Melinda Smith told us about that yellow Hummer. I started thinking I was being given the runaround, but I tried to give them the benefit of the doubt. I think the only reason we got the thumb drive is because some highly organized secretary took care of what she saw as a request that hadn't been responded to. I think our request had been flagged because nobody was supposed to respond."

"That sounds conspiratorial," Abbie said.

"I know." Clarke scraped the bottom of the paper bowl to get the last remnants of rice and beans. "I don't like it. I don't like it at all. And, you know what? If I hadn't worked with airport security before, I might have been able to believe Henderson's story about them being overworked and understaffed. They're not. On top of that, there's the clear lie about the boss traveling. There are just too many things to think it's a coincidence."

"For a moment, let's assume you're right and what happened was not simply the result of extraordinary incompetence or an office so understaffed that it takes months to do what should take days. Who would have an interest in us not seeing the security footage? Who would have the ability to keep us from it?"

"I have some ideas," Clarke said. "I don't like any of them."

Abbie sipped her lemonade. "What are you thinking?"

"We have to figure out what's going on in Costa Rica. It looks like Steve was stealing money from investors. Then there are all the people he already owed money to before the Celestial Times Shares project. If we think of this in nonreligious terms, we could make a list of just the people who lost money to Steve. Given the blood atonement angle, though, we probably should include the possibility that someone thought Steve was breaking the Law of Consecration by stealing from the Church. I did a little research and read about some stories—not very credible ones—of pioneers 'atoning' for stealing cows back in the day of Brigham Young. I wouldn't think taking money for private resorts near temples would constitute withholding money intended to further the Lord's interests on earth, but some people might."

Abbie was impressed with Clarke's research. The two of them picked up their trays and deposited the remnants of their lunches into the square trash cans near the restaurant's exit.

"Let's go figure out Costa Rica, then," Abbie said.

TWENTY

Clarke and Abbie spent the rest of the day trying to get through to the right people in Costa Rica. It was an exercise in frustration. The telephone numbers they had were out-of-date or disconnected, and the few times they did reach an actual human being, the person who could have helped them was out of the office.

Abbie heard Clarke's stomach growl for the third time. She looked at the clock. They had gotten carried away and hadn't realized that the rest of the office, with the exception of the one officer whose turn it was to take the night shift, had left.

"Let's call it a day," Abbie said. Clarke agreed.

By the time she got home, Clarke's wasn't the only stomach growling. Abbie opened her fridge feeling equal parts dread and hope: dread that there wasn't anything edible inside and hope that she'd forgotten some leftover that would take no time to reheat. Her dread had been well-founded. Abbie emptied the contents of a container of Icelandic yogurt into a bowl and poured a generous amount of muesli on top.

She was sifting through her mail as she ate her dinner when her phone buzzed. It was John.

"I know it's short notice. Dad wants to be at Pineview at the crack of dawn. There's some special bird he wants to add to his life list. He's become quite the birder. We'll swing by after. It'll just be breakfast. You have to eat anyway. We'll be gone before you have to leave for work. I promise."

"I really don't have the time; this case is going nowhere and it's my fault. There's something I'm missing. On top of that, it seems that everything I try to get done is taking me four times as long as it should. If I were a conspiracy theorist, I'd say someone was trying to make my job harder. Even my partner thinks so."

Abbie felt conflicted. She'd love to see John, but there was no food in the house, so putting something together for breakfast tomorrow morning would be an effort. Plus, even though she had managed to chat with her dad at John's the other night without raising her voice, she felt her chest tighten just thinking about seeing him again so soon. Abbie was never sure if he'd say something that would trigger her. Even though she knew on an intellectual level that she needed to forgive him for not being there at the end—forgive him for putting the Church before family—she hadn't been able to move that understanding in her head to a feeling in her heart.

"We won't stay that long. I promise. I know you just saw Dad and it went okay. I was surprised when he called me today to ask if I'd mind driving up tomorrow. He claimed it was about the birds, but you know how Dad asks for things without really 'asking' for them? Well, he wanted me to see if we could stop by. Breakfast was my idea. I figured that would make it easy for you to escape if things get heated. You can completely say you have to get to work."

Abbie didn't answer.

"So, breakfast?"

Abbie was still thinking.

"Would it make a difference if I told you Flynn was coming along?" John asked. "He'll need to eat breakfast, too."

John had always been able to read Abbie. She hadn't really given Flynn much thought since she'd seen him at John's—except, if she was honest with herself, she wouldn't mind seeing him again. Evidently, John knew that.

"You still there, Abs?"

"Yes."

"Did I mention Flynn's divorced?"

No, Abbie thought, *you didn't.* She wasn't sure if that made her feel better or worse.

"It was ugly at the end, but for the best. Even I have to admit it." That was a lot for John to say. Her brother had married his high school sweetheart in the Provo temple and was now father to five beautiful, happy kids. Abbie adored them all as much as she adored his wife. "We're on for breakfast then." John said these words as a statement, not a question.

"I didn't say that," Abbie said.

"Sure you did. See you in the morning. Seven thirty–ish. The birds Dad wants to see do their thing early . . . Abs, if it makes a difference, I can pick up doughnuts."

"No, I think I can manage breakfast for four," Abbie said.

"I love you," John said.

"Love you, too."

Abbie opened up her cabinets, hoping that somehow she'd have the ingredients for breakfast magically appear in her kitchen. Reality was less helpful. She knew John would happily bring breakfast if she asked, but Abbie wanted to do something nice. There wasn't enough food in the house for one person, let alone four.

It had been a while since she'd cooked for more than herself. She'd once hosted brunches, dinners, teas, and cocktail parties in the City and at their place upstate all the time. They'd liked entertaining. As Abbie tried to find a recipe for a prosciutto strata she'd used to make all the time, she felt the familiar pleasure of planning food for friends and family. Was it an *Epicurious* recipe or from *The New York Times*? She read through three recipes with the ingredients she could remember before she found the right one. She jotted down a list of what she needed on her phone and headed to the grocery store.

An hour later, she was back in the kitchen with fresh-squeezed orange juice, whole milk, cream, arugula, fresh mozzarella, basil, tomatoes, garlic, pine nuts, prosciutto, eggs, and hearty bread that was not a day old, but, Abbie hoped, would hold up to being layered with the prosciutto, cheese, pesto, tomatoes, and arugula. She'd also bought the best of the berries that were on offer.

The strata had been one of her signature brunch dishes. Even when the bread wasn't quite up to snuff, the combination of warm melted mozzarella with prosciutto, pesto, and tomato remedied any baguette-related shortcomings. Fresh berries served as a nice counterpoint to the hearty morning dish. In New York, the berries had been the food of choice for Phillip and Abbie's ultra-thin female friends, who partook of food only when social engagements required it. Tomorrow, the berries would be dipped in the crème fraîche mixed with brown sugar and vanilla without any thought to calories.

Abbie poured an egg mixture over the layers in a deep white ramekin, took the last sip from her glass of a very crisp New Zealand sauvignon blanc, and put the strata into the fridge. She thought about all the times she'd made this before: for close friends staying the weekend upstate; for larger groups the morning of the New York City marathon. She'd never done adult things, like hosting a brunch, in her home state. She'd left after her senior year in high school and had never returned for more than a brief visit. Even the summer after her freshman year, she'd managed to find an internship in Manhattan and stayed with a friend whose parents had an enormous apartment on Central Park West. This would be the first time she would be having her dad over for a meal as a grown-up here in Utah.

Abbie placed four dark-gray place mats made from some sort of indestructible recycled material on her dining room table. She pulled open the top drawer of her pale wood sideboard and counted out four pale-gray linen napkins. They had been carefully ironed one night after she'd first moved in. It was when Abbie hadn't started work yet and had found herself watching a reality TV show she was embarrassed to be watching. As penance, she had ironed all her linens as she indulged in that guilty pleasure.

After she finished setting the table, she stepped back to look at what would be the first table she'd set for company since Phillip died. *Nicely done.* Phillip didn't always articulate that he appreciated Abbie's attention to detail, but she liked to think he did. She looked at the table again, then grabbed some kitchen scissors from a wooden block and walked outside into the dark. She didn't have many options, but she was able to find some pretty leaves. She snipped them short and arranged half a dozen shot-glass-sized vases in the center of the table.

She surveyed the result of her efforts. Now, with the addition of leaves and wild flowers scattered among the place settings, it looked like one of her tables.

She needed to get to sleep. She was going to have to get the strata in the oven with enough time for it to bake and rest before the guys arrived. Abbie headed upstairs to wash her face and brush her teeth. She pulled on soft, well-worn flannel pajama bottoms and a tank top. Abbie opened the windows. The room was chilly for the tank top, but she slept better when it was cool. Her mother had been a big believer in the health benefits of fresh air. Every Saturday when her mom did her heavy housecleaning, she'd throw open the windows unless there was a blizzard or a rainstorm. Even then, her mom would weigh the risk of getting the windowsills wet against the advantages of fresh air. Abbie doubted there were any demonstrable health benefits to giving houses a good airing out or sleeping in rooms with open windows, but the habits of childhood were hard to break.

★★★

"Good morning!" John gave his little sister a big hug. "Smells good. I guess we can eat the doughnuts I picked up later."

Abbie smiled, but knew John had probably picked up delectable pastries and an assortment of yogurt and fruit just in case she hadn't managed to pull anything together for breakfast on such short notice. Undoubtedly, there was breakfast for four in the cooler in the trunk of his car.

Flynn gave Abbie a hug as he came in. "Thanks for doing this. I know John sprung us on you at the last minute."

"Any good birds?" Abbie directed the question to all of them, but suspected that only her father was really interested. John had learned the names of birds but had never been one to pore over bird books trying to identify something he'd spotted for the first time.

"Yes!" her father responded, with an enthusiasm he reserved only for birds. "A female osprey and a bobolink. I was hoping to spot a horned grebe, but no luck this morning." Even though her dad was dressed for birdwatching, he still looked every bit a professor: carefully ironed khaki pants and a blue flannel shirt somehow looked as formal as if he were in wool trousers and a blazer. His pale-blue eyes shone through his round glasses. They were still bright eyes, but they had dimmed some since her mom had died.

"It's good to see you, Abish. I'm glad John arranged this." Abbie thought she heard some warmth in her dad's voice, but she sensed there was something else, something that made her a little uncomfortable. Abbie brushed it off as a knee-jerk reaction and shifted her focus to breakfast.

"I'm famished," John announced on cue. "Can we eat?"

"Please, help yourselves." Abbie waved at the table, which now had a large white ramekin at its center with a pie server resting on a plate to the side. Pesto was drizzled over the concentric circles of tomatoes beneath golden cheese. To one side of the strata were a bowl of strawberries and cappuccino-colored crème fraîche; to the other side was a slender crystal pitcher of orange juice.

"I have milk, too, and coffee and tea, if anyone would like." Abbie knew neither her father or brother would take her up on coffee or tea, but she didn't know about Flynn.

"I'd love some coffee," Flynn said.

Abbie poured Flynn a cup of coffee and set a shiny silver carafe on the table.

Flynn raised his cup. "A toast to our hostess for treating us early-morning birders to such a feast."

John raised his glass of orange juice. He was grinning. Abbie's dad looked awkwardly at his glass, but raised it after a moment.

By eight in the morning, the entire strata, meant to serve up to ten people, had been devoured. One lone strawberry lay in its bowl. The bowl of crème fraîche was wiped clean. Flynn and John were laughing about the morning and recounting stories that would have been funny to only those present at the time.

"Abish, can we talk?" Abbie's dad asked.

Abbie was surprised by how serious he sounded, but then remembered that John had told her their dad had been the one to orchestrate this breakfast. Abbie wondered if her dad knew John had told her he was behind this early-morning meeting.

"Of course," Abbie said.

Her dad remained silent.

"Would you like to go somewhere private?" Abbie lowered her voice.

"Yes, that would be good."

"We're not good enough company for you?" John teased when Abbie and their dad stood up from the table.

"Exactly." Abbie winked at her brother.

Abbie showed her dad into her study on the other side of the kitchen. It had French doors leading onto a stone terrace with a large outdoor dining table. The view was up the mountainside into the trees. Like the rest of the house, the office was uncluttered and gave an appreciative nod to Scandinavian design. Her dad sat down on a slate-colored upholstered chair in the corner, but did not put his feet on the matching ottoman. Abbie sat in her desk chair but turned it away from the desk so she could face her dad.

"I don't want to alarm you, but I think it's important to tell you about a recent conversation I had with Port."

It had been a long time since Abbie had heard that name. Port was an old family friend. Abbie had no idea how long he and her dad had known each other, but she did know their friendship predated her parents' marriage. She also knew their friendship had survived some very serious disagreements about Church doctrine. In Abbie's mind, her father was a conservative apologist, but from the perspective of BYU and most Church leaders, her father was just barely on the right side of being a tolerable progressive. Port and his family had spent many Sunday dinners with the Taylors when Abbie was little. Most of the time, the kids would be excused to play and the wives would clean up while Professor Taylor and Port engaged in lengthy discussions about the scriptures.

Port was a secret nickname. It was a reference to Orrin Porter Rockwell, also known as the "Destroying Angel of Mormondom," the famous bodyguard to both Joseph Smith and Brigham Young who was known for his skill as a gunfighter and his fierce loyalty to the Church. During grand jury questioning for the attempted assassination of the governor of Missouri, Porter Rockwell had argued he was not guilty because he "never shot *at* anybody, if I shoot they get shot!" Not too many people knew the current Second Counselor to the President's nickname—which had absolutely nothing to do with his actual name—but Abbie did.

"Okay, Dad," Abbie said. "I'm listening."

"Yesterday, I can't remember when exactly, I came into my office, and my assistant, you know, the very bright graduate student who is going on to get his PhD in religious studies at Stanford . . . anyway, he told me he'd been getting calls all morning. Someone was upset that I wasn't returning my cell phone calls."

"Okay?" Abbie wasn't sure where her dad was going with all this. She was trying not to be impatient, but she did need to get to work.

"Port told me he wanted to speak to me about my daughter, the detective."

Abbie felt her chest tighten. Why did Port want to talk about her?

"He told me he was going to ignore my role in, and these are his words, 'disseminating untruths about the history of changes made to the temple ceremony and who may or may not have supported said changes' and the Strengthening Church Members Committee file on you and me. He said he wanted to talk to me about your investigation in Pleasant View and what conclusions you may or may not have drawn from the ME and the airport. I don't know what those last references mean, but I imagine you do."

Even though her dad was not making a big deal about the SCMC comment, the threat was not lost on Abbie. As a professor at the Y, her dad's career was dependent upon supporting the Church. She knew there were professors in other departments—sociology, political science, psychology—who'd ended up on the wrong side of a disciplinary hearing because their academic research seemed to be at odds with views held by some of the Brethren. They not only lost their religious affiliation; they lost their jobs.

"It has taken the Church years to escape the public-relations nightmare of the penalty oaths. You know that younger members and new converts often misunderstood those oaths when they went for their endowments in the temple. They found them disturbing rather than uplifting. Your investigation could destroy all that hard work the Church has done to make the gospel more appealing. The Church has spent time and money to improve its image. Port said I'd faint if I knew how much the 'I'm a Mormon' advertisements on New York City taxicabs cost."

"What does Port want?" Abbie asked. She felt anger bubbling inside her. Her dad had shown, again, that he was putting the interests of the Church ahead of the interests of his family. Abbie was trying her best not to let her face reflect what she was feeling. She doubted she was doing a very good job of it.

"He was vague. You know how Port is. You must be discrete. It's important this case stays out of the press, or what do they call it? The case needs to stay out of social media. It's important not to bring up doctrines that could upset members of the Church, let alone cause a ruckus among anti-Mormons who happily make anything into a scandal."

All of a sudden Abbie understood why her work on this case had been harder than it should be. It wasn't just because Henderson was squeamish about the temple clothes and the throat slitting that looked a little too much like blood atonement for his comfort. Her mind flashed to all those closed doors and quiet phone calls. Had Henderson been informing someone from that very first morning in the basement closet? Was Port why she'd had to dash out of Zion Commerce with Smith's financial information before the receptionist could catch up with her? Was Port the reason it had taken an overachieving secretary to get the footage from the airport? Clarke's conspiracy theory didn't seem so baseless.

"Dad, are you talking about a blanket we-don't-want-any-bad-PR, or is there something more?" Given that Port had found out about the airport and ME information almost as soon as she and Clarke had, Abbie had a sick feeling that Port's interest went beyond the routine "we don't want bad press."

"It seems the victim was overseeing some real-estate ventures for the Church. The man was not as upstanding as one would hope. His personal shortcomings shouldn't be allowed to reflect badly on the Church."

"Are you serious, Dad?"

Her dad closed his pale-blue eyes. "Yes. Abish, It would not be good to give anti-Mormons a chance to rehash things that are no longer relevant. Please make sure this case stays under the radar."

Abbie's desire to keep her composure evaporated. "No one has picked up the story anywhere. I'm not in the business of talking to reporters." Her words were clipped. She sounded annoyed and she didn't care.

"I know. I told Port that."

"Did you tell him you would talk to me?" Abbie asked.

"Yes, I did. I think it's the right thing to do."

Abbie was happy she hadn't eaten much of the strata. She was feeling a little nauseated.

"Dad, did you even go bird-watching this morning, or was that just a ruse to deliver Port's message?"

"Yes. Yes, we did go out looking for birds. I just needed to talk to you, too. I don't take orders from Port."

Abbie wanted to respond, "But that's exactly what you're doing," but she stopped herself. Something in her dad's tone made her think twice. She could see it in his tired eyes. Maybe this entire conversation had been hard on him, too.

"Dad, is that all?"

Professor Taylor took off his glasses and cleaned them with a soft cloth he pulled from his shirt pocket. Abbie saw the movement for what it was: a stalling technique.

"Dad? Is that it?" Abbie asked again.

"The last thing Port said to me was, 'This needs to go well.' "

Abbie didn't ask her dad to interpret the statement. They both knew the words were meant to be a threat.

TWENTY-ONE

It was a relief to pull into the parking lot of the Pleasant View City Police Department. John and Flynn had cleaned up breakfast while Abbie and her dad were having their conversation. John had read the tension as soon as Abbie opened the door to her study. He and Flynn had said quick good-byes. Her dad hadn't given her a hug and she hadn't wanted one.

When Abbie walked into the station, Clarke was already on the phone, trying to get through to the police in Costa Rica. Clarke's Spanish was excellent. He wasn't one to brag, but when he had mentioned that his Spanish was "okay," that was a laughable understatement. Clarke had served his mission in Peru. Abbie later discovered that while Clarke was at the MTC, the acronym for the Missionary Training Center, he had been known as a linguistic whiz kid.

After the frustration of the day before, neither Abbie nor Clarke expected to make much progress anytime soon, but they were pleasantly surprised when an officer in San José returned their call. Abbie picked out a word here and there as Clarke engaged in a lengthy conversation in Spanish.

"So?" she asked after he put down his phone.

"The detective I spoke with, Officer Segura, actually knew who Smith was because Segura grew up in a town not too far from San José, a place called Jacó. Anyway, Jacó's a kind of vacation town. Turns out, that's where Smith bought a rather expensive place on the beach. According to Segura, Smith and his wife were big spenders."

"Wife? Melinda told us she had never been to Costa Rica, but Bowen mentioned Smith's wife. I didn't know what to make of that. Now we have someone else talking about her."

"Yeah, but there's something about Segura's description of the wife that makes me think he wasn't talking about Melinda Smith," Clarke said. "He described the wife as young and quite beautiful. Not to be unkind, but I don't think even the most generous person would describe Melinda Smith as either young or beautiful."

Clarke would never be unkind, but Abbie had to admit he was right. "So any idea who this 'Mrs. Smith' actually is?"

"Segura was certain she was American. He said she was blonde and liked to wear a bikini. He thought he might be able to find a picture because the Smiths liked to go out and even went to some local fund-raisers. I gave him my email in case he found photos."

"What about the bank account information?" Abbie asked.

"If we go through official channels, it could take months or even longer. We'd have to send a letter rogatory, which is some kind of legal request from a court here to a Costa Rican court that compels the bank to release the information. My Spanish is okay, but discussing legal issues is a bit out of my comfort zone, so I could've misunderstood some of what was said. Segura thinks because it's a murder investigation, he can make a few calls and get us the information we need through unofficial channels."

"That'd be great," Abbie said. "Did he know anything about the temple in San José or about Celestial Time Shares?"

"He knew all about the temple, but he hadn't heard anything about Celestial Time Shares or any kind of Mormon resort," Clarke said.

"Great work!"

Clarke couldn't hide a shy smile at Abbie's compliment. In just a few phone calls, he had managed to move the investigation forward in a way Abbie could never have done on her own. She was feeling optimistic that they'd have information from the Banco de Costa Rica soon.

Clarke's phone beeped. He looked down.

"It's from Segura."

Abbie waited while he read the email and opened an attachment.

"Hmmm, this is odd. Segura sent an article from a newspaper about a Mormon leader visiting in San José for a temple rededication ceremony. There's a picture of a few Apostles and Elder Bowen in front of the temple. It's from the week before Smith was killed."

Clarke handed his phone to Abbie. Sure enough, it was Bowen, smiling in front of the San José temple six days before Smith was killed.

★ ★ ★

"I need to run this by Henderson first." It went against every fiber of her being to ask permission before interviewing a suspect who had lied to her. The day had flown by with their conversations with the police officer in Costa Rica. It was past five and Henderson's office was dark. Abbie dialed Henderson's number, but it went straight to voicemail. She tried to resist the pull of confronting Bowen with the picture of him in front of the temple in San José. She told herself that nothing would change if she waited until tomorrow, after she'd had a chance to ask Henderson's permission. She really tried, but in the end, Abbie simply could not resist. There would be a steep price, but she was willing to pay it.

"Do you want to sit this one out? I'll take the heat from Henderson," Abbie said.

"No. I'm coming with you." Clarke's tone was unequivocal.

Dusk was a beautiful time to drive to Bountiful. The outline of the jagged peaks of the Oquirrh Mountains in the west looked as if they'd been torn from black construction paper and placed on top of a watercolor of deep blues, pinks, and purples. Clarke drove south on I-84. Abbie had wanted to drive in the police car instead of arriving more discreetly in her Rover. She wanted to send Bowen a signal.

Neither Clarke nor Abbie spoke during the entire drive from Pleasant View to Bountiful. Bowen was not going to appreciate his surprise visitors, and Henderson was going to be furious as soon as he found out about the interview.

Abbie worried Clarke might regret his decision to come with her, but she respected him for it.

A few moments after Clarke rang the doorbell at the Bowen residence, an athletic teenage boy with thick, dark-blond hair and the good looks of his father answered the door.

"Hello?" the boy asked.

"Hello," Abbie responded. "We're here to see your dad. Is he home?"

"Yeah." The boy turned his head back inside and yelled, "Da-ad! It's for you."

He then turned back to face Abbie and Clarke. He wore the confidence of a boy who excelled at sports in a culture that valued athletic prowess. Abbie heard a man's footsteps. The boy opened the door more widely: Elder Bowen stood in front of Abbie and Clarke. He wasn't able to conceal his distaste for the unwelcome guests on his doorstep. He recovered quickly, but not quickly enough to hide his initial reaction.

"Detective Taylor, I wish you'd called. We're in the middle of a family dinner," he said, as though this excused him from whatever had brought the police to his door.

Abbie smiled broadly. "Oh, Mr. Bowen, this won't take long. Why don't you just step outside so we can talk without disturbing your family?"

Bowen was caught off guard again, but before he could respond one way or the other, his son made the decision for him. "Dad, I'll tell Mom you have to talk to some people. Church stuff, right?"

Without waiting for his father to respond, the boy

walked back inside the house. Bowen stepped outside, quietly shutting the front door behind him.

"Mr. Bowen, last time we spoke, you told me you had never been to Costa Rica. Now, we have this photo of you in San José taken less than a week before Steve Smith was killed." Abbie turned her phone toward Bowen so he could see the article and the picture. She watched a number of emotions flicker across his face: anger, defiance, arrogance, and contempt. He settled on defiance.

"Your chief of police hasn't requested that I answer confidential questions about Church matters unrelated to Steve Smith's murder. I've been cooperative in order to help with this regrettable situation. But now, you ambush me here at home with my family. Precious time I get too little of. If you wish to speak with me, please have Russ call me or, better yet, ask Russ to call my attorney. We can set up a mutually agreeable time to speak. Now, I think you should leave so that I can get back inside to my family."

Bowen glared at Abbie as he spoke. He didn't turn to go back inside but watched Abbie carefully, waiting for her to react. Abbie could sense he expected her to back down. Instead, Abbie lifted the outside corners of her lips toward her eyebrows. It was subtle, but it was enough of a smile that Bowen could not contain his rage at her lack of deference. He looked as if he wanted to hit her.

"You are correct to point out that Chief Henderson is my boss," Abbie said calmly, "but surely you know that as the sole detective of the Pleasant View Police Department, I have the authority to interview whomever I see fit whenever I see fit. You have every right to refuse to speak with me here, of course, which means we can make the long drive back to the police station in Pleasant View. Then, you can call your attorney and I will call the district attorney. We can take it from there. Would you like to explain to your family that your 'Church business' is going to take you the rest of the night, perhaps into the early morning hours?"

Abbie let this statement hang in the air. She watched as the color drained from Bowen's face. He said nothing.

Abbie continued, "It seems to me, given your position in the Church, it might be uncomfortable for this to become an official interview. Local papers might get interested. I've done my best to keep this investigation discreet, as your dear friend Chief Henderson has asked me to, but if you force me to take you to the station in our police car, I can hardly be blamed if an enterprising young journalist, from *The Trib* perhaps, takes an interest."

Bowen's gaze softened. He had not gotten where he was by fighting losing battles. He smiled, but this time it looked like an authentic attempt to extend an olive branch. At the very least, Bowen was demonstrating that he understood it was time to change course.

"There's no need to turn this situation into something it's not. We seem to have gotten off on the wrong foot," Bowen said. "Why don't we walk around to the patio in the back? We can sit comfortably and discuss whatever questions you have there."

She and Clarke followed Bowen around the side of the house to a red brick, herringbone-patterned patio with wrought-iron furniture and cushions Abbie thought looked as if they had just arrived from a Frontgate catalog. The backyard, not surprisingly, was exquisitely landscaped.

"May I offer you some lemonade?" Bowen asked. "My wife made some from scratch for tonight."

"That would be lovely," Abbie responded. Abbie saw Clarke relax a little. She could tell he had no interest in watching any more of her confrontation with Bowen.

Abbie and Clarke sat down. A teenage girl soon appeared, carrying a pitcher of lemonade and a plate of raspberry crumble bars. She carefully put down the tray and poured three glasses of lemonade. She smiled at Abbie and Clarke and went back inside, shutting the French doors behind her without making a sound.

They were starting over. Bowen was on notice not to underestimate Abbie again.

"Let's start at the beginning, Mr. Bowen. Tell me everything you know about Steve Smith, Celestial Time Shares, and what's going on in Costa Rica."

"I take it that you've spoken to Eduardo Morales, the manager at the bank in Costa Rica." Bowen's tone had changed from that of a lecturing Church leader to that of a helpful colleague. Abbie didn't give any indication that they had not spoken to the Costa Rican bank manager.

"I should have told you that I visited the Banco de Costa Rica when I visited the temple in San José a few weeks ago. When we first spoke, I was convinced that this business venture in Costa Rica could not possibly have anything to do with Smith's death."

Clarke took a bite of a raspberry crumble bar, swallowed, then asked, "Elder Bowen, you've been to Costa Rica before?"

"I've been to Costa Rica too many times to count. I served my mission in Chile, so my Spanish is fluent. Whenever the Brethren feel they need someone from Salt Lake to be in Spanish-speaking Latin America, I'm usually the first choice. My most recent trip had been on the calendar for months. I was there officially for the temple rededication, but"—Bowen turned to face Abbie—"I did take the opportunity to check on Steve's progress."

"What did you find out?" Abbie asked.

"I made a few discreet inquiries, but everything pointed in the same direction. You probably already know that Steve hadn't bought any property, none of the local contractors had heard of the project, and, to top it all off, according to the bank manager, almost all the investment money had been transferred into various personal accounts offshore."

"This is not at all what you told me last time we spoke," Abbie said.

"I know." Bowen shrugged. "I wish I could pretend there was some good reason for what I told you, but it is really exactly as I said. I didn't think this business project had anything to do with Smith's death. I still don't."

"What you did was lie to a police officer during the course of an investigation," Abbie said. "Can you explain to me exactly how you were able to access Smith's information in Costa Rica? I would have thought his accounts were private."

"We have connections that allow us to access information that might otherwise be confidential," Bowen replied. Abbie didn't ask who the "we" Bowen was referring to was. She was pretty sure she knew, and she didn't relish the idea that Bowen had unfettered access to other people's financial information, but she didn't doubt that he did.

Bowen continued, "I was told Steve had used some money to buy a rather extravagant villa in a village outside San José. I also heard the rumors about Steve's young, gorgeous wife. I know Melinda Smith, not well, but we have met. I think quite highly of her, but I wouldn't describe her as young."

Clarke raised his eyebrow.

Bowen continued, "When I left Costa Rica, I was angry, both about the business and about what looked like Steve's apparent infidelity. As you know, temple marriage is an eternal covenant with our Heavenly Father. Breaking the Law of Chastity is not something to be taken lightly. When I got back to Utah, I called Steve." Bowen took a sip of lemonade and carefully placed a raspberry crumble bar on a napkin in front of him. "Steve told me there was nothing to worry about. He assured me the project was on schedule."

"And what about his villa and wife?" Abbie asked.

Both Bowen and Clarke inhaled at the same time. Sex was not an easy topic for Mormons to talk about, especially extramarital sex. The fact that Abbie was herself a woman made it even more uncomfortable for the two men she was sitting with.

"Well, that was not the easiest part of my conversation with Steve," Bowen said. "I asked him about the house first, probably because that was more comfortable than a question about the covenants he made in the temple with his wife."

"And?" Abbie asked.

"Steve told me there'd been a mix-up at the bank about the money he'd wired from a variety of accounts in Utah. He told me he wasn't at all surprised about what I'd been told. According to Steve, the Banco de Costa Rica is a financial mess. Steve said the bank had confused personal and business accounts, but he was straightening everything out. He even chuckled at the thought that he would need investor money to buy such a 'simple house'—those were his words to describe the villa."

"Did you believe him?" Clarke asked.

"You know, I did." Bowen sighed. "I still do. Steve wasn't a detail guy. It wouldn't surprise me if he'd initially had issues with paperwork and accounting, but I don't think Steve would steal money. I really don't."

"But you were angry. At some point you believed Steve could have stolen from you."

"Sure, I was mad, but I was mostly mad because it didn't look like Steve had made any progress on the project. I think Celestial Time Shares is going to explode. It's a high-risk investment, but I truly believe that providing Latter-day Saints a way to travel the world, combining spiritual work and temporal R&R, is brilliant. I was angry because I was being selfish. The sooner this first project is finished, the sooner we're all going to start seeing great returns. Steve was the guy to get the job done and I wanted him to do just that."

Was Bowen right about the likelihood of financial success?

"And what about the young and attractive wife?" Abbie circled back to this key question.

"Steve told me that was a misunderstanding about his PR assistant. He told me she was an old family friend, someone he'd known since she was a kid. He said she was more like a daughter than anything else. She'd just graduated from college—Weber State, I think—and she needed a job. He acknowledged they spent a lot of time together in Costa Rica and that she stayed with him at his home, but she had her own bedroom and bathroom. He assured me their relationship was completely appropriate."

Abbie was skeptical that the relationship had indeed been "completely appropriate." Why would their Costa Rican colleague have called this young woman Mrs. Smith unless Smith was pretending he was married to a woman who wasn't Melinda when he was in Costa Rica? Someone wasn't telling the truth. Had Smith lied to Bowen or was Bowen lying to her?

TWENTY-TWO

Who was the young Mrs. Smith?

Abbie sat at her kitchen counter sipping her second cup of coffee. It had been late by the time Clarke and she had made it back from Bountiful. Abbie crawled directly into bed, but tossed and turned all night until her alarm went off the next morning. She was hoping the coffee would give her some energy. She hadn't slept through the night since they'd found the body. She'd worked in homicide in New York, so she was very comfortable with death, even gruesome death. Something about this case, though, was getting to her. Even though the list of possible suspects was long and seemed to be growing, Abbie knew that the person who killed Steve Smith had done so because he needed to atone for his sin. What was the sin? That Abbie couldn't figure out. She was dealing with a person who had an unwavering faith in the way the world worked—the way God worked—that Abbie had once found comforting herself. This was a person who was certain they knew right from wrong. This was a person who had no doubt.

Abbie swallowed the last bit of coffee in her mug. She

wasn't shocked by Smith's apparent infidelity, but she felt disappointed because of it. She hadn't known the dead man, but she'd seen the wife who'd devoted her life to him and their family. Even if Melinda Smith was not the most endearing of characters, she was a woman who had lived for her husband and children, just as she was supposed to do. Despite all her skepticism, Abbie was fond of the idea of a happy Mormon family. "Family is forever." If you followed the rules, your family would endure eternally.

Abbie pictured Smith in his temple clothes. If he was having an affair, he was certainly not honoring those covenants he'd made in the temple.

Sexual sin was an abomination; that's what the Church taught. Thoughts of her first "chastity night" drifted into her mind. A disapproving, middle-aged woman had greeted the group of thirteen- and fourteen-year-olds from Abbie's ward. Before saying anything, the woman took two pieces of bubblegum out of her bag. She unwrapped one piece and handed it to a teenage girl seated in the front row at one side of the room. She handed the second piece—still in its original wrapper—to a girl in the second row on the other side of the room. She then asked the girls to pass the gum to the person sitting at the other end of the row. A boy sitting in the first row ended up with the unwrapped piece of gum. In the second row, another boy got the gum still in its original wrapper.

"Go ahead and chew your gum," their teacher instructed the two teenage boys. The boy with the unwrapped gum refused. He tossed his gum into a trash can in the corner of the room. The other boy happily unwrapped his piece of gum and popped it into his mouth and chewed.

What a lesson about virginity.

Abbie could still feel the heat in her cheeks from discussing heavy petting with stern-looking adults in a church classroom. Remaining morally clean was an important aspect of being an LDS teenager. Abbie, like a lot of her friends, had worn a CTR ring to remind her to "Choose the Right." The ring was the LDS equivalent of the WWJD rings other Christians wore to remind them to ask "What would Jesus do?" when faced with a moral dilemma.

Abbie's phone buzzed, bringing her out of her memories and back into the present, the present where she still didn't have a lead suspect in Smith's murder.

"Do you have a minute to talk?" Clarke asked.

"Sure, what's up?"

"Segura just emailed me a picture of Steve Smith and the person he was calling Mrs. Smith—"

"Really? That's great!" Abbie interrupted Clarke, but she couldn't contain her excitement. "Can you start checking the picture against our databases? Maybe also check out pictures of students at Weber State and Utah State? I'm on my way in right now."

"Taylor," Clarke said slowly with sadness in his voice, "we don't need to do any of that. I know her. Her name is Jessica Grant. She's in the singles ward with me. She was head cheerleader at Weber High, I think. She just finished up her degree at Weber State."

Abbie heard Clarke's disappointment. Someone he knew was not living up to the LDS code he himself lived by. Abbie didn't for one instant doubt that Clarke was worthy of his temple recommend. She was certain he started and ended each day kneeling in prayer.

"You know we need to talk to her as soon as we can," Abbie said.

"Yeah, I know. I was thinking about that. She lives at home with her parents. I think it would be best to talk to her someplace other than her family's living room. I don't think we want to bring her to the station. That'll scare her. I was thinking I could call her and ask her to meet us at Nielson's. We could sit outside."

Clarke hadn't taken this kind of initiative before, but he'd clearly thought this through. He was probably right about how to approach what undoubtedly would be an uncomfortable situation.

"Sure. I think you're right. Go ahead and give her a call." Abbie thought she could hear a little pride in Clarke's tone as he said good-bye. She probably didn't tell him he was doing a good job often enough. The fact was, he had been doing a good job, even when doing his job was uncomfortable for him. She made a mental note to try to give him more positive feedback.

A few hours later, Abbie and Clarke were sitting at a table out in the sunshine at Nielson's—a place known for its frozen custard and thick made-to-order shakes. Clarke was devouring his German chocolate shake studded with pecans and large flakes of coconut and swirled with thick ribbons of caramel. Abbie had a bottle of water. Jessica Grant was ten minutes late. Then Clarke waved. Abbie turned her head and saw a young woman walking toward them.

She looked as if she'd walked straight out of central casting for the role of sexy girl next door: five foot six with long, blonde hair messily pulled into a ponytail. She was wearing skinny jeans and a fitted turtleneck. Despite being modestly dressed—technically not an inch of skin was showing—Jessica Grant managed to draw every male gaze in visibility range to the shape beneath her tight jeans and formfitting sweater.

"Hi, Jessica," Clarke began. "I'm so sorry we've got to talk to you like this, but you probably know Steve Smith has been killed. We need to speak to everyone who knew him well."

"Killed? I didn't know . . . I thought. Oh, that's awful." For a moment Jessica looked distraught. Then she smiled again and her face lit up. "Jim, please call me Jess. I don't think anyone's called me Jessica since kindergarten." She giggled a little nervously.

Kindergarten wasn't that long ago, Abbie thought, looking at the girl, who was evidently in her early twenties. Without the eye makeup and lipstick, Jessica could easily have passed for eighteen, maybe even seventeen.

"Okay, Jess." Clarke smiled. "I think you know I'm a police officer. This is Abbie Taylor. She's the detective for the Pleasant View police." Abbie still hadn't gotten used to being "the detective." In New York, she'd been one of a veritable army of investigators. If there was ever something you were unsure of, there were plenty of people to ask for advice. Someone had always seen something before. Here, the truth was, Abbie was "the detective." With a population of less than ten thousand and a low crime rate, Pleasant View needed only one person to investigate wrongdoing.

"Jessica," Abbie said in a voice she hoped sounded both empathetic and authoritative at the same time, "we've been told that you knew Steve quite well. Is that true?"

Jessica looked at the ground. She didn't say anything, but tears started rolling down her cheeks. She dabbed underneath her eyes with a tissue she'd pulled out of her Louis Vuitton shoulder bag. A gift from Smith? Abbie wondered. Abbie watched the young woman regain her composure. Something about Jessica looked very familiar to Abbie, but she couldn't place what it was. *Why did this girl look so familiar?*

"Yeah. I knew Steve," Jessica said.

Abbie caught Clarke's eye and nodded her head almost imperceptibly. Abbie had told Clarke on the drive over that he should take the lead in this interview if it seemed Jessica was uncomfortable. Clarke understood Abbie's signal. He scooted a little closer to Jessica on the bench around the table.

"Jess, I know this is going to be really hard, but I think you can help us find out what happened." Clarke sounded like he was talking to a frightened child. Maybe he was.

Jessica looked into his eyes and nodded.

"Let's start at the beginning. When did you meet Steve?" Clarke asked.

"Steve gave a talk at Sacrament Meeting about a year and a half ago. He was such an amazing speaker. I don't know if you were there that Sunday, Jim, but it was so inspiring. He spoke about how his mission had changed him. How he knew the gospel changed people's lives. He was so close to our Heavenly Father. It was . . . it was . . . just so powerful. I was prompted by the Holy Ghost to go up and thank him for coming. I never do things like that, but I did that Sunday."

Jessica's eyes were starting to tear up again. She pressed a tissue underneath them, careful not to smear her makeup. Clarke waited and then asked, "Did you see him after that?"

"Yes." A brief smiled flitted across the girl's lips. She looked down at the table. "He came to one of our volleyball games. I'm pretty good, and we won. He came up afterwards and congratulated me. He offered to give me a ride home. I was planning to walk, but it was a little cold that night."

"And after that?" Clarke asked.

"At first I thought it was just a coincidence. We kept bumping into each other at different things at church. I know he's in the bishopric, so I wasn't surprised to see him at stake conference, but there were other times, too. After a while, it seemed like more than just chance. It seemed like we were meant to see each other."

Jessica hesitated. Clarke put his arm around her like a big brother would. "Jess, I know this is hard, but we need to know everything." In New York, Abbie doubted this scene could ever have happened, but this was a small town in Utah. Clarke wasn't doing anything more than putting a person at ease, a person who was very close to the case. Not only had she probably been sleeping with the victim, but she was involved with Celestial Times Shares in Costa

Rica. If there was a center in the intersecting circles of the Venn diagram of this case, Jessica Grant was definitely right in the middle of it.

Clarke's instincts were on the money. Jessica started speaking, and this time the words tumbled out.

"Steve was so in tune with the spirit, you know? He was in the bishopric and everything. I felt so safe with him. When he asked me to help him with his work in Costa Rica, I knew it was what Heavenly Father wanted me to do. Steve thought I would be wonderful as the public-relations director for Celestial Time Shares. Since the project was just getting off the ground, he didn't want me to talk about it. He told me that I should just tell my family and friends I was going to Costa Rica as a Church volunteer to help teach English. He bought me a ticket and I left in the beginning of March last year. Steve was already there. He had this beautiful villa on the beach. We spent the entire spring there together. It was magical. He treated me like a queen. It was so hard to come back and pretend none of it happened."

"Did you know . . ." Clarke hesitated briefly before finishing the question. ". . . that Steve was married?"

"Of course." Jessica nodded. "I've known Steve my whole life—our families are friends. I knew him and his family. He told me Melinda wanted a divorce. Things hadn't been good between them for years, but they were staying together until their youngest kids were a little older. They had prayed about it. Steve wanted to make sure he could take good care of his family and his wife, but he felt prompted by Heavenly Father that I was supposed to be his new wife and we were supposed to start a family. It was important to me—to both of us—to get married in the temple. I didn't care if Steve didn't get a temple divorce. Melinda didn't want one. I understand that. It'd be important to me, too, if I were in Melinda's shoes. I mean, it makes sense to want to stay sealed to the man who's the father of your children. Being married for eternity and sealed with your family after you pass through the veil, well, that's the most important thing in the world to me. Steve knew I couldn't wait forever though; you know, I'm already twenty-two. We needed to get married soon." Jessica sighed. Her shoulders drooped. Being a twenty-two-year-old unmarried LDS woman in Utah was awfully close to being an old maid. As strange as it sounded to outsiders, that's the way a lot of young women felt.

"Were you going to meet Steve in Costa Rica again this year?" Clarke asked.

"Yeah," Jessica said. "He said he'd call when everything was ready. He wanted to get Celestial Time Shares up and running this year."

"Jess, did you ever see Steve here in Pleasant View?" Clarke asked.

"Well, we saw each other at stake conference. We bumped into each other once at one of my sister's barbecues. She entertains a lot and she's worried I'm not meeting enough eligible LDS men, so she invites me to everything where there are single RMs."

Abbie knew all about the desire to marry a Returned Missionary. Having gone on a mission signaled a certain degree of worthiness. When Abbie had married Phillip, her parents had finally had to acknowledge she wasn't coming back to the Church. Her mom had always been more open to Phillip than her dad had been. She'd actually liked him. Her father had begrudgingly admitted he was a good man, but once they were married, he'd never missed an opportunity to point out that her union with Phillip would end at death. Sooner than anyone had expected, it turned out.

Jessica continued, "I finally had to tell my family I was getting married in the temple soon, but I couldn't talk about it yet," Jessica said. She reached for another tissue from her bag and scooted a little away from him. Instead of looking at Clarke, she looked down at the table.

"Steve and I tried to remain chaste. When we were in Costa Rica, it was different somehow. It was natural to express our love for each other because we were living in the same house like we will when we're married in the temple for real."

Abbie noticed how Jessica had gone back in time to when there was a possibility that Steve Smith might actually divorce his wife and marry her. A scenario that probably had always been unlikely, but was now impossible.

"Up here," Jessica said, "well, his wife was here. Steve and I tried, we really tried, to wait until the divorce was final." She took a deep breath. "We loved each other. We prayed about it together. Steve and I both heard the still small voice of the Holy Ghost letting us know it was okay for us to be together even before we could get married in the temple, because we were already spiritually married."

"Did anyone know about you and Steve?" Clarke asked.

"Uh . . . no." Jessica hesitated. "Steve hadn't told his

wife about me yet. He said it was like when Joseph Smith didn't tell Emma right away that he'd already been sealed to other wives. Emma wasn't ready. Melinda wasn't ready; her heart wasn't open yet. Steve was going to tell her when she was ready to hear that their union on this earth had come to an end. He thought she would be ready soon. He told me they hadn't shared a bed, you know, really shared a bed, in years."

Abbie sensed Jessica was holding something back. Not about what Steve had told her about Melinda. Abbie assumed that either Steve had lied outright or Jessica had heard only what she wanted to hear. Abbie was picking up on something else in Jessica's pause before she denied that anyone knew about their relationship. Jessica did not strike Abbie as an emotionally self-sufficient woman. This was a young woman who needed validation. She had girlfriends she relied on to tell her what she should wear and what she shouldn't eat. Jessica Grant was not a person who would have been able to maintain an affair with a married man for over a year without confiding in someone. Abbie let that point go, though. It was not the time to interrupt. Clarke was doing a wonderful job keeping the conversation flowing.

"When was the last time you saw Steve?" Clarke asked.

"I saw him a few weeks ago. I was helping my sister with her kids." Jessica went on, "Steve was with his kids, so we couldn't really talk."

"You didn't see him at all after that?" Clarke asked.

"I might have, but only a few times. He called me before he left for Costa Rica. He told me he loved me and couldn't wait for us to be together again. He was super excited to do Heavenly Father's work. We were both excited about starting our life together. We were going to start our family right away. Steve said I'd be a great mom."

Clarke waited a moment before asking one last question. "Jess, have you been through the temple? Not just for baptism for the dead, but have you had your endowments?"

Jessica shook her head.

Abbie knew she had a good poker face, and she relied on that skill now. She gave no indication of how impressed she was that Clarke had asked about temple endowments. Faithful Mormons would never divulge specific details of these temple rituals because they believed they were sacred. Without having had her own endowments, Jessica Grant wouldn't have known how to properly dress Smith's body in his temple clothes, unless she was the type to research temple rituals. Abbie looked at the former cheerleader in front of her. She didn't think she was the kind of person who would spend spare time on research of any kind, let alone on Church rituals.

Well played, Clarke.

TWENTY-THREE

After their conversation with Jessica Grant, there was no doubt they had to talk to Melinda Smith again. There was more to Steve Smith than the picture his widow had painted of the ever-loving husband, supportive father, and devout member of the Church.

"Do you think Melinda knew about Jess?" Clarke asked as they opened the doors of the squad car to drive to the Smith house.

"I don't know," Abbie said.

"I know people have different sides of their personalities. Like, for me, I have my friends I play basketball with and different friends I like to talk to about books," Clarke said. "I know you hear stories about people having secret lives, but I thought it was just the sort of thing that happened in movies or maybe if you lived in Hollywood. Not something that would happen here. I've known Jess for years. I never ever would've guessed. I thought there had to be some other explanation when I saw that picture Segura sent. It makes me feel kind of sick."

"I know," Abbie said as the two of them climbed into

the car. Neither one of them said anything else for the entire ride. Abbie felt ill. Luckily, Clarke didn't seem to notice; he looked as if he was feeling just as queasy as Abbie did. It was as though they both sensed in a very concrete way just how unpleasant this conversation was going to be. When they stood at the front door, Abbie heard yelling and someone crying inside. Clarke rang the doorbell.

"Shut up!" someone shouted from inside the house, loudly enough that you could probably hear the voice all the way to the street. A few moments later, Smith's widow opened the door. Melinda looked frazzled. Her blonde hair had been raked back with fingers into a plastic clip. There were awkward bumps of hair where the top strands had been pulled more tightly than the hair underneath. Nearly an inch of dark-brown and gray roots was showing. Melinda was wearing an oversized button-down shirt that hit her right across her ample hips with turquoise Capri pants that had probably fit her better about fifteen pounds ago. Her feet were bare, and the nail polish on her toes was chipped. Coarse dark hairs sprouted from beneath her thin arched eyebrows. It looked as if she had slept in her makeup.

"Let's sit in the kitchen, if you don't mind," Melinda sighed when she saw the two police officers.

Abbie and Clarke followed her into the kitchen. In stark contrast to the house they had seen on their first visit, the current version of the Smith residence was a study in emotional collapse. Half-eaten Pop-Tarts were stacked haphazardly on plates with dried ketchup and congealed melted cheese. There were bowls with soggy cereal and smudged glasses with a few swallows of chocolate milk or orange juice left in them. An open pizza box soaked in grease with a few pepperoni slices of unknown vintage was stacked precariously on the counter. Melinda didn't seem to notice any of it.

"Sister Smith, we need to ask you some delicate questions. Is the kitchen private?" Abbie's voice was soft, almost gentle. Even if she knew that an affair with a younger woman was one of the oldest motives for murder in the book, she couldn't help but feel some sympathy for this woman whose life had disintegrated in the space of less than a week.

The widow's tired eyes registered some surprise, but not enough to alter her apparent exhaustion. "No, I guess not. You can hear everything here. We can go into the dining room and close the doors."

Melinda shuffled across the family room adjoining the kitchen and opened French doors into a dark dining room. She walked around an enormous mahogany table to the other end of the room and shut another set of French doors that led directly to the entry hall. A sideboard and colossal china cabinet matching the table loomed on either side of the room. The walls were a deep red. Unlike what Abbie had seen on the walk to the kitchen, this room was spotless. Aside from a garish silk flower arrangement in the center of the dining table, there was nothing cluttering the horizontal surfaces here. Melinda slumped into one of the heavy leather dining chairs. Abbie took the seat across from her and Clarke sat down next to Abbie.

"Melinda, do you know a young woman named Jessica Grant?" Abbie asked.

"Yeah." Melinda exhaled and looked visibly relieved. "We've known Jess since she was a baby. Very sweet girl."

"Do you know if your husband knew Jessica?"

"Of course he did. Our families have been friends for years. Steve and I watched her grow up. She was almost like a daughter," Melinda said.

The widow looked at Abbie, then at Clarke. He averted his gaze and stared down at the table. He still looked a little nauseated.

Abbie had gone over a number of ways to soften the question she was about to ask. Nothing she had come up with sounded good to her, so she just came out with it. "Did you know your husband and Jessica spent last spring in Costa Rica together, where Jessica was known as 'Mrs. Smith'?"

The color drained from Melinda's face. If someone had asked Abbie to describe the widow's complexion at that moment, she would have said pale green.

"Excuse me," Melinda mumbled and staggered from her chair. The widow opened the French doors and dashed to what must have been the powder room. Abbie heard a door close and then the sound of retching. A few minutes later, she heard a toilet flush followed by the sound of running water. When Melinda returned to the dining room, her hair was damp and the remnants of yesterday's makeup had been washed off her face, revealing a splotchy complexion.

Melinda sat back down in her chair. She looked Abbie directly in the eye and whispered almost inaudibly, "No, I didn't know that."

"These are going to be tough questions," Abbie said.

"I'm sorry, but we need to ask them. Did you know Jessica was away last spring?"

"Sure. She told all of us she was going to spend the spring in Belize or something doing some kind of internship or church service thing."

"Did you ever notice any evidence of romance between your husband and Jessica?" Abbie asked.

"No," Melinda answered. "Steve was friendly, sure. As a member of the bishopric, he occasionally had to speak to the local singles ward where Jessica went to church, but Steve, but Steve, he wouldn't . . ." Melinda couldn't finish whatever thought was in her head.

"Had your husband ever been unfaithful before?"

"No . . . well, I guess I don't know." Melinda looked defeated.

Abbie knew it might be too much for a woman to digest both her husband's death and his infidelity at the same time. The air in the room felt thick and heavy. Melinda shut down. She stared at some point in front of her, her eyes glazed. Either Abbie was witnessing a stellar performance or Melinda Smith really hadn't suspected her husband of cheating. At this point, there wasn't much more to ask.

Abbie said quietly, "We'll let ourselves out."

Melinda didn't move. She didn't say anything. Clarke shut the door silently behind them, leaving the shell-shocked widow sitting in her dark dining room with its blood-red walls.

TWENTY-FOUR

Abbie and Clarke decided to split up the work for the rest of the day. With Clarke's facility for Spanish, he could do research on Costa Rica Abbie couldn't. Abbie needed some time alone to think. This case was taking its toll. Abbie felt the pressure of time. It was already Saturday, five days since they'd found Smith's body, and they were nowhere. Clarke wanted to go to church in the morning, so they'd agreed to meet up in the early afternoon on Sunday.

What were her dad's words . . . 'personal shortcomings' that had nothing to do with the Church? Was Port worried about Smith's shady business techniques or his adultery? Did Port know about both? Did Bowen know? Or was there something else entirely that Abbie and Clarke hadn't discovered yet? Was Jessica the only one who had caught Smith's eye? Abbie's mind was in rapid-fire mode. There were too many questions and not nearly enough answers.

Helga Boalt had told them Smith had leered at her friends. The Bishop had listed four young women. And, now, of course, there was another reason to look at Melinda Smith, even if the widow had seemed genuinely shocked by the news. Jessica also had a reason. She'd wanted to be married in the temple and start a family. At twenty-two, she was feeling the discomfort of not being married in a community where many of her friends were probably working on their first or second children. Would a spurned young lover who expected marriage be angry enough to kill? There also was an entire army of fathers and brothers who might have reason to be protective of either the cheated-on wife or the seduced young lover. Her dad's warning from Port—was that what it was?—added another strange dimension to this case.

A night in bed had done nothing to slow down the whirling thoughts in Abbie's head; she needed to go for a run. There was nothing like the rhythm of running to calm her overactive mind. She changed into her work out clothes, tied the laces on her shoes, and headed for the door. Given how poorly she'd slept, she was surprised by how energetic she felt once she started moving. Fifteen minutes into the run, her head began to clear.

She wondered what time church started at Smith's ward, Ben Lomond 7th. She could watch the people Smith had shared much of his life with in a routine setting. When she reached the halfway point of her run, she checked her phone to see church start times. Ben Lomond 7th started with Sacrament Meeting at nine. She scrolled through her playlist to a song with a fast beat and made it home in good time.

Abbie carefully looked over her closet for a dress that would be appropriate for church. To the right side were the high heels: Louboutins, Pradas, Aquazzuras, and at least a dozen others. To the left were evening dresses, mementos of a life she no longer lived. There were pretty chiffons in jewel tones, an off-the-shoulder Herve Leger, a crystal-encrusted Carmen Marc Valvo sheath. In front of her were what she'd once called day dresses, along with blouses, blazers, skirts, and trousers. Everything was hung according to category from lightest to darkest in color. Abbie knew she had a slight obsessive-compulsive thing going on when it came to organization, but she protested when anyone said she was a neat freak because she always had at least one closet that was a complete disaster. She liked her life to be tidy, but when given the choice between cleaning and skiing, she'd always choose the latter.

With the exception of what she'd worn to Smith's funeral, Abbie hadn't worn most of the clothing hanging in her closet since she'd moved back to Utah. She hadn't been able to leave these clothes in New York because they reminded her so much of her life with Phillip. Now, these fashionable pieces just looked silly to her. The time when she'd believed this abundance of expensive clothing and accessories reflected something about who she was seemed like a distant memory. Now all these exquisite evening bags, shoes, and beautifully tailored clothes just looked like a lot of unnecessary stuff. She had the overwhelming urge to throw the lot of it into garbage bags right then and donate it all to Deseret Industries, but that would have to wait. She looked at her phone. She didn't have much time if she was going to get to Sacrament Meeting.

The clothes she lived in now were all a variation of a single uniform, slim trousers and fitted shirts worn with flats, but LDS women didn't wear trousers to church. Abbie searched her day dresses. She found an understated Michael Kors sheath dress with bracelet sleeves and a boat neck top that hit just above the knee. It was tailored and, while lovely, perfectly forgettable. She then scanned the top shelf, where her handbag collection was arranged. Each bag was in its own dust cover with a picture of it pinned to the outside. She chose a navy Chanel that lacked the interlocking *C*s to coordinate with the modest dress she'd picked. She hoped nobody would recognize either the dress or the bag, because she didn't want to stand out any more than she knew she did just by virtue of her physique and auburn hair.

Abbie combed her hair into a low ponytail and put on small drop pearl earrings. The only other jewelry she wore was her plain gold wedding band on her left ring finger. She stepped back and looked at herself in the mirror. Yes, she looked ready for church.

Abbie picked up her old matching set of the Bible and Book of Mormon with her name embossed in italic gold letters on the fronts. She didn't know why she had saved them, but she had. She was glad to have them now, because they would give her something to do with her hands. They'd also give her cover at church if she wanted to pretend to be reading the scriptures.

Abbie walked through the glass door at the back of the church with a few minutes to spare. This was the church where she'd met Bishop Norton in his office after Smith had been killed. Then the hallways had been silent; now those same halls were full of gaggles of noisy kids. Abbie doubted "gaggle" was actually the collective noun for groups of young children and teenagers, but if it wasn't, it should have been. Behind the children dragged tired-looking mothers trying to keep them quiet. The teenage girls were attempting to look cool in modest tops and skirts hovering just below their knees. Most of their efforts had clearly been spent on either straightening or curling their long hair and then rimming their eyes with liner. Many wore obviously fake lashes. The teenage boys' nod to rebellion was to wear their ties askew and leave wrinkled button-down shirts untucked.

Abbie entered the chapel and slid into the last bench. She watched a few men with overly coiffed hair make their way to the front of the chapel. They sat on the elevated section facing the benches where the congregation sat. A sour-looking woman who looked older than Methuselah started playing "I Know That My Redeemer Lives" as people in the congregation shuffled to their seats. Just before it was time for Sacrament Meeting to start, a harried family of seven scooted into the bench in front of her. The man was in his late forties with thinning hair and a prosperous belly. He promptly started to doze. His wife, whose makeup had been applied with a generous hand, gave her toddler Froot Loops in a small plastic container as soon as they were settled. The elementary-school-age kids elbowed each other with enough vigor to probably cause some pain. Whenever one of them said "ouch," the others would mock-reverently whisper "shush." The mother, who was occupied with keeping the toddler quiet, could do nothing but glare at them. At the other end of the bench, two teenage daughters sat silent and sullen.

"Good morning," Bishop Norton said. "It's such a joy for me to look out and see all of your friendly faces. We all know that our time on this earth will be marked by trials and tribulations, but as members of the Church, we also know that if we follow God's plan, we have nothing to fear. He has shown us the way. Please take comfort in that even as you may be going through your own personal struggles. Today we can count the many blessings we receive when we follow our Heavenly Father's plan." The Bishop then turned to a gray-haired man sitting on the dais. "Brother Gallagher, would you please give the invocation?"

Abbie folded her arms, bowed her head, then discreetly looked around the room. She saw the Smith family. Melinda was with her children and two men who looked as if they could be her brothers. The Smith kids were squirming some, but no more than most of the other kids their age.

On the other side of the chapel, Abbie saw Jessica Grant. She was wearing a dress with spaghetti straps. The dress showed off Jessica's well-toned arms and signaled the fact that she wasn't married, because if she had been wearing garments she couldn't have worn those thin straps against nothing but her sun-kissed skin. Married women could only wear a dress with spaghetti straps if they wore a modest T-shirt covering their cap-sleeved garments underneath.

Abbie wondered why Jessica was here. She'd thought she went to the singles ward with Clarke. It was apparent she was sitting with a large family. Abbie couldn't see the faces, but she could tell that most of the family shared the same thick honey-blonde hair Jessica had.

Bishop Norton stood again after everyone murmured "amen." He introduced a younger man who had just returned from his mission. He talked about how wonderful it was to see how the gospel transformed people's lives. He concluded with the common refrain, "I bear my testimony that I know this Church is true, and that our Prophet is the true Prophet of God."

After another speaker and a few hymns, it was finally time for the closing prayer. Abbie heartily joined the other members in saying amen, but probably not for the same reason as everyone else.

Abbie watched as people moved to their next meeting. She opened her Book of Mormon, hoping that reading would give her some time to watch people without being noticed. With a stroke of luck, a large group of tall boys walked past her just as Jessica Grant stood up. Jessica was standing with Sariah Morris. They both had the same blonde hair, the same soap opera good looks. Then Abbie realized the obvious: Sariah and Jessica were sisters. It wasn't an uncommon age difference in families with five or six kids.

Sacrament Meeting, it turned out, was about as much church as Abbie could stomach. What had seemed like a good idea on her run didn't seem like such a great idea now. There really wasn't that much reason to stay. Instead of sitting for another two hours—Relief Society and Sunday school—Abbie started navigating her way through the busy halls to make her escape at the back exit of the church.

"Sister Taylor! What a surprise to see you here." Abbie

recognized the voice immediately. It was Chief Henderson. "I didn't know you were a member of this ward."

"Hi, Chief. No, uh, I'm not a member of this ward, but I thought I just might drop by today to get a sense of where, uh, . . ." Abbie decided midsentence that it might not be a bad thing if Henderson thought she was there as a prodigal daughter seeking redemption instead of as a detective trying to get a new perspective on her case.

"We're not members of this ward either—we're in the Pleasant View 11th—but my wife's niece is teaching her first Relief Society lesson today. She wanted to be here for support." Henderson turned and tapped on the arm of a woman engaged in an animated conversation with another older woman.

Before Abbie could figure out a polite getaway, she was facing Henderson's wife with her well-hairsprayed hair. She was wearing a calf-length floral dress and sensible white shoes.

"This is Abbie Taylor," Henderson said. "You know, the detective I told you about."

The woman smiled as if she had only heard wonderful things about Abbie, which, Abbie knew, could not possibly be the case.

"Hello, it's so nice to finally meet you. We've admired your father's writing for years. My brother took a class with him at the Y years ago. Inspiring is what he called it. He stills talks about it to this day. Are you going to Relief Society? My niece is teaching this morning."

"Yes," Abbie smiled, enthusiastically, she hoped. "Do you know which room it's in?" There was no sense in fighting the inevitable. Abbie could sit through an hour of Relief Society.

Henderson's wife grinned broadly. "Right here." She turned to her husband. "Sweetheart, I'll see you later." With that, Abbie was ushered into a room and found herself sitting on a padded folding chair next to Henderson's wife in the front row.

Oh, well, so much for escape, Abbie thought.

After singing "Precious Savior, Dear Redeemer," the young woman leading the lesson stood up. The lesson was on how LDS women could better support their husbands in these challenging latter days. A middle-aged woman at the back of the room with a loud and nasal voice shared a personal story about how her husband had guided her family through a period of financial difficulty through prayer and following the promptings of the Holy Ghost. Now they had a new car and a houseboat in Lake Powell.

Abbie heard the door open at the back of the room. Behind her two women whispered, "Excuse me." Apparently there were no seats in the back and the two had to walk to the front of the room. They smiled apologetically as they scooted past Mrs. Henderson to the two seats to Abbie's left. It was Jessica and Sariah. Sariah murmured "Sorry" when she brushed against Abbie's knees before she sat down. After she sat, she touched Jessica's forearm with the tenderness of a mother. Jessica placed her hand on top of her older sister's and squeezed it. Then, absent-mindedly, she started playing with a delicate gold chain around her neck. Abbie glanced at Jessica, who was doing her best to pretend she didn't recognize the detective. It was then that

Abbie saw something sparkle at the end of the necklace, but as soon as Abbie looked again, Jessica had stopped fiddling with the chain.

Abbie didn't really pay attention to the substance of the lesson. She sang when she was supposed to and smiled when the other women laughed at some mildly amusing comment about men being men. Then she bowed her head for the closing prayer and said amen.

On autopilot, Abbie exchanged pleasantries with Henderson's wife. It couldn't hurt to make a good impression. After Henderson's wife left, Abbie stayed behind outside the chapel doors. She opened her scriptures again and pretended to be reading.

"She can't be completely surprised. I mean, after all the people he didn't pay." Abbie pretended she wasn't eavesdropping on the two strangers. She kept her head down, staring at whatever two pages her scriptures had fallen open to. The woman and her friend evidently didn't mind being late for Sunday school.

"There's no way it was anyone in the ward. I bet it was one of those guys who work on the construction jobs here and then move on," the other woman said. Abbie had to strain to hear what the women were saying. She tilted her head slightly so that her ear was directly in line with the women's mouths.

"You know"—the first woman leaned in—"I heard someone saw him with—"

"Hello, Bishop," the second woman said brightly.

That was the cue for the gossip to end, and it was also the cue for Abbie to get out of the meetinghouse before she was drawn into a conversation with the Bishop about why she was there in the first place. Abbie ducked out the closest side door just as her phone buzzed. It was her dad.

"Abish, I'm in Ogden. Is there any chance you have time to meet for lunch now?"

Abbie was surprised by the question, given how their last conversation had gone. Her father was not one for apologies. Abbie couldn't help but wonder if he had another message from Port. But despite her misgivings, it was still her dad.

"Actually, I do have time," Abbie said. She hoped she wasn't going to regret it.

TWENTY-FIVE

"Yes, some more water would be nice," Abbie said to the young server with long curly hair pulled into a loose bun. He looked like he'd spent the morning either hiking or mountain biking before coming here to earn just enough cash to support the cost of his outdoor hobbies. He was part of a tribe of such people who moved to the state for skiing, climbing, mountain biking, and a whole slew of new extreme sports. Many of them supported their athletic endeavors by waiting tables when they weren't in the mountains.

Abbie had been sitting at the table for at least ten minutes. This was not her dad's kind of restaurant. It served local produce, fish, and wild game. They made their own breads and pasta, or at least that's what the menu stated. And everyone who worked here had at least one visible tattoo. Her dad must have chosen it because he thought she'd like it. She appreciated the gesture.

People were drinking wine a few tables over. Abbie was debating ordering a glass. She knew her dad would consider it an affront. She really would have liked a glass of something, but she nursed her water with a slice of lemon instead.

Finally, her dad arrived. Abbie watched the hostess direct him to their table. "Hello, Abish. You look well." The moment he sat down, the waiter appeared and asked him if he'd like to see the wine list. She could see his discomfort.

"No, thank you," her dad answered. He then turned to his daughter. "How are you settling in?"

Abbie wasn't sure how to answer this question. Her dad was acting as if the Port conversation hadn't happened. He was not good at small talk, especially with her. She was really wishing she had that glass of wine right about now.

"Fine," Abbie said. She was racking her brain to come up with more than a one-word answer. "I never stopped missing the mountains here. It feels like heaven to see them every day now." She turned the conversation toward her dad. "How are classes going?"

"Very well, thank you."

"Any interesting research?" Abbie asked.

"I'm working on a paper for the Religious Studies Center concerning the period of early statehood after the 1890 Manifesto." Her dad didn't need to explain what the 1890 Manifesto was to his daughter. It was President Woodruff's statement disavowing the practice of polygamy and telling members of the Church to abide by the law of the land. The Church had sent a number of cases to the Supreme Court with the purpose of establishing the practice as protected under First Amendment free exercise of religion. The Supreme Court, it turned out, did not find that polygamy was protected under the Constitution.

Small talk wasn't Abbie's strength any more than it was her father's. Her mom had been the social butterfly of the family. She could charm everyone in the room at parties or conferences. It didn't matter who you were or where you came from, Hannah Taylor would make you feel like you were the most interesting person she had ever met. It wasn't an act, either. Abbie's mom had genuinely found something to like in everyone.

Abbie took a sip of her lemony water in silence. She didn't know what to say to bridge the awkward gap between her dad and her, and she was grateful when the young waiter returned to take their orders. It was a welcome, if momentary, diversion. Her dad asked for the stroganoff, and she ordered the elk with risotto.

After the waiter left, her dad said, "I've known we've needed to talk for a long time. John's been after me for a while to meet you for lunch on neutral territory. I think we need to clear the air."

Abbie wondered if he was going to talk about Mom. They never had. Not at the hospital, not at the funeral, not at any of the family get-togethers with her brothers and sisters. They'd never said a word.

"I know you blame me for not being at the hospital when your mom died."

Abbie felt her stomach clench. Her heart started beating hard and fast. Even after three years, the anger was fresh. She didn't want to speak.

"Abish?"

"I don't know what to say." Abbie said the words slowly, willing herself to remain calm. Even so, she knew her voice sounded harsh.

"John thinks you need to tell me how you feel. I know that sounds sentimental."

"You don't want to talk about this?" Abbie asked.

"Well, it's not that I don't want to talk about it, it's just, well, I think things like this work themselves out naturally over time. I don't think they need to be picked apart in conversation."

That was true. Her father didn't think emotions needed to be, or even should be, expressed. Abbie shared some of his reticence to discuss one's internal world. She was not one for self-indulgent melodrama.

"John thinks it's been long enough. He told me that if things were going to have worked themselves out between us, they already would have."

Her older brother was probably right.

"You should have been with us those last five days." Abbie spoke in a monotone. She was trying to keep her voice moderate, but it wasn't. Each word was clipped and had an edge you could cut stone with.

"I know you think that."

That was it? His best response was not to admit he'd been wrong, but only to admit that she thought he was?

"No, Dad, everyone thinks that! It was bad enough that you were always gone while we were growing up. You left Mom to do everything and then had the audacity to think that your sheer presence at Sunday dinner or for forty-five minutes every evening before you abandoned us all again made you a good dad. It didn't. You weren't. But I accepted it. We all did. Even Mom. She loved you and she knew your work was important to you, so it was important to her. But, when we all knew we were at the end . . . she was in so much pain, but she was with us. We could talk. We even laughed. And you weren't fucking there. Not for any of it, because of what? Some stupid Church thing that you did like a lapdog because some Apostle asked you—"

"Abish." Her dad said her name quietly. She hadn't raised her voice that much, but she had used the word "fucking." Abbie inhaled and then exhaled. He was right: the word had been uncalled for.

"Dad, you abandoned Mom when she was dying? Every morning, she asked where you were. For days we covered for you. We said you had this obligation or that obligation. What was so important that you were not at your wife's bedside for the last five days of her life?"

Her dad looked crumpled. He didn't say anything. The waiter returned with their food, but instead of explaining the intricacies of their dishes, as one would expect in a restaurant like this, he turned and left, mumbling something about them enjoying their meals.

"I thought I had more time," her dad said with a sadness that probably would have melted anyone else's heart.

"More time?" Her tone was harsh, but she couldn't seem to help it. She'd vented to John and to Phillip, but she'd never talked to her dad about those last days. There had been nothing but hostile silence on the subject. Now that the topic had been broached, Abbie was flooded with fresh grief and anger. Even as the adult in her struggled to find forgiveness or understanding, the little girl who had lost her mom wanted to lash out. "What could have been so important that you would risk that precious time? The doctors were clear. They said—"

"The doctors said we probably had two or three weeks."

"And you think that makes it okay? What the hell is wrong with you?"

"Port asked me to fly to upstate New York," her dad said. "There had been a discovery of some documents. The person who owned them wouldn't let them out of his sight. The Church didn't want to acquire them unless we were certain they were authentic. There was the flight, then the drive. It just took so much time."

"And why couldn't that wait? If those documents had been around since the 1800s, they could wait another month."

"Well, that was it. There were other bidders involved. Port didn't want other people to have them if they were real."

"Do you even hear yourself?" Abbie asked.

Abbie stabbed at her elk. It was rare and probably delicious, but she had no appetite.

"You have to understand, these were very sensitive documents," her dad said.

"My God. If you still think that a bunch of papers that could have embarrassed the Church were more important than being with Mom, then you're . . . you're . . . I don't know what the hell you are."

Abbie took a long drink of her water, again wishing it were wine or something even stronger. Anger radiated from every cell in her body. She wasn't proud of the resentment she'd been nursing since her mom had died, but she felt justified in her judgment. She was right. He was wrong.

She looked up from her glass of water. Her dad seemed to have shrunk before her eyes. She'd never seen him like this. They had a long history of verbal sparring, albeit usually without Abbie swearing. Every conversation started with an opening gambit. The goal was checkmate or to force the other to knock down his or her king.

Her dad reached across the table and touched his daughter's hand.

"Is there any way I can make this right?"

Abbie was caught off guard by her dad's vulnerability. She had clung to her anger so long that unclenching was almost as painful as the anger itself.

"Did Port know how sick Mom was?" Abbie asked.

Her dad looked down at his plate, as untouched as Abbie's was. "Yes."

"Yes? Let me get this straight, Port knew he was asking you to leave your wife's side while she was dying so you could fly across the country to make sure those damn documents didn't contain anything that could embarrass the Church? Is that right?"

Abbie's dad nodded.

"This is the same Church that spends millions of dollars on PR campaigns and 'I'm a Mormon' ads instead of, oh I don't know, helping the poor and the sick? I mean, we've already established no one gives a damn about the dying. It was more important to protect the Church's image than for you to be with your wife during her last days on earth."

"We thought there was more time . . ."

"To hell with you."

Abbie stood up.

"Abish, please, I was wrong."

Abbie had never heard her father admit he was wrong about anything. Ever.

"You're right. You're right about all of it: about the rush to authenticate the documents, about the money the Church spends on PR, about Port asking me to leave Hannah and, most of all, about me leaving her and all of you."

Abbie sat back down.

"I love your mother. She was the only person in the world who understood me and loved me anyway. Since that day I boarded the plane for New York, my world has been gray. The color hasn't come back. I wake up every morning knowing I missed those last days where I could have held her hand and kissed her hair. The only solace I have is in knowing I'll be reunited with her. I know we are married for all eternity."

Abbie didn't believe in marriage for "time and all eternity," but at that moment she understood why it was so important for her dad to cling to his faith. Five days wasn't all that bad in the scheme of forever. Abbie didn't share her father's need to believe, but she understood it. She felt the anguish of his regret.

Abbie's heart broke. She saw her dad for who he was: a

man who loved his wife, and now she was gone. She knew what it was like to love someone, to think you would always have a chance to take back that thing you said when you were annoyed, to rely on tomorrow to make things right. Abbie had loved Phillip and he had loved her, but they were human. They both had said things—done things—they would have liked to make better if there had been time.

"Dad? Do you still miss her?"

Her dad had tears in his eyes, but he didn't answer.

"You know," Abish went on, "she used to send me Valentine's Day cards every year up until the very end. Sometimes funny ones and sometimes mushy ones, but I always got one, no matter what."

Her dad shook his head. "I didn't know that."

"When we were little and you'd go away for a conference, Mom would make breakfast for dinner. We'd have pancakes and chocolate sauce, strawberries, maple syrup . . . whatever we wanted. We'd eat on the floor in the family room watching TV." Abbie smiled, but tears were rolling down her cheeks. Her dad handed her his neatly folded and pressed handkerchief.

"I don't think I ever told you," Abbie said as she dried her eyes with her dad's square of cotton, "but my first semester in college, I completely bombed an English essay. It was dripping in red ink. I was devastated. I locked myself in a bathroom stall and just cried and cried. I was convinced I was going to be kicked out and my life would be over. Then Mom called like she always did on Thursday night. She calmed me down, told me I could do it, and then spent the rest of the night helping me figure out how to rewrite the essay—word by word. We were up all night."

Her dad reached across the table. This time he took Abbie's hand in his own and answered her question. "I miss her. I still really miss her."

Damn it. I still miss her, too.

TWENTY-SIX

Abbie texted Clarke and told him to take the rest of the day off. They could start early in the morning instead of Sunday evening. The day had taken its toll. Abbie opened a bottle of Schramsberg Blanc de Blancs and poured a generous amount into a heavy crystal tumbler. Some people reserved bubbly for celebratory occasions. Abbie, though, was a firm believer in the words, apocryphal or not, of the great Lily Bollinger: "I drink champagne when I'm happy and when I'm sad. Sometimes I drink it when I'm alone. When I have company, I consider it obligatory. I trifle with it if I'm not hungry and drink it when I am. Otherwise, I never touch it—unless I'm thirsty." She took a sip of the champagne (or, sparkling wine, if you were going to be persnickety about the French claim to the regional name). The bubbles had the effect she was hoping for. They gave her a little space to relax.

She wasn't proud of the language she'd used with her dad. She knew she'd said some things more to hurt him than to release her anger, which didn't exactly make her feel as if she'd handled the conversation as well as she could have.

But for the first time since her mom had passed away, there wasn't a wall between them. As difficult as that lunch had been, Abbie was grateful it had happened.

After a second sip, Abbie couldn't deny how exhausted she was. Her eyes felt sandy and her body was drained. She might as well go to sleep. She set down the glass of pale golden bubbles, climbed the stairs to her room, and crawled into bed. Sleep must have come quickly, because when her phone buzzed, it was pitch black outside.

Abbie squinted at her phone. She blinked her eyes a few times so that she could read the name of the caller.

"Clarke?" Abbie said.

She was still groggy.

"There's been another death. You need to get over here right now."

"Where?"

"The Grants' house. It's Jess," Clarke said.

"I'll be right there."

★ ★ ★

By the time she arrived, Jessica's parents were sitting with Henderson in the living room. The dead girl's father had his arm wrapped around his wife's shoulders, as if he could somehow protect her. Silent tears were streaming down the mom's cheeks, but she wasn't making a sound. She just sat there, suffering in silence. Henderson glanced at Abbie and nodded his head her way, almost imperceptibly, acknowledging her.

Abbie walked up the half-flight of carpeted stairs to Jessica's bedroom. The room was all pink flowers and white wicker. There were high school dance pictures stuck in the frame of the full-length mirror in the corner of the room. Jessica's white vanity was overflowing with drugstore makeup and tools to dry, straighten, or curl hair. Blue and red pom-poms hung over the vanity mirror. There was a white dresser against a pink-and-white striped wall. On top were a few bottles of perfume, some trophies with gold or silver figurines of girls holding pom-poms, and a stack of magazines titled *Celestial Shine*. On the other side of the room was a desk somewhere underneath piles of clothes and papers.

The nightstand was as cluttered as the rest of the room. There was a large framed picture of a family hanging over the desk. Abbie recognized the parents downstairs in their much-younger versions, along with children who were all adults now. There was also a dark-orange prescription bottle with a childproof white cap.

A white twin bed jutted from the wall into the middle of the room. Above the headboard hung a pale-pink poster of the Linda Gay Perry Nelson poem "My Three White Dresses"—not a poem Abbie would have chosen to frame. The poetess celebrated a woman's life by reducing it to the three times she wore a white dress: the day she was blessed as a baby, the day she was baptized into the Church, and the day she was married "without stain" in the temple.

Jessica's body lay on top of the bed. She was dressed in a white cotton nightgown that reached her ankles. Her face was pale as paper, her arms folded across her stomach. You could see her silver CTR ring on her right hand, the same hand that was holding the bowie knife. A deep gash ran under her chin from her left ear to her right. Blood stained the pink floral sheets and pillow.

"Do we have any idea about time of death?" Abbie asked the on-call ME.

"Not more than a few hours."

"Would you care to venture a guess about whether this was self-inflicted?" Abbie pressed.

The ME looked at Abbie and arched his right eyebrow. "No, I wouldn't. I've seen too many gory suicides to think this couldn't be done by someone's own hand. It's amazing what teenagers are doing now. They'll have a better idea once they look at her in Taylorsville."

Jessica's room reminded Abbie of a tableau in *Romeo and Juliet* she'd seen years ago at the Shakespeare Festival down in Cedar City. Juliet had been played by a beautiful actress with long, brown hair that hung in loose curls down her back. The actress had worn a demure white ruffled nightgown in the final suicide scene. When she plunged the dagger into her chest, dark-red stage blood spread tragically down the pristine white fabric. The image had been so unsettling that, years later, Abbie still felt the visceral reaction she'd had when the scene was performed on stage in the replica of the Globe theater in southern Utah.

"It looks staged to me," Clarke said as if he had read Abbie's mind. He'd been taking pictures of the room for a while now. He looked haggard and much older than his twenty-something years. He looked as if he'd aged a decade since she'd seen him yesterday. Young people's deaths did that to you.

Abbie left the commotion of Jessica's room and walked

back downstairs. Henderson had left the grieving parents with a number of their grown children.

"Her mom found her," Henderson told Abbie in the hallway outside of the parents' earshot. "They last saw her early this morning before church. They were heading to Bountiful, where one of their granddaughters was playing the organ in Sacrament Meeting."

Henderson looked broken. "I know we just saw her at church this morning. Apparently she met up with some friends for lunch. We're still trying to get everyone's stories straight to get a reliable timeline. Her parents didn't get back from Bountiful until late. They went to bed without checking on her, but her mom peaked into Jessica's room when she woke up in the middle of the night to get some water."

"So the last time her parents saw her alive was Sunday morning, but you and I saw her at church around noon?" Abbie asked.

"Yes," Henderson said.

"And we're figuring out the rest of the timeline right now?"

"Yes. The Grants may be clearer on all these details in the morning. Right now I think they're in shock."

"Did you ask them about the prescription for Ativan?" Abbie asked.

"What?"

"There was an empty bottle of Ativan on the nightstand. The prescription had been filled two days ago. It should have been nearly full," Abbie said.

"I didn't notice it," Henderson said.

Abbie couldn't blame him. Everyone on the scene looked

stricken. Children and young people were the hardest deaths to deal with. They just seemed wrong. Abbie didn't know a cop around, regardless of toughness, who didn't feel at least a hint of grief when a young person died of unnatural causes.

"You can go ahead and talk to them if you want, but keep it short. We can always talk to them later," Henderson said. "I need to get some air."

Abbie stepped aside in the narrow hallway to let Henderson pass. She had never seen him look so deeply sad. She walked into the living room. The Grants were collapsed on the sofa in what could only be described as despair.

"Brother and Sister Grant, I'm so sorry. There are no words," Abbie said. She reached out to touch the mother's shoulder. Abbie knew all the thoughtless things people said to a person grieving the loss of a loved one. In the last few years, she had been on the receiving end of some pretty callous comments. She had vowed never to say anything like "It was for the best" or "She's in a better place." It was amazing the things that came out of people's mouths.

The air in the living room was heavy. Utah didn't have high humidity, so it wasn't as if the air really could feel oppressive the way it could in places like Florida or even New York in the summer. This felt like the house itself knew something terrible had happened.

"Detective," Jessica's father said, interrupting the silence. "What can we do to help you?"

"I don't want to burden you now with too many questions, but I have a few. You last saw Jessica this morning before you left for church?

"Yes. She was still in bed, but we had to leave early to make it to Bountiful," Sister Grant said. "She was texting some friends on her phone. I kissed her good-bye."

"When did you get home?"

Jessica's father answered, "Around ten fifteen, I think. We had dinner at my son's and then drove back. We thought Jessica was asleep, so we didn't look in on her."

"Thanks," Abbie said, then asked, "Can either of you tell me how long Jessica had been taking Ativan?"

Both parents looked surprised.

"Ativan?" Jessica's dad asked.

"It's a prescription drug to reduce anxiety," Abbie replied.

Jessica's parents looked genuinely perplexed.

"I don't know anything about it. I didn't know she felt like she needed . . ." The mom's eyes filled with tears. Abbie wished she could have spared them the question, but she couldn't.

Abbie glanced across the room and saw two of Jessica's brothers. They exchanged a look. They knew about the prescription.

"Thank you. Again, I'm so sorry for your loss." There really was nothing else to say to parents who had just walked in on the gruesome remains of their youngest daughter.

Clarke came downstairs. "I've finished with the pictures."

"Okay," Abbie said. "Let's talk to the brothers."

Abbie and Clarke walked over to the two men Abbie had seen react when she'd asked Jessica's parents about the Ativan.

"I know this is a really hard time, but the sooner we know the basic facts, the sooner we can figure out what happened."

"Sure," the older of the two said. "Maybe we should go outside."

Clarke and Abbie followed the brothers into a small kitchen and through a back door.

"Did either of you see your sister today?" Abbie asked.

"I didn't," Tom, the older brother said, then looked at Jake, his younger brother.

Clarke piped in, "Jake, did you see Jess today?" Clarke then turned to Abbie. "Jake and I were at Weber State together," he said.

"I saw her in the afternoon. Probably around four. After church."

"How did she seem to you?" Abbie asked. She didn't think this death was any more a suicide than Steve Smith's had been, but it was premature to rule anything out.

"Like Jess. All unicorns and rainbows." Abbie couldn't help but notice a little sarcasm in his voice. It seemed jarring under the circumstances.

"What do you mean?" Abbie asked.

"Nothing. Only that Jess kinda lived in her own world. She was a bit of a princess waiting to be rescued," Jake said.

Abbie turned to Tom. "Do you agree?"

"I wouldn't have put it that way, but yeah, Jess was the baby of the family, and she acted like it. We all loved her and protected her. By the time she was born, our parents had already had four of us. They were tired. They gave in to what she wanted a lot more than they had with the rest of us." Tom didn't sound angry or jealous, just matter-of-fact.

"Had either of you noticed a change in her mood in the last few weeks?" Abbie asked.

The two looked at each other.

Clarke spoke up. "Listen, we don't know what we're dealing with right now. The more you can tell us, the better." Abbie felt a shift in the brothers' demeanor. Clarke had read the situation correctly and said the right thing.

"Okay, so, Jess was kind of giddy two weeks ago," Jake said. Tom nodded his head in agreement. "She wouldn't tell me what was going on, which was a little weird because we were really close, since we're the only two who live at home and she's only sixteen months younger than I am. Anyway, she was kind of floating on air. Then, I don't know, about a week ago, she just took a dive. My mom was worried. She wasn't eating again."

"What do you mean, she wasn't eating again?" Abbie asked.

Jake looked at his older brother as if he were asking permission. Tom closed his eyes slowly, which, apparently, was all the permission the younger sibling needed.

"Okay, there was a while in high school, a couple of years maybe, when Jess was sort of anorexic. It never got so bad that all her hair fell out or anything like that, but it was bad, bad enough that she had to go away for a summer to some special center to learn how to eat. It was really expensive, too. Luckily, our sister had money and paid for the whole thing. Anyway, now whenever Jess is going through a rough patch, we're all on high alert about her eating. We know how to spot it when she cuts up food on her plate, pushes it around, but never eats it. We know to look for the excessive exercising. You know, all the stuff you have to be aware of when an anorexic relapses."

"Any idea why she went from being on top of the world to not eating?" Abbie asked.

"No," Jake said.

Abbie turned to Tom. "Do you have any idea what happened?"

"I wish I did," he said. "My guess would have been that it had something to do with a guy, but I don't think she was seeing anyone."

Abbie saw something register on Jake's face. "Was she dating?" she asked.

Jake looked at the ground and shrugged his shoulders. "I don't know." He was lying, but Abbie had a feeling he was not going to open up in front of his older brother.

"So, what do you know about the Ativan?" Abbie asked.

This time Tom spoke first. "We all knew about it. I mean, not our parents, but all of us." Abbie understood "us" to mean Jessica's brothers and sister. "After the anorexia scare in high school, we all were keeping an eye out for her. There was a point in her sophomore year in college when things were going badly. She was struggling with her grades and it didn't seem like she could keep up. Our dad's a teacher. Doing well in school matters. Jess was not really an academic, so she always had a hard time. Anyway, Sariah—that's our sister—saw the signs first. We had a sort of sibling meeting and decided the best thing would be to get Jess in to see a therapist. She got the Ativan then and has been taking it ever since."

"Your parents don't know about it?"

The two brothers shook their heads at the same time. "They're kind of old school. They don't think you should ever need to see a psychologist for anything. You should be able to deal with all your emotional problems on your own or with the help of prayer and church. Jess needed more help than that," Jake said.

"Do you know if she was seeing a therapist again? For more than just refilling prescriptions?" Abbie asked.

"I don't think she was, but I don't know. I don't live here," Tom explained. Jake didn't say anything.

"I don't think there's any good way to ask this, but do either of you know anyone who'd want to hurt Jessica?" Abbie looked at each of the brothers.

"Not a soul," the older brother said.

Jake piped in, "Jess may have been irritating with all her fairy tale stuff, but everyone loved her. Nobody could ever even stay mad at her."

"Okay. Thanks for your help. I'm so sorry for your loss. We'll be in touch soon." Abbie handed them each her card. "Please reach out to me or Jim if either one of you remembers anything or thinks of anything that might help us."

Abbie and Clarke had started to walk back toward the kitchen when Jake asked, "You don't think she killed herself, do you?"

Abbie looked back at Jessica's brother. "At this point,

I don't have enough information to know. Do you have any reason to think she might have?"

"I don't know what a person is like when they're suicidal, but Jess was pretty despondent this past week. Whatever happened was major. She seemed really hopeless. I don't think she had it in her to kill herself. She wasn't like that, but she was worse off than even the lowest point of her anorexia. Not every second, sometimes she even seemed normal, but this week was the worst I'd ever seen."

"Thank you," Abbie said. "I think we should let you be with your parents. It might be a good idea if none of you sleep here tonight. I know we'll have officers in Jessica's room for most of the night."

Tom assured Abbie and Clarke that everyone would be staying at his place for the foreseeable future. By the time they returned to the living room, the rest of the family had arrived—Sariah Morris and a man who, judging by the family resemblance, must have been the middle brother.

They were praying.

TWENTY-SEVEN

When the alarm went off, Abbie decided sleep was more important to her health than an early morning run. In the cruel way that only alarm clocks manage, the snooze alarm buzzed only a few seconds later, even though the clock maintained it had been ten minutes since it had last made its presence known. The citrus scent of her grapefruit shower gel did nothing to make her feel alert. Jessica's death had crawled into Abbie's head. Last Sunday, Smith had died. They had found his body the next morning. This Sunday, Jess had died. Abbie felt accountable for Jessica's death. If Jessica had killed herself, could Abbie have prevented it? If Jessica's death was a homicide, would she be alive if they'd caught Smith's killer? There wasn't a scenario Abbie could think of that relieved her of the dreadful weight of responsibility.

Abbie stopped in the local coffee and bagel shop on her way to work. She needed caffeine. The coffee was tolerable. The bagels weren't, but they would have to do.

She walked into the station. "Good morning." Her voice sounded as exhausted as she felt. Clarke was already at his desk studying the pictures he had taken just a few hours earlier. Abbie handed him an orange juice and large poppy bagel with cream cheese, red onion, and smoked salmon.

"Thanks." Clarke unwrapped the bagel and took a large bite. His desk, which was usually littered with candy bar wrappers and the remnants of whatever snack he had just eaten, was detritus-free. He had to be hungry.

"We need to talk to Jessica's parents again. Can you track down where the older brother lives? We need to know whether they had any idea about Jessica's relationship with Smith."

Clarke swallowed the bite of bagel he was chewing and said, "Sure, I'll call Jake."

Abbie walked to her office. The normal sounds of the station were muted. Sadness had muted the day-to-day noise of police work. It felt wrong to smile.

Abbie had just managed to sit down and take her first sip of coffee when Clarke appeared in her doorway.

"We can head over there now. Jake said they're not doing so well, but that's probably to be expected."

"Okay. Let's go, then."

Clarke climbed into the passenger side of the Range Rover. He served as navigator, and a few minutes later they arrived in front of a split-level house in an older neighborhood in Pleasant View. The entire street was lined with modest-looking, well-maintained houses, probably built in the 1950s and 1960s. There was an older-model Lincoln Town Car parked in the driveway and a brand-new GMC pickup truck.

A woman answered the door.

Abbie introduced Clarke and herself, then said, "Thank you. I'm sorry we have to intrude, but it's better that we talk sooner rather than later, as difficult as it is."

"Come in," the woman said with as much friendliness as the situation permitted.

Jessica's parents were sitting in the living room. There were a few young kids spread out on the floor reading and coloring. The woman who'd answered the door corralled them into the kitchen with the promise of baking brownies.

Abbie glanced around the room. The furniture was well taken care of, but it was neither new nor particularly well made. There was an upright piano awkwardly placed near the doorway so that you had to walk around the bench in order to enter the room. There were several hymnbooks stacked on top of the piano and a book of children's church songs balanced against the music rack. A large framed photo of the Logan temple was hanging on the wall over a brown paisley sofa. Between the two windows overlooking the front yard was the Gary Kapp image of Joseph Smith's First Vision, depicting a glowing Heavenly Father and Jesus Christ hovering above the ground in the woods of upstate New York where Joseph Smith had encountered the divine beings for the first time. The rest of the room looked as if it could have been a living room in any similar neighborhood in the state. Someone, probably the woman who'd answered the door, had stenciled "Families are Forever" above the doorway to the kitchen. There was a bookcase with copies of the scriptures filling the bottom two shelves, but the top shelf held much older books. Abbie stepped closer to get a better look. There were some early editions: a hymnbook, a Book of Mormon, and a copy of the fourth volume of *The Journal of Discourses*. Abbie had grown up with an extensive library of first and early editions of LDS books. Even though she didn't believe these books were divinely inspired, Abbie retained a reverence for all books, especially old ones.

Once the kids had scampered into the kitchen, Abbie turned her attention to Jessica's parents. Jessica's father was holding a well-thumbed copy of his own brown leather Book of Mormon.

"Brother and Sister Grant, we're so sorry for your loss. I wish we could spare you this conversation, but under the circumstances . . ." Abbie didn't feel the need to finish the sentence.

Jessica's mother, an older woman whose mostly gray hair was cut in a short bob that showed off her still tight jawline, was what many would call a "handsome woman." Her husband, whose hair was entirely gray, wore it closely cropped in a manner that made Abbie wonder if he had served in the military before becoming a teacher.

"Do you know what happened?" Jessica's father asked.

"We're still waiting on results from the Office of the Medical Examiner concerning Jessica's death. As soon as we know something, we'll let you know," Clarke said.

"Your son Jake lives with you?" Abbie asked.

"Yes," the father answered.

"He said he last saw Jessica around four o'clock."

"That makes sense. He would have gone to church and then to visit the young lady he's dating. She lives in Logan."

Abbie nodded to Clarke, who jotted down something in his small spiral notebook. He was going to have to confirm Jake's whereabouts.

"This may seem like a strange question, but did you know Steve Smith?"

Jessica's parents looked at each other.

"Well, yes," the husband replied. "We've known the Smiths for a long time. Steve's dad and I were at Weber State at the same time. It's so sad about his death."

Something in his tone made Abbie think that Jessica's parents didn't know his death was a homicide.

"Brother and Sister Grant, you may not have heard, but the medical examiner determined that Brother Smith's death was a homicide," Clarke announced. Evidently, he'd picked up on this misapprehension as well.

"We thought . . . we thought it was a heart attack," Jessica's mom stammered. Jessica's father put his hand over his wife's and squeezed it.

"We're trying to get a full picture of Steve Smith. Did you know him well?"

Jessica's father shook his head. "Like I said, I knew his dad. I'm sure our families had contact. The kids, I mean. I'm sure there were high school football games where our kids overlapped, but I don't remember any of the Smith kids having been friends with our kids. Do you, dear?"

"No, different circles of friends. I think the Smiths were more liberal. Not to say they weren't good people . . ."

Jessica's mom seemed to regret having passed judgment on the Smith family. She added, "Once the Smiths moved to Pleasant View, we would see the family at stake conference. I probably did some Relief Society work with Sister Smith."

"So, Steve Smith never visited you at your house?" Abbie asked.

"No." Jessica's parents answered at the same time. Then her father said, "I don't mean to be difficult, but what does Brother Smith's death have to do with Jessica? You don't think they're linked, do you?"

"At this point in time, we're not ruling anything out," Abbie said. "Do you remember the last time you saw Brother Smith?"

"I don't know," Jessica's mother said. "It must have been at stake conference, but I'm not sure. I don't specifically remember seeing him." She looked at her husband. He shook his head. "No, I couldn't say either. As I said, it's not like we were close."

"Do you know if Jessica was friendly with him?" Abbie asked.

"I can't imagine she would have been," Jessica's father said. There was something in his tone that put Abbie on alert. Clarke had again opened his notebook and wrote something down.

"Did Jessica ever mention him? You know, like he gave a talk at a Young Adults evening? Maybe a ride home?" Clarke asked.

"I don't remember her ever talking about him or anyone in the Smith family, for that matter. Do you, dear?"

Jessica's mom turned to her husband, who was still holding her hand.

"No, I'm quite certain I never heard her talk about him."

Clarke closed his notebook. Abbie saw he was trying to decide whether Jessica's parents were telling the truth. She could see in his face that something wasn't sitting right with him.

Abbie took over. "This is just routine, but I need to confirm again where you were on Sunday before you found Jessica."

"We were at church with our son's family in Bountiful." Clarke took the name and address of the son.

"And what about last Sunday morning?" Abbie asked.

The couple looked at each other. Jessica's father said, "Most Sunday mornings we're at home until church."

Jessica's mom stood up and walked to the kitchen. She returned with a dark-blue day planner. "I don't have anything written down for last Sunday. Sometimes we have things to do. I help out an elderly sister in the ward who sometimes needs help getting ready for church. After so many years of doing these things, Sundays sometimes blur together."

Abbie stood up, along with Clarke. She looked at the bookcase again. She was debating whether *The Journal of Discourses* might be a first edition.

"Ah, you recognize that?" Jessica's dad said as he watched Abbie's gaze.

"Yes, my father's a historian."

"William Taylor? I wondered, but I didn't want to pry.

You can tell him it's a second edition of Volume Four. Heber Jeddy Grant was my grandfather."

Heber J. Grant had been the seventh President of the Church. The name "Jeddy" stuck somewhere in Abbie's head. If she were speaking, she would have described the feeling as having a word on the tip of her tongue. As it was, she had a thought stuck between synapses. *What connection wasn't she making?*

TWENTY-EIGHT

Abbie had to stop at the grocery store on the way home. It was already dark and she was exhausted, but today was her mom's birthday. She had to pick up some birthday candles and cake. Every year on her mom's birthday, Abbie would end the day by lighting a single green candle (her mom's favorite color) and eating at least one slice of German chocolate cake washed down with a tall glass of cold milk. Over the years, it had become harder and harder to find German chocolate cake. Last year, Abbie had had to bake one herself. As she stared through the glass in the bakery section of the grocery store, all she could see were cakes iced in white or brown or depicting neon characters from the latest children's movie.

"Sweetheart, can I help you?" Abbie looked up to see an older woman wearing a white coat with her hair pushed up into a hairnet.

"I'm looking for a German chocolate cake. You don't by any chance have one?"

"Let me take a look in back. We do have a nice chocolate cake with vanilla frosting here."

“Thanks, but it needs to be German chocolate.” Abbie heard herself and realized the cake didn’t “need” to be anything. In fact, she didn’t need cake at all. The fact that she knew she was being irrational did not lessen her compulsion to have a German chocolate cake. The woman had been in the back of the bakery for what seemed like an eternity. Abbie started wondering if she should check the baking aisle for cake mixes. At this hour, there was no way she could bake a cake from scratch.

“Here you go!” The woman in the hairnet emerged from the back carrying a white box. “It’s the last one. Would you like anything written on it?”

“No, that’s okay.” Abbie watched the woman begin to tape the sides of the box and then changed her mind. “Actually, could you write ‘Happy Birthday, Mom’ in green?”

“Sure thing. It’ll just take me a second. Green?”

“Yes. Thank you.” Abbie exhaled. Her unreasonable anxiety about not having her mom’s birthday cake was draining from her body. She’d be home soon. She could shower away the day and sit down to a dinner of cake, milk, and champagne. Her mother would not have partaken in the champagne, of course, but Abbie knew she wouldn’t mind. In fact, her mom would probably have pointed out that Brigham Young oversaw the production of “Dixie wine” in the southern part of the state.

Abbie followed the familiar twists up Ogden Canyon in the dark. She kept her brights on the entire drive because there was no traffic heading the other way. She had turned the Rover onto her gravel driveway and headed up toward the cabin when her stomach dropped.

Lights were on in her bedroom and downstairs in the living room and kitchen. Abbie watched as two male figures moved in and out of view. Apparently they hadn't heard the car. She removed her foot from the brake and let gravity drag the Rover down to the road. She glided to the shoulder around the bend and parked.

It didn't take long for her eyes to adjust to the dark. She started walking up the driveway without any light, trying her best to be as silent as was possible on gravel. There was a back door into her study if she could manage not to set off the motion-detecting lights. She crouched behind a white Mercedes parked in front and considered the best way to get into the house without being seen.

Neither man had bothered to cover his face, but she couldn't identify either one from where she was. One was in a suit and tie; the other was wearing a flannel shirt. Flannel Shirt looked big. His hair was cropped. He had the thick neck and obvious muscular build of a man who either worked in private security or was an amateur body builder. Either way, he did not look like a guy you wanted to mess with. Suit Man looked familiar, but in a way that white men with expensive haircuts and well-tailored suits all did.

Abbie took the long way through the trees around the back of the house. She had eluded the motion detectors so far. At the moment, she was glad for that, but as she thought about it, she made a mental note that she should have the security system upgraded. If she could get past it, anyone could. She was almost certain she had set the alarm before she left that morning. She hadn't gotten a call from the security company, and there was certainly no alarm going off right then.

Abbie watched the man in the suit disappear, and then she saw the lights in her study go on. Suit pulled out his phone and started taking pictures of the papers on her desk. He was careful. He went through the stacks of her father's notes, but put them back as he found them.

Abbie moved a little closer to try to get a look at Suit's face. In the process, she must have triggered one of the motion detectors. The outside lights came on suddenly, casting strange shadows in the darkness. Abbie crawled behind a juniper bush, but not before Suit looked up. She could see him say something, but she couldn't make out the words.

The front door slammed. Heavy footsteps interrupted the nighttime quiet. Then Abbie saw Flannel Shirt walking slowly in her direction. The lights were shining out into the trees. Abbie could see the shadow of the man heading toward her, but she couldn't see him from her hiding place behind the thick evergreen shrubbery. She didn't move. She didn't breathe. She was prepared to shoot, but hoped it wouldn't end that way.

"I don't see anything! Could it have been a deer?" Flannel Shirt was standing just in front of her juniper bush. Abbie probably could have reached out and touched him through its branches.

Suit came to the door that led from her study onto the stone patio. He opened it and stepped outside. The light attached to one of the trees hit his face. It was Bowen.

"I thought I saw a person, but I could be wrong. I've got what I need. Let's go."

"Whatever you say, sir." Flannel Shirt looked directly at Abbie, but apparently couldn't see her. He turned around and walked back toward the driveway. Abbie watched as the lights in her house went out. She heard car doors open and close. She waited behind the bush long after they drove away until she heard nothing but silence.

Abbie hiked down the driveway. This time she pulled her phone out of her pocket and pressed the flashlight icon. She moved the light around the Rover and across the road. Nobody was there. The turnoff to her driveway was empty.

Abbie climbed back into the Rover and drove up the dirt road. She parked in the same place where the white Mercedes had been just a few minutes earlier. She picked up the grocery bag with the cake and candles and walked up the stairs to the cabin. When she unlocked the door, the alarm started beeping. Her stomach dropped for the second time that night. She entered the code and the beeping stopped.

She set her mom's birthday cake box on the counter. She inhaled the faintest hint of citrus and moss—Eau Sauvage. Abbie doubted Flannel Shirt was a Dior man. She then walked through the entire house and turned on every single light, even the ones in the closets. She inspected every place Bowen and his goon could have been. If she hadn't actually seen them in her house, she would never had known they'd been there. Everything was exactly as she had left it that morning. *Including the alarm.*

TWENTY-NINE

Abbie lifted her head from the kitchen counter when she heard her clock beeping upstairs. The cake, a single candle with a blackened wick in its center, was on the counter along with a glass of milk. Abbie had managed a single bite last night, but her appetite had vanished in the aftermath of her unexpected guests. She was so on edge that she had simply sat in the kitchen trying to figure out what Bowen and Flannel Shirt were looking for. She couldn't get it out of her head that they knew her alarm code. She also knew she couldn't say a word to anyone at work. If she mentioned this to Henderson, it would confirm all the anti-Mormon conceptions he already had about her. He not only wouldn't believe her; he'd be convinced she was on a witch-hunt to discredit LDS leaders.

A shower and a thermos of hot coffee would have to power her through the morning. Abbie caught her reflection in the bathroom mirror. There was no denying she looked the worse for wear. She opened a drawer and took out her heavy-duty concealer. She rubbed some blush along her cheeks and tried to convince herself no one would notice she looked like death warmed over.

Her phone buzzed.

It was a text from Clarke: WE CAN TALK TO JESS SIBS.

Abbie pushed last night's events to another part of her brain. She texted Clarke she was on her way. She looked at the screen on her phone. She had texted John last night, but it was late and he hadn't responded.

By just after eight in the morning, Abbie was sitting in the passenger seat next to Clarke. They were going to see Jessica's brothers. The Grant siblings had circled the wagons at Tom's house.

The front door was open when Abbie and Clarke arrived. A young woman with three toddlers in tow was leaving.

"Thank you so much for the lasagna and salad," said the woman Abbie now knew was Jessica's sister-in-law, Tom's wife.

"Of course," the young mom said. "I'm so sorry for all of you. We all adored Jess." The mom turned and saw Clarke. "Hi, Jim."

Clarke greeted the woman warmly and explained he was there on official business. Jessica's sister-in-law ushered Abbie and Clarke into the family room, where the brothers were talking about the obituary. She whispered, "Mom and Dad are napping upstairs. You won't need to talk to them right now, will you? They've been having a really hard time with this. We haven't been able to get them to rest until now."

Abbie assured the sister-in-law she wouldn't interrupt Jessica's parents' sleep. She and Clarke sat down in the large family room, which was a half-flight of carpeted stairs down from the living room where they had been the day before. The room was a mishmash of hand-me-down sofas and easy chairs that had seen better days. The walls were painted a shade of lavender that was a little too bright for Abbie's taste. Jake motioned for Abbie and Clarke to sit on the sofa facing the window. The middle brother had been typing on his laptop. A "first draft" of the obituary, he explained. He snapped the computer shut and turned his attention to the newcomers.

"We're trying to get a better picture of Jessica. Any detail, however unimportant you think it may be, might end up being critical. The more information you can give us, the better."

"Of course," Tom said.

"Do any of you know if your sister was seeing anyone?" Abbie asked. She hadn't believed Tom and Jake's denials the night before. She was hoping that in this setting, with all Jessica's brothers present, they would realize that honesty was the best policy.

Jake looked to his brothers, the oldest first and then the middle. For an uncomfortably long moment, no one said anything. Then Tom spoke up. "I don't think she was seeing anyone seriously."

"What about not seriously, then?" Abbie asked.

The middle brother said, "You know, we didn't keep track of Jess's social life. I'm sure she was dating, but she wasn't engaged or anything."

"So, you're saying you think she was dating, but none of you thought it was serious and none of you know who she was seeing?"

The brothers nodded.

Abbie was about to call them out when Clarke spoke up.

"Listen, we know Jessica was seeing someone seriously. I think you all know she was, too. It's not going to be helpful for us—and it certainly is not going to be good for you—if you don't tell us what you know."

Tom looked at his younger brothers, then back to Clarke. "Okay, we sort of were aware that she had this crush on Steve Smith."

"Do you care to elaborate on that?" Abbie asked.

This time, Jake spoke up. "I saw her with him. I wasn't sure at first, but then I saw them kissing. Not a father–daughter kind of peck; it was a real kiss. It was wrong on so many levels."

"And you two? Did you see Jessica with Steve Smith?" Abbie asked.

"Yeah," the other brothers admitted.

"Did any of you talk to Jessica about it?"

The brothers shook their heads. Then Tom spoke up again. "Jake saw her. At first, we didn't believe it. Brother Smith was a family friend. It didn't seem possible. Even Jake started to doubt what he saw after some time passed. We decided we'd better figure out if there was anything going on before we talked to Jess about it."

"And how exactly did you do that?" Abbie asked.

Tom said, "We didn't exactly spy on her, but we followed her around a few times. They'd meet up and spend an hour or so together at one of Jess's friends' house. None of us know what they did. Maybe they were just talking."

"Do you think they were just talking?" Abbie asked. She emphasized the word "you." No one who was paying attention could have missed the skepticism in her voice.

"No," the brothers answered in unison.

"Did you end up confronting Jessica about it?" Clarke asked.

There was silence. This time the middle brother spoke up. "Jess is really close with Sariah. We thought this was the kind of conversation that would be better between sisters."

"And what happened?" Abbie asked.

"Sariah talked to Jess," Tom said. "It turned out Jess had a major crush on Brother Smith. He was aware of it and was counseling her. He'd been trying to help her meet someone at her ward. It sounded to me like whatever Jake saw was a schoolgirl crush. You know, Jess coming on to Brother Smith, not the other way around."

"Did you know Jessica spent several months last year with Smith in Costa Rica?" Abbie looked at each of the Grant brothers after she asked the question. Whatever strengths the brothers had, playing poker was not among them. It was obvious this was the first time they'd heard that their baby sister had spent months last spring with Steve Smith in Costa Rica. The middle brother said, "Uh, yeah, we knew about it. She was doing some kind of work down there. It was her first real job after college."

"We knew she was working in Central America," Jake added.

"Yeah, I'm not exactly sure what she did day-to-day,"

Tom added, "but it was a good chance for her to get some work experience."

All three brothers were supporting each other in the lie they were making up on the spot. Abbie had no idea why. She glanced at Clarke. He seemed to be thinking exactly what she was.

"And that didn't bother you?" Clarke asked. "The idea that your little sister, who was nursing a crush on Steve Smith, spent months alone with him in a beachfront villa in Costa Rica?"

"No, it didn't," Jake said. "Jess wouldn't do anything that would prevent her from getting married in the temple. Brother Smith is a happily married member of the bishopric in his ward. He wouldn't break his temple vows."

"Did you ever talk to Smith directly about Jessica?" Abbie asked.

"There was no need to," Tom said. "Jess believed in fairies and unicorns. It wasn't out of character for her to imagine things or even convince herself they were true. We'd all seen her have crushes on her teachers in high school and even a few professors in college. This was exactly the sort of thing she'd do. We knew it would pass. There was no need to bother Brother Smith about it. He knew what was going on and was handling it."

Clarke jotted something down in his notebook. The brothers glanced his way. Abbie thought she detected slight discomfort on all their faces.

"Can you all tell me where you were last Sunday morning?" Abbie asked.

"I got ready for church, then I went to church," the middle Grant brother said.

"Same," Jake and Tom echoed.

"Can anybody verify that?" Abbie asked.

The brothers looked a little irritated, but Clarke diffused the situation. "Guys, we have to ask these questions just so we can rule everyone out. It's standard."

The middle brother answered, "My family can tell you I was getting ready and then everyone at church can tell you I was at church."

Again the others said, "Same."

"And what about this Sunday after church?" Abbie asked.

"When Jess passed away?" Tom asked. "You can't possibly think we had anything to do with that? I mean, are you even sure Jess didn't do this to herself? I hate to say this, but she was rather dramatic. She's made attempts before when she didn't get her way."

"We're not ruling anything out at this point," Abbie said, "In the meantime, as a matter of course, I need to know where you all were."

The middle brother confirmed he'd been at church for most of the afternoon. After that, he'd had dinner with his family and his parents before they drove back home. Tom had also been at church for the early part of the afternoon and then spent the rest of the evening at home with his family. Jake had been at home and then gone to visit a friend—he didn't call her his girlfriend—until he got home. Everyone gave Clarke relevant names and addresses for homes and churches.

Abbie and Clarke said their good-byes and left the brothers to work on the obituary. As soon as they closed the front door behind them, Clarke said, "They're lying about knowing Jess was with Smith in Costa Rica."

"I know," Abbie said, "but why?"

THIRTY

Luckily, Clarke had already looked up the address for Sariah before they talked to the brothers. It was only a few minutes before they pulled up at the curb in front of the house in Ben Lomond Circle. Abbie was hoping to get to the older sister before the brothers had a chance to text or call her about what they'd said.

When they arrived at the sister's house, they were greeted by the sight of two young kids playing soccer in the front yard. There was a minivan parked in the driveway with its back door open, revealing bags of groceries and probably a dozen two-liter bottles of soda.

"Go ahead and kick!" the girl yelled. "The goal's between the rock here and the flowers over there." She spread her arms and grimaced in a vain attempt to look menacing. Both she and her little brother had dirt on their knees and grass stains everywhere. The boy set the ball carefully on the lawn and walked back a few paces. He ran as fast as he could and kicked. The older girl dove to the right and managed to catch the ball as she landed on the ground.

"And that," she announced triumphantly, "is how it's done."

"I'll get it next time." Her brother grinned. Then he turned to the two grown-ups walking up his front walkway. "Are you here about Aunt Jess?"

"Yes, we're policemen. I'm Detective Abbie Taylor, and this is Officer Jim Clarke, of the Pleasant View City Police Department. We're here to speak to your mother," Abbie answered, not shifting her tone to the singsong voice many women used when talking to young children.

"She's inside," the girl said. "We're getting ready for Grandma and Grandpa and all the cousins. They're all coming over here. My mom says the change of scenery will be good for everyone."

The front door was open. Abbie couldn't see anyone, but she could hear someone moving around in the back of the house. Sariah Morris walked into the entrance hall from a side door. She was carrying a basket with several large containers of baked goods. At least two of them had tape on them identifying the containers' owners.

"Oh, hello, I didn't hear the doorbell." Sariah was wearing slim chocolate-brown trousers that hit at her slender ankle. Her sweater was lightweight pale-pink cashmere. On her feet, she was wearing coffee-colored velvet moccasins. Her hair was down. The layered cut let her thick honey-colored hair fall in loose waves around her face. She was wearing makeup—a little perfectly smudged brown eyeliner, blush, eyebrow powder, concealer, and lip gloss—but it had been so subtly applied that Abbie was pretty sure Clarke thought Sariah had woken up looking like she did right then.

"We didn't ring it. I hope you don't mind," Clarke said by way of apology.

"Not at all," Jessica's sister said.

"We can see you're busy, but—"

"We're all meeting with the Bishop at the church in forty-five minutes to go over the funeral. Then everyone's coming here." Sariah was trying to keep her voice friendly, but you could hear in it the tension of a woman who had too much to do and too little time in which to do it. "Is there any way this can wait?"

"I'm afraid it can't. We'll try to be as quick as possible," Abbie said.

"Okay." Sariah pulled out her phone and started typing. Abbie heard the whoosh of a text and then, after a few more typed words, a second whoosh.

"I needed to let everyone know I'll be a little later than I'd promised." This time, Abbie noted, the irritation in Sariah's voice was not so well disguised.

Sariah showed them into the living room. Abbie had expected this house to look like every other house she'd seen in the neighborhood. Something imitating the houses on *Real Housewives*: shiny wood, oversized furniture, and coordinating couches, chairs, and curtains—desperate to show off the good taste and wealth of the families who lived there. This house was different. The entry hall floor wasn't marble; it was reclaimed wood. The furniture was understated. There was a large framed photograph of the Salt Lake Temple hanging over the mantle, but the frame wasn't ornate gold, and the photograph was in black and white. The coffee table looked as if it had once been part of a barn door. On top of it, there weren't any orchids or expensive books on art. Instead, there was a simple ceramic milk jug overflowing with wildflowers and three volumes of *The Journal of Discourses*.

"First editions?" Abbie asked.

"One is; the other two are second editions. My family originally owned the entire twenty-six volumes of the first publication. Over the years, the set has been divided up as we each inherited different volumes. I've been slowly trying to get a complete set again. I did manage to find this second edition of the fourth volume at a yard sale in Grantsville." A beep interrupted the conversation. Sariah looked down and read something on her phone, then asked, "What is it you want to know?"

"We'd like to hear your perspective on your sister's relationship with Steve Smith," Abbie said.

Surprise flashed across Sariah's face. Maybe she hadn't spoken to her brothers yet. "I'm not sure what you mean by the word 'relationship.' "

"Oh, I think you do." Abbie didn't want to give Jessica's sister any time to think about her answer.

With deliberate calm, Sariah said, "If you're talking about the crush Jess had on Brother Smith, sure, I knew about that. I wouldn't have called it a relationship, though. The Smiths are dear family friends. Our kids are roughly the same ages and hang out together a lot. We're in the same ward. Melinda and I trade carpooling duties, things like that. Our kids do a lot of the same activities. You know, soccer, dance, cheerleading, Scouts. Jess developed some sort of infatuation with Steve. We all saw it for what it was: another one of her fantasies. She had a thing for older men in positions of power: teachers, professors, even her doctor once."

"You're telling me that Jessica didn't spend several months with Steve Smith in Costa Rica?"

"Oh, I'm not saying that at all," Sariah answered. "In fact, I think that's where the whole absurd obsession started."

"There wasn't anything physical going on?" Abbie asked.

"Goodness no."

"You sound fairly sure about that," Clarke said.

"I am," Sariah said.

"Did you ever discuss this 'crush' with Melinda? Since you were such good friends . . . ?" Abbie asked.

"Of course not. Nothing good could have come of that. I knew Jess's infatuation would pass as soon as she started dating someone seriously and got married. Melinda had enough on her plate with Steve getting this project in Costa Rica going. It was hard to be a single mom for months at a time. It never even crossed my mind to burden her with my little sister's silly infatuation."

"We've spoken to Melinda. It doesn't seem like she shares your certainty that this was a one-sided schoolgirl crush," Abbie said.

"Melinda's been through so much. I imagine she's so broken that she can't think straight. Give her some time and she'll realize that whatever fantasy Jess made up in her head about Steve was just that: a fantasy. As I'm sure you've heard from everyone who knew her, Jess lived in her own little world."

Abbie was trying to get a handle on Sariah Morris. The woman was hard to read. She either was telling them the truth—or her version of the truth—or, unlike her brothers, was a supremely good liar.

"How was Jessica after Smith died?" Abbie asked.

"I think she was coming to her senses, finally. After Steve, well, after what happened to Steve, Jessica couldn't keep up the delusion about him."

"Was she seeing anyone else?" Clarke asked.

"Not that I know of, but I wouldn't be surprised. Jess may have been a bit dramatic from time to time, and she did have her fantasies, but there was no escaping the fact that she was beautiful. There was no shortage of handsome returned missionaries who were interested . . . as you probably know, Jim." Sariah gave Clarke a knowing glance, perhaps expecting him to agree with her. Abbie noticed that he did not.

"Your brothers mentioned that Jessica had attempted suicide before," Abbie said.

"That's a bit of an overstatement, I think. Once she took pills when she didn't get voted junior prom queen. She was one of the princesses. Another time, she took a razor to her wrists, but the wounds were so superficial that there was no real danger of anything except the bloodstains on what she was wearing. I don't mean to sound cold. Jess was the baby of the family. We all loved her more than anything, but we weren't blind to her tendency to be a little melodramatic from time to time."

"Would Steve's death have caused her to do anything, as you say, melodramatic?" Abbie asked.

"Well, yes, probably," Sariah said. She looked at Clarke again and added, "You have younger sisters, so you know what I mean."

Clarke shrugged. "Where were you last Sunday morning?"

Sariah looked shocked. "Are you asking me where I was when Steve Smith was killed?"

"Yes. It's routine," Clarke responded. The friendliness that usually warmed his voice was absent.

"I went for a long run. I'm training for the Ogden marathon. I got back just in time for church."

Sariah looked like a runner. She was slender, with the taut muscles of someone who probably logged at least twenty-five miles a week.

"And what about this Sunday afternoon?" Clarke asked.

"I was at the church, then came back here with my family. We had dinner, and I went to bed early because I had my sixteen miles in the morning and I was exhausted. I had been asleep for hours before Mom called about what happened." Sariah paused for a moment, then asked, "Do you think Jess did this to herself?"

"We're not ruling anything out at this point," Abbie said. "Do you think she could have?"

Sariah's eyes filled with tears. The first tears Abbie had seen from the sister. "Yeah, this is the sort of thing Jess would do, but she wouldn't have expected it to work. She would have expected someone to rescue her."

THIRTY-ONE

"Let's stop in at the Shooting Star." Abbie clicked her seat belt as Clarke started the car. They'd been talking to the Grant family all day and Abbie was famished. If the sounds coming from Clarke's stomach were any indication, he was, too.

"Uh . . . okay," he said.

Abbie had thought about making this suggestion for quite some time. In a state where most people don't drink coffee or tea, let alone alcohol, the art of spending an hour or two just talking was not well practiced. A little alcohol lubricated conversation. Without it, people became antsy after the superficial niceties had been exchanged. But, if there was a place in the northern part of the state conducive to open and unguarded conversation with or without alcohol, it was the Shooting Star Saloon.

The place was the oldest continually running bar in Utah, according to the owner. It was known for great burgers and the occasional ghost of an old cowboy. Abbie's sisters would not set foot in the place because liquor was served, but she'd had a few dinners there with John. She liked it. It was the perfect level of shabby that made her feel right at home.

Abbie was gambling Clarke would feel at home, too. She wanted them to have a chance to talk. It was important to relax, even if only for the amount of time it took to eat a burger. They needed to debrief and brainstorm. They had two bodies and were getting nowhere fast. She blamed most of their lack of progress on herself. She wanted—needed—a place where she could exhale. She had to have an hour or two away from all the descendants of the same pioneers she came from—those hardworking converts from Britain and northern Europe who had crossed the Atlantic and thousands of miles of the United States on foot or by wagon to this Zion in the American West. Phillip had once come across her high school yearbooks and joked how the entire school, with a few Samoan and Tongan exceptions, looked the same. He wasn't wrong. She was surrounded by her people, except she wasn't one of them anymore.

Abbie sensed she was missing something. Part of her was still "processing" the conversations with her dad. Processing was a word a therapist would use, but it seemed appropriate. She wanted to forgive him for the time he'd missed with her mom, but then he had gone and done Port's bidding, just like always. Was he capable of saying no? As long as her dad believed he and her mom would be together for eternity if he did what the Church wanted, as long as he felt compelled to follow all the rules, Port would have power.

On top of all that, Abbie had to admit to herself that it was taking an inordinate amount of emotional energy to suppress her anxiety about the break-in. She was processing that, too. It was bad enough that it had happened, but knowing that Bowen had her security code was plain unnerving. Had he been in her place before without her knowing? What else in her life did he have access to? And, the most disconcerting question of all, why?

The bartender recognized Abbie and nodded his head in her direction when she walked in. She and Clarke took a booth in the back and ordered burgers, which would be served in plastic baskets lined in paper along with a generous serving of potato chips. They each ordered root beers.

"What's your take on the Grant family?" Abbie asked.

"I hate to say this, but I don't think they're telling us the truth. I don't know why they're pretending they knew about the trip to Costa Rica, but I don't think they did. At least, I don't think the brothers knew Smith had been there. As to the rest of it, I feel like we're getting half-truths or half-lies. I don't like it. I also don't know what to make of the suicide angle. The fact that they all think it's possible is kind of weird." Clarke took a gulp of root beer from the icy mug.

"You knew Jessica. Is the picture her siblings are painting accurate?" Abbie asked.

"It sorta is. Jess was beautiful. You couldn't *not* notice her. The reason she wasn't married wasn't because she didn't want to be married and not because she didn't date. She had a reputation for being difficult. She went on more first dates than anyone I knew, but they rarely led to a second. She had unrealistic ideas about life and about herself. I'm not saying I think she made up the whole thing about Smith, but it's completely conceivable that she embellished."

"What about suicide?" Abbie asked.

"I hate to say this, but her sister is right on the nose. Jess could pull a stunt like this, but not with the expectation that she'd actually die. She'd be convinced someone would save her and then everyone would make a big fuss," Clarke said.

The burgers arrived in all their greasy, salty glory. The smell of the meat alone compelled both of them to take larger-than-polite bites. It took Abbie longer than Clarke to chew and swallow the mix of soft hamburger bun, ground beef, cheese, ketchup, and iceberg lettuce lining the bottom bun to prevent the juiciness from turning it into a soggy mess. By the time Abbie took a swallow of her root beer, Clarke was already halfway through his burger and had waved to the waitress that he'd like a second.

"How do you explain Melinda's response to the news about the affair?" Abbie asked. "It seemed to me that she responded like a woman who believed her husband had cheated on her with Jessica."

"I wonder if Smith had cheated on her before. Not to be mean, but if I looked like Melinda, I'd wonder what my husband was doing spending all that time with young single women, even if it was at church activities."

Abbie took another bite of her burger. "Do you think Smith and Jess were actually having an affair? Jess certainly made it sound that way."

Clarke swallowed and thought for a moment. "I'd say there's an eighty-five-percent chance they were . . . at the very least, something happened in Costa Rica. Granted, it's not clear how far they went. I mean, there are a lot of things two people can do without, you know, actually having, uh . . . you know . . ."

"Yeah, I know," Abbie said.

"I do have an idea how we can find out."

"I'm listening," Abbie said.

"You may not have noticed all the cheerleading pictures in Jess's room when we were there. Jess's best friend, Meghan Silver, was a cheerleader with her in high school. I think they shared an apartment for a while in college. They were always together at church. If there's anyone Jess would have talked to, it'd be Meghan."

"I take it you know where Meghan lives?" Abbie asked.

"Yeah, I do."

If it hadn't been so dark in the Shooting Star, Abbie would have sworn Clarke was blushing.

Abbie finished her burger, and Clarke was popping the last bite of his second Star Burger into his mouth when both their phones buzzed.

It was Henderson: NEED TO SEE YOU ASAP.

★★★

"There's something you have to see," Henderson said as soon as Clarke and Abbie walked into the station. He handed Abbie an evidence bag with a pale-pink sheet of paper inside. "It's the suicide note."

Someone had typed out the words "I'm so sorry, but this is the only way" in Courier font, all italics. There was no signature.

"I thought tech didn't find anything on Jess's computer," Abbie said.

"They didn't. Tech went through everything on her computer and phone. There wasn't anything there. I looked through the papers on Jess's desk again this afternoon while you were talking to the family and found it." Abbie thought Henderson sounded relieved, but also a little surprised. As nice and tidy as this note made the case, Abbie could tell even Henderson didn't quite believe his luck.

Abbie had gone through every piece of paper in Jess's room. Twice. She couldn't possibly have missed a suicide note, could she?

"Are there any prints on it?" Abbie asked.

"Yes, Jessica's," Henderson answered. "I've already spoken with her mother. She told me Jessica liked to use this pale-pink paper whenever she had to print something out." Given the girlishness of Jess's bedroom, Abbie had no trouble believing Jessica Grant used pale-pink paper. She probably dotted the *i* in her signature with a circle or maybe even a heart, Abbie thought, even if she felt a bit judgmental for thinking it.

"That girl's desk was a disaster," Henderson said. "It's not hard to see how we might have missed it."

"Is there any way this isn't a suicide note?" Clarke asked. "The words themselves could refer to a lot of things."

"Yes, but this note makes sense. Jessica Grant wasn't the sweet innocent girl we all thought she was. The most straightforward theory is usually the right one, even if it forces us to admit some uncomfortable truths about people we thought we knew. Jessica realized Smith was not going to marry her and carefully planned revenge. Then the guilt became too much to bear, and she ended her own life, too. We had a bowie knife in both places, both Smith and Grant were dressed in white, both deaths looked like what you'd wear for your wedding . . . well, you get the idea. It's not hard to think the same person was responsible for both."

Abbie generally believed in the principle of Occam's razor: among competing hypotheses, the one with the fewest assumptions should be selected. Henderson was not sounding at all unreasonable. In fact, there really was no demonstrable flaw in the theory. Sure, as far as suicide notes went, this was thin. There was no signature and it had not been left in a place where it could easily be found. On the other hand, if her brothers and sister were to be believed, Jessica was given to dramatic gestures. If she had expected to be rescued that night, maybe the suicide note wasn't entirely necessary. Still, something about the note and the idea of suicide didn't sit quite right with Abbie. The idea that Jessica had killed Steve was improbable not only because Jessica was not a person to meticulously plan anything, let alone a murder, but also because Jessica hadn't had her endowments. She wouldn't have known how to dress Steve in his temple clothes.

"Is there any way someone could have planted the note?" Abbie asked.

"I wondered about that," Henderson said. "You secured the crime scene yourself, and the room was cordoned off. Of course, we didn't have an officer at the scene around the clock, but we did set the alarm on the house. I had to enter the code this morning. I think it's pretty unlikely anyone tampered with the room."

Henderson was probably right. It was not likely anyone would have tampered with the scene after they left. Abbie wondered if her resistance to the note had more to do with the fact that she had missed a key piece of evidence than it did with the suicide theory itself. From everything she and Clarke had heard that day, a dramatic suicide attempt was exactly the damsel-in-distress move Jess's siblings had come to expect.

"We were on our way to interview Jessica's best friend when you texted. Do you mind if we follow through with that?" Abbie asked.

"Seems like a waste of time at this point, don't you think?" Henderson was looking at his computer screen. The conversation was over.

Clarke said, "It may be, but I feel like we owe it to Jess's parents to follow through."

That was brilliant. Invoking Jessica's parents put Henderson in a position where it would be difficult to turn down their request.

Henderson sighed. "Okay, you two go interview the friend, but with the suicide note, I want this whole thing wrapped up by Wednesday. We don't need to spend taxpayer money on an investigation into a murder-suicide." Henderson looked directly at Abbie. "Final report on my desk by Wednesday end of day. This case is closed as far as I'm concerned, even if it's a very difficult result for both the Smith and Grant families."

Abbie and Clarke stood up at the same time. "Yes, sir," they said. They had the rest of tonight and tomorrow. And whatever they could do before the end of day on Wednesday. That was not enough time. Not even close.

Abbie followed Clarke to his squad car. They buckled up in silence. Once Clarke had pulled out of the parking lot, Abbie asked, "Do you think Jess was capable of killing Smith and then killing herself?"

Clarke didn't answer at first. He drove as though he hadn't even heard Abbie's question. Then he said quietly, "No. I don't."

THIRTY-TWO

Clarke rang the doorbell at another one of the McMansions in Ben Lomond Circle. The house was a smaller one for the neighborhood, but still too big for the narrow plot of thick, green grass that surrounded it. A few trees stuck out from the centers of dark brown circles punched through the front lawn. None of them was taller than six feet and none of them had trunks wider than Abbie's arms.

Abbie and Clarke hadn't been standing at the door long before a middle-aged woman with a flour-speckled apron opened the door. She smiled when she saw Clarke.

"Jim, I'm so glad to see you. Meghan didn't tell me you were coming by, but she really could use a good friend right about now."

Meghan's mom stopped talking when she saw Abbie.

"Sister Silver, this is Detective Abish Taylor," Clarke said. "She's the detective for the Pleasant View City Police Department."

"Oh. You're here as a police officer." The woman spoke her thoughts out loud as she began to comprehend why Clarke was actually on her doorstep.

"We'd like to speak to Meghan. Is she up for it?" Clarke asked.

"I think so." The mom wiped her hands down the front of her apron. "She'll be happy to see you, no matter why you're here." The woman's familiarity with Clarke was not lost on Abbie.

"Why don't you sit in the living room? I'll go get her."

Abbie and Clarke had just sat down when Meghan walked in. Her eyes were rimmed with red and slightly puffy, but even that couldn't disguise her thick dark lashes and well-arched brows. She was a beautiful girl: tall, with a long narrow waist, pale creamy skin, impossibly high cheekbones, and perfect bow-shaped lips. She was Jessica's brunette counterpart. She walked straight to Clarke and put her arms around him. He reciprocated immediately, but pulled away when he saw Abbie stand to greet Meghan.

"Meghan, we're here to talk about Jess," Clarke explained. "Let's sit down."

Everyone did as instructed. Clarke asked Meghan to tell them about Jessica.

"We've—we'd—been best friends since the summer before seventh grade. She practically lived here in high school. We shared an apartment when we were at Weber State. We were talking about getting an apartment together again if we didn't get married soon."

"Did you see her on Sunday?" Abbie asked.

Tears welled in Meghan's eyes, but she inhaled slowly and maintained her composure. "No. She decided to go to church with her sister. She did that sometimes instead of going to our ward. We were planning to meet at Nielson's for Diet Cokes later in the afternoon."

"Did you go?" Abbie asked.

"No. Jess texted me sometime around four to say she couldn't make it."

"Did she tell you why?" Clarke asked.

"No. I figured some guy had asked her out or she just decided she wasn't up for it. She wasn't really feeling social. I was super happy she was at church. That was a good sign."

"Do you know what time she texted you?" Abbie asked.

Meghan reached for her phone, which she'd set on the coffee table. She scrolled through her texts. "Four seventeen PM."

"And no other texts after that?" Clarke asked.

"No."

"You said you thought Jessica may have gone out with someone on Sunday. Was she seeing anyone seriously?" Abbie asked.

"Not really; I mean, she wasn't officially engaged or anything." Meghan's eyes lingered on Clarke. It crossed Abbie's mind that Meghan was holding back because she was there.

"Was she unofficially engaged?" Clarke asked.

Meghan didn't say anything.

"I know you may feel like you don't want to tell us something because you don't want to betray a trust. I get that," Clarke said. "I also understand you might not want to tell us things that other people might judge. We're not going to judge. We want to find out what happened to Jess. The best way for you to be a friend right now is to tell us what you know. Even the things you promised not to tell or even little things that might seem unimportant. The more we know, the easier it will be for us to understand what happened."

"You won't tell anyone what I tell you?" Meghan looked concerned, nervous even.

"We're not interested in spreading rumors or gossip," Abbie answered. "Our investigation is confidential. You don't need to worry about your friends or family—or Jessica's friends or family—hearing what you tell us, but we do need the truth, all of it."

Meghan looked at Clarke. He nodded.

"Okay." Meghan uncurled her legs from underneath her and climbed out of the chair she was sitting in. She closed the French doors that led to the entry hall. No one would be able to overhear what was being said now.

"Do you know who Jessica was seeing?" Clarke asked.

"Yeah," Meghan answered. There was less hesitation in her voice now. "She was engaged to Steve Smith. It was a secret. He asked her to marry him when they were in Costa Rica working on some project for the Church. He gave her an engagement ring. It was a huge pink diamond, really expensive. She always had it on. She put it on a thin gold chain she wore around her neck so you couldn't see it under her top. It looked just like she was wearing a necklace."

A memory of something sparkly flickered in Abbie's mind. She remembered Jessica playing with a delicate chain when they'd been in Relief Society on Sunday.

Meghan went on, "She was so excited. They were going to get married in the Logan temple as soon as Steve got his divorce."

Meghan's voice dropped to almost a whisper when she

said the word "divorce." Even though the Church accepted divorce, it still wasn't something anyone took lightly.

"Had they set a date?" Abbie asked.

"Yeah, but it was super secret. Jess said Steve had the divorce papers and was planning to talk to his wife a few weeks ago. Jess called the Logan temple from my room for wedding times, like, two weeks ago."

"Did you ever see Jess and Steve together?" Abbie asked.

"Yeah. I was sort of their messenger," Meghan said.

"What do you mean?" Abbie asked.

"Steve lives just a few houses away from here. It was really easy for us to run into each other 'accidentally.' If Jess had something she wanted to give Steve, she'd just text us. I could go for a run or Steve could walk the dog. It was pretty easy to bump into each other. Once, when the weather was really bad, they met here. No one was home, so it was safe."

Abbie tried her best to look as if this was completely normal. Clarke, on the other hand, was clearly having trouble pretending there was nothing wrong with a married man old enough to be Jess's dad arranging clandestine meetings with her.

"When you say they met here, what do you mean?" Abbie asked.

"You know." Meghan looked at her shiny blue nails. "They wanted to have some time together, some private time. You know?"

Abbie nodded. It was clear Clarke understood, too, but wished he didn't.

"What happened after Steve passed away?" Abbie asked.

"It was awful. For a few days, Jess didn't eat anything. I mean, like, nothing at all. It was all I could do to get her to drink Diet Coke. Her mom called me because she was really worried."

"Did her mom know about Steve?" Abbie asked.

"No! She didn't have a clue, but she was always on top of what Jess was eating, ever since her anorexia in high school." Abbie remembered her own high school days and the pressure to be pretty and thin. She remembered the girls who pushed food around on their plates but never ate anything. Apparently things hadn't changed that much in the years since. There was a lot of pressure on young women to be attractive. Utah had more plastic surgeons per capita than any other place in the country, including LA and New York.

"Did she say anything to you when Steve died?" Abbie asked.

"She didn't." Meghan shook her head. "She didn't say anything about it at all. I thought it was kind of weird. I think she was in shock."

"Did you know Jess was taking Ativan?" Clarke asked.

"Yeah." Meghan didn't seem surprised by the question.

"Do you know if she ever took more than she was supposed to?" Abbie followed up.

"No, she was really responsible about it. I'm on it, too. I used to take Xanax, but my doctor changed me to Ativan. We were both super scared about overdosing, so we were really good about only taking as much as we were supposed to."

"This is a tough question, but I need to ask it. I'd like

you to take your time before you answer," Abbie said. "Do you think Jessica could have taken her own life?"

"No way! Sure, she was messed up about Steve dying. I mean, really, the whole thing with Steve was messed up."

You can say that again, Abbie thought.

"You know though, I tried not to judge. She was my best friend. I was going to be there for her no matter what. Suicide? No. Jess would've found someone else to marry. She knew that."

"Do you know if she had ever tried to hurt herself before?" Abbie pressed.

"Jess could be dramatic sometimes, but she never did anything serious. You know? She never did anything that couldn't be fixed."

"Can you think of anyone who would have wanted to hurt her?" Abbie asked.

"No way. I mean, like, sure, there were girls who were jealous. Jess kind of always got what she wanted. People were nice to her, and guys would do anything for her. So, yeah, there were people who resented that, but nobody would ever actually want to hurt her. They'd just say mean things about her behind her back."

"Things like what?" Abbie asked.

"You know, like she wasn't that smart or she was kind of flaky. She lived in her own little fantasy world of rainbow sparkles. Stuff like that."

"Do you happen to know where Jess was the day Steve Smith died?" Abbie asked. "That would be last Sunday before church."

"I don't know where she was before church, but she

was at church with us." Meghan looked across at Clarke. "We sat together in Sacrament Meeting."

Clarke nodded.

"If you think of anything that seems like it might be important, please call me or Officer Clarke." Abbie stood up. "I know this was hard. You were a very good friend to Jess. She was lucky to have you in her life."

Clarke stood up and so did Meghan. Abbie could tell Meghan wanted to give Clarke another hug but was holding back because she didn't think it was appropriate. Meghan's eyes were watery as she watched the two of them walk to the door. Then she suddenly blurted out, "This might not be anything, but there was something weird last Sunday at church. I think I saw that General Authority, the one who does all the media stuff for the Church. You know, Elder Brown . . . no, that's not right . . . Elder Boon? I swear I saw him before Relief Society talking to Jess."

Abbie took this bit of information in without even batting an eye. "Thank you. That's exactly the kind of little detail that will help us figure out what happened. If you remember anything else, let us know."

As soon as they were both in the car and couldn't be overheard by anyone, Clarke asked, "Did we find a pink diamond engagement ring in Jess's room?"

"No," Abbie said. "We didn't."

THIRTY-THREE

"Flynn's not using his place. You're staying there until we figure out what happened here." John's voice was stern.

Abbie wondered how long he had been waiting in front of her cabin. He was two thirds of the way through the book he was reading. Abbie knew from years of being his little sister that, when he sounded like this, there was no sense in disagreeing. He handed her a piece of paper. "Here's his housekeeper's number. She's expecting to hear from you. She'll meet you at the house and give you the keys and security code. I think you should leave your Rover in the garage there. Flynn has cars. He said take whichever one you want."

Abbie threw her arms around her big brother. The day had not given Abbie much time to tend to thoughts of the break-in. Now that she was opening the door to her home where Bowen had been about twenty-four hours ago, she couldn't ignore how raw her nerves were. She was grateful John was there.

"Get what you need for a few days. Do you want me to come upstairs with you?"

She was a cop. She didn't need her big brother holding her hand while she packed an overnight bag. "No, it's okay."

"I'm coming anyway," John said as he followed her upstairs. Abbie smiled as she exhaled.

She pulled a carry-on suitcase from her closet and started packing. She kept the matching small duffle bag packed with travel-sized versions of all her toiletries and duplicates of her tooth and face brushes. In less than twenty minutes, she was done. She grabbed a large canvas tote bag hanging from the inside doorknob of her closet and dropped her dad's research on blood atonement inside.

John carried her things to her car. "Why don't you call Flynn's housekeeper now and tell her we're on our way over?"

Abbie did as instructed. The woman who looked after Flynn's house had the voice of an indulgent grandmother and assured Abbie she would be waiting for her. Mr. Paulsen, she said, had already given her instructions.

After Abbie finished talking to Flynn's housekeeper, John said, "I'll follow you over there." As much as Abbie knew she was capable of taking care of herself, she was relieved John was so protective.

Abbie turned onto Ritter Drive, then onto a long private driveway overlooking a field with a few horses she could see in the faint light of dusk. As she passed one of the trees midway down the drive, outdoor lights switched on, evidently set with motion detectors. She pulled in front of the three-car garage.

A barrel-shaped woman with a contagious grin and short gray curls waved from the front door. It was painted forest green, as was all the trim and shutters of the classic white clapboard house. The house was grand for its era, but in comparison to the McMansions of Ben Lomond Circle, a real-estate agent now would describe it as "understated" and "gracious." There were two full stories and a pitched roof with dormers.

John pulled up behind Abbie, hopped out, and took her two bags from her car to the front door. He introduced himself to the woman standing at the door. He turned and gave Abbie a hug.

"I'm sorry to run, but I've missed half of Harrison's performance already. I need to get home. Text me tonight before you go to sleep."

Abbie hugged her brother tightly. "Thank you." She didn't want to let him go, but she released him so he could catch the end of his son's musical.

The woman said, "Hello, Abbie. I'm Margene. It's so nice to meet a friend of Flynn's. Let me take you to your room so you can drop your bags; then I'll show you around the house."

Abbie followed Margene up the highly polished wooden staircase to the second floor as the older woman chatted away. "Flynn mentioned that you're a morning person, so we thought it would be nice for you to be in one of the bedrooms facing east." Margene entered a perfectly appointed room decorated in shades of pale blue. Abbie wasn't an expert in antique furniture but had a feeling that each piece was a mint-condition original. There was a full-sized four-poster bed facing a fireplace, a chaise longue and small side table inlaid with wooden flowers and leaves in front of a large window overlooking the field outside. To the side of the door stood a chiffonier with an arrangement of fresh white roses and sprays of baby's breath.

"Flynn always makes sure there are fresh flowers if the guest rooms are being used." Margene walked across the room to a door on the side of the bed. She opened it and turned on the light. It was an all-white bathroom with Carrera marble tile. "Adding small bathrooms for each bedroom was the only real structural change Flynn made from when his grandparents lived here. It took some effort, but it does make for a more comfortable stay." Abbie had to agree. There was a single white rose in a small bud vase sitting on the side of the pedestal sink.

"I'll take you downstairs so you know where everything is, and then I'll leave you be. Flynn mentioned you're a detective and probably need a good night's rest. I made dinners for the rest of the week. I'm not sure how long you're planning to stay. They're all in the fridge, labeled with heating instructions." Margene turned on the lights in the kitchen. The cabinetry was white, the floor classic black-and-white tile, and the counters and backsplash were white subway tile. The appliances were brushed stainless steel—a toaster, coffee maker, and an electric tea kettle—but they didn't look as if they'd had much use.

"I don't drink myself," Margene said—although Abbie already knew that—"but here's the wine fridge." The older woman then showed her through to the walk-in pantry and pointed to a door. "This leads down to the cellar. There's quite an extensive wine collection, or so I'm told. Flynn said to help yourself to anything." After a quick tour of the ground floor, the laundry area, and the garage, Margene gave Abbie a tutorial on setting the security system.

"You should set this external system as soon as I leave. I was given strict instructions that you do so. Also, you'll need to pull your car into the garage."

The older woman said good night, adding that she didn't live very far away and that if Abbie needed anything, anything at all, she should not hesitate to call. "I've been looking after this house and the Paulsen family for longer than you've been alive, my dear."

Abbie punched in the security code as instructed. She walked to the garage. When she turned on the lights, she saw a navy Karmann Ghia parked behind the first of the three garage doors. She entered the security code again and opened the garage door. Above the light switch was a pegboard with three neatly labeled keys hanging from hooks. How could she possibly resist the Karmann Ghia? She carefully backed the car out and pulled her old Rover into its spot, which was a bit of a squeeze. After closing the garage door and reentering the security code, she felt the muscles between her shoulders and neck finally release some of the tension that had been building up for the last twenty-four hours.

Abbie opened the wine fridge. There was a bottle of Domaines Ott Rosé, which was calling out to her. She found a waiter corkscrew in a drawer lined in dark-green felt along with some bottle stoppers for still and sparkling wine. Abbie opened the bottle and poured the pale-peach liquid generously into a stemless glass. After a few swallows, Abbie acknowledged her growling stomach and opened the fridge, where she found a plastic-wrapped plate of poached salmon, cucumber dill salad, and thick spears of asparagus. All of it could be eaten cold.

Abbie emptied her wine glass and poured a second one while enjoying what turned out to be one of the best dinners she'd eaten in a long time. The silence of the house set so far back from the road gave her the space to think, really think, for the first time since the break-in. The conversation with Meghan didn't support the murder-suicide theory in the least. Abbie couldn't think of any reason why Meghan would have lied about the engagement ring. If there was an engagement ring—even a missing one—it meant there was an engagement, which cast a new light on everything.

Abbie took another sip of her wine. Jessica's was not the only ring that was missing. Another image flashed in Abbie's mind: a strip of thick white skin on a man's hand where a wedding band had once been. Hadn't the dry cleaner mentioned something about Smith wearing a garish platinum band with diamonds?

After unpacking her things, washing her face, and brushing her teeth, Abbie crawled under the covers. She set her phone to charge when she saw two messages. One was from John. She quickly texted a reply, saying she was well and safely ensconced in Flynn's house. The second was from an unknown number with an 801 area code. She listened to the voicemail. It was from a Dr. Lars Eriksen, the ME who'd been assigned to Jessica's case. He'd finished with the autopsy and suggested that Abbie might like to speak in person at her earliest convenience.

Abbie texted Clarke to let him know that she was going to Taylorsville first thing in the morning because the ME had asked to see her. Clarke texted back immediately: THAT'S WEIRD, ANY IDEA WHY? Abbie responded that she wasn't sure. This was true. She wasn't sure why the ME wanted to speak in person, but as she drifted off into much-needed sleep, Abbie had a pretty good guess.

THIRTY-FOUR

After years of living in Manhattan, where it could take an hour to travel just a few miles, Abbie relished being able to drive forty miles. She parked Flynn's Karmann Ghia in front of the gray-brick, steal-and-glass structure that was the newish Office of the Medical Examiner for the State of Utah. Clarke had called Abbie before she left Riverdale to see if she wanted him to meet her there, but they both agreed that, given Henderson's deadline, it would make more sense for Clarke to go over the Smith financial documents again to make sure they hadn't missed anything. Clarke wasn't any more convinced Jessica was Smith's killer than Abbie was.

Dr. Eriksen was expecting her. Although mornings generally were reserved for autopsies, he had left instructions at the front desk that Detective Taylor should be taken to his office as soon as she arrived. Abbie hadn't been waiting long when he opened the door behind her and walked around to his desk. He was a tall man in his mid-sixties—trim and athletic. Abbie suspected he spent a lot of time on the slopes.

"Thanks for seeing me," Abbie said. "I know you guys are understaffed and overworked."

Eriksen smiled. The deeply etched lines around his eyes deepened. He wore his thick silver hair short.

"Thanks," he said. "I imagine you guys are overworked, too."

Abbie shook her head. "Nothing like you." Drug overdoses had become an epidemic in Utah in the last few years. It was well known that the Office of the Medical Examiner was completely understaffed when compared to other states.

"Can you give me a layperson's overview on Jessica Grant?" Abbie asked.

"Sure. Your victim bled to death after her throat was slit, which also deprived her brain of oxygen."

"Were there any hesitation cuts?" Abbie asked.

"No, but I don't know why there would be. You weren't thinking this was a suicide, were you?" Eriksen asked.

"A suicide note has been found."

"It wasn't a suicide." Eriksen's tone was calm and certain.

"No room for doubt?" Abbie felt her heart skip a beat at the prospect that she was right about Jessica's death.

"No. First of all, as you already pointed out, there were no hesitation cuts. Second, there's the amount of lorazepam in her system. She was probably unconscious when her throat was slit. Finally, and most importantly, there's the angle of the wound. My best guess is that whoever cut her throat was standing over her."

"You'd testify to that?" Abbie asked.

"Sure. I don't think it's a close call. You'd have a

difficult time finding a reputable ME who'd come to a different conclusion." Eriksen said.

"Even though we found her holding a bowie knife?" Abbie asked.

"Sure. The knife found in her hand is the knife that killed her, but she couldn't possibly have done it herself."

This wasn't a neat and tidy murder-suicide after all. This was a second murder. Whoever had killed Smith had come back for Jessica. Why?

"Was she pregnant?" Abbie asked.

"Yes," Eriksen said. "How did you know?"

"Just a hunch."

"Given how thin she was, it didn't look that way, but she was just into the second trimester of her first pregnancy," Eriksen said.

"Is it possible to determine who the father was?" Abbie asked.

"I already have. I had a hunch, too."

★★★

Abbie texted Clarke the moment she got to the parking lot. JESS PREGNANT. SMITH THE FATHER.

Dr. Eriksen promised he'd email the report to Henderson immediately. Henderson was not going to be happy about it. The murder-suicide theory was just so clean—no loose ends, no reason to keep digging, everything tied up with a nice little bow. But after Henderson read the report, there would be no room for argument.

About an hour later, when Abbie walked into the station,

she felt tension in the air. Clarke gave her a nervous glance when she walked in and then looked right back at his computer screen.

"Taylor, Clarke." Henderson spoke their names crisply, but there was no hiding the anger in his voice.

Abbie followed Clarke into Henderson's office. Neither one sat.

"Clarke told me what this Eriksen guy concluded. I called him immediately to get the report because, of course, such a report would change the complexion of this case," Henderson said. "It's highly irregular for an ME to speak to a detective on a case before sending the report here, by the way." Henderson glared at Abbie.

Because this was Abbie's first murder case in Utah, she had no way to know whether what Dr. Eriksen had done was irregular or not, but Abbie didn't think Henderson was waiting for a response from her, so she stayed quiet.

"By the time I finally got through to someone who could help, your Dr. Eriksen had been called away because of a family emergency. No one in Taylorsville can find any report by Eriksen on Jessica Grant."

Why had Henderson called Dr. Eriksen "your Dr. Eriksen"?

Clarke spoke up. "You're telling us that after I told you about Taylor's text, you called to get a copy of Eriksen's report, but so far, no report is forthcoming?"

"That's exactly what I'm telling you. I'm also telling you both that unless and until I get such a report that verifies that the manner of death for Jessica Grant was homicide and that she was pregnant with Steve Smith's child, the course of this investigation does not change. I want this entire mess cleaned up by Wednesday."

"But, sir, in all likelihood there's just some kind of filing error. You know how overworked they are. In the interest of justice, we need to wait until we can all go through the report." The moment Clarke said the words *in the interest of justice*, Henderson's face went a deep shade of red.

"In the interest of justice? Officer Clarke, the interest of justice is served when we follow where the evidence leads and close a case expeditiously. We have suicide note, a teenage girl with a history of mental issues who had made attempts before and who, by her family's own account, was nursing some kind of crush on a respected member of this community. I don't know what your definition of justice is if it's not—"

Henderson's phone buzzed three times. It was sitting on his desk facing Abbie. Henderson glanced down to grab it and put it in his pocket, but not before Abbie read the three rapid-fire text bubbles: ME AWAY FOR WEEK . . . REPORT GONE . . . IS CASE UNDER CONTROL? THX.

Abbie averted her eyes before Henderson looked back up from stuffing the phone in his pocket.

"You two do what you need to do to write this up," Henderson said. "We need to give two families closure. I intend that we do exactly that."

Clarke followed Abbie down the hall and to her office. He closed the door behind him.

"I don't know what's going on. I've never seen the chief like this before," Clarke said.

Abbie sat down. Clarke took a chair across from her desk and asked, "Did you see what the texts were? I tried to read, but there was a glare on the phone from where I was standing."

Abbie told Clarke what she'd read and then told him who'd sent the message: Kevin Bowen. At first, Clarke said nothing. In the silence, Abbie worried he thought she was making it up. If Abbie hadn't seen it with her own eyes, she would be doubting what she'd just seen herself.

"That explains a lot," Clarke said finally. "I mean, why we've had so much trouble with this case, the chief closing the door to his office all the time, why he's so on edge . . ."

"There's something else you should know," Abbie said. Then she told Clarke about the break-in.

★★★

Clarke was furious about what had happened, but after he calmed down, he agreed that there was nothing to be gained by telling anyone else about the break-in, at least not at the moment. He did, however, insist on personally setting up a new security system at Abbie's. They spent the rest of the afternoon rereading every piece of paper they had on both the Smith and Grant cases.

They reviewed every interview, every photo, every piece of evidence. Clarke wondered if he could convince someone at Dr. Eriksen's office to let him look for the missing report. He did his best at flirting with the young receptionist who had shown Abbie into the office that morning. In the end he got her telephone number, but was told that until Dr. Eriksen returned from his family emergency, there was nothing she could do.

"Let's get some dinner," Abbie said after she heard Clarke's stomach growl for the umpteenth time. He wouldn't complain, but they could both use some food and a change of scenery. "How about Rainbow Gardens? That should cheer both of us up."

Abbie let her mind wander as Clarke drove to the restaurant. Neither of them spoke. Clarke was probably still processing the events of the day. Abbie was trying to figure out what she wasn't seeing in this case. It occurred to her that even though her family's history stretched back to the early days of the Church, she wasn't part of that history anymore.

Abbie knew she inhabited an unpopular space in Utah. It was easier to live here if you had never been a member of the Church than it was if you had left the Church. Not everyone saw Abbie's choice as a personal one. Some saw her decision as a rebuke; others saw it as a sign of moral weakness.

This might be why she was missing something about this case. Steve Smith and Jessica Grant had been active members of the Church. They'd shared their lives with everyone around them. They'd gone to church with the same neighbors every Sunday. They'd known who had been called to leadership positions, who went to the temple regularly, who went on expensive vacations, who bought new cars, and who had second homes in St. George. Regular visits from home and visiting teachers meant the Bishop knew who was having surgery, who was hiding a coffee pot in their kitchen, and who was having money or marital trouble. Nothing was private for insiders, but the world was difficult for an outsider to penetrate. Abbie wasn't entirely an outsider, but she wasn't exactly an insider either: she was an apostate.

Clarke and Abbie walked into Rainbow Gardens. The place didn't ever change. The black-and-white tile floor with kelly-green accents had been there for as long as anyone could remember. The hostess greeted them and sat them beneath the branches of a large, healthy ficus trees in the inner part of the restaurant.

A teenage waitress with a challenging complexion appeared at their table. "What can I get you?"

They ordered their sandwiches along with two Mormon muffins with extra honey butter.

As soon as the teenager left, Abbie said, "I want to know about Jessica Grant's and Steve Smith's families. I think we're missing something."

"I don't know if I know anything helpful. Both families have been here forever. The Grants are the Grants of the prophet Heber J. Grant. I think his father—by that I mean Heber J.'s father—was close to Brigham Young. Jess's parents have lived here in this general area a long time, but I don't know exactly how long they've lived in Pleasant View. Smith's family lived in Ogden when he was a kid. I think he went to Bonneville. His family goes back to Hyrum Smith, but I'm not exactly sure how."

"Either family have problems with the Church?" Abbie asked.

"You mean being inactive?" Clarke looked as if he didn't understand the question.

Abbie rephrased it. "No, I mean, were there any times

when the Church changed course to become more progressive and family members resisted? You know, like some of the people who don't like the new variations of garments or don't like the changes in the temple ceremony or have trouble with young women being able to serve missions at nineteen?"

"Both families are Iron Rods. I don't know anyone in either family you could call a Liahona, with the exception of one of Jessica's uncles who moved to California and, rumor is, came out as gay. Nobody in her family talks about it."

Clarke was using LDS vocabulary for a way some people categorized members. The terms had come from a talk given by a prominent Church leader in the 1980s. A person who was an Iron Rod looked to the scriptures for answers and followed Church leaders without question; a person who was a "Liahona"—the compass Lehi had used when he fled Jerusalem for the New World—felt there might be room for more personal revelation and questioning. People joked that Liahonas were just future former Mormons.

"Do you think there would be anyone in either family who thinks that taking the penalty oaths out of the temple ceremony was a mistake? Anyone who might believe, at least in theory, that there could be a need for blood atonement?" Abbie asked.

"You know this is a touchy subject, but I've been thinking about it a lot. It's hardly like anyone will talk about what we do in the temple. After we found Smith's body, I did a little research on the temple ceremony." Clarke paused for a moment and took a deep breath. "By the way, I feel pretty bad about the whole thing with the identification."

This was the first time Clarke had directly brought up the fact that everyone but Abbie had known who the victim was from the moment they saw him. Clarke went on, "The chief cut me off when I wanted to tell you who Smith was. When you were looking through the clothes, he told me that even though it seemed like we all recognized Steve Smith, it was best in situations like these to wait for formal identification. At the time, I just figured that was right. I'd never been involved with a homicide before. I didn't know better, even though I knew it didn't feel quite right not to tell you."

Abbie had swallowed a bite of her bran muffin with the honey-sweetened butter. "Thanks for explaining."

"I'm not trying to explain, I'm trying to apologize. Not being honest was wrong. I'm sorry."

Abbie could see that the years at church learning repentance—real repentance—were hardwired in her partner. Clarke felt bad about what he'd done. He had probably prayed about it. Amid all the things Abbie had left behind when she left the Church, she had kept the practice of repentance. Abbie no longer prayed to a god when she felt she'd done something she wished she hadn't, but the ritual of acknowledging fault, making amends, and doing everything possible to not repeat the same mistake again was a ritual that comforted Abbie, even when it was difficult. Perhaps especially when it was difficult. While an apology didn't erase history, it made things better and sometimes, like now, it created the foundation for a stronger friendship.

"It's okay," Abbie said. Clarke looked relieved, and grateful.

"So, here's what I think," Clarke said. "There's some

anecdotal evidence of blood atonement actually happening in the mid-1800s; you know that. The Church has tried to distance itself from the practice and the theory, but Joseph Fielding Smith defended it in the 1950s and Bruce R. McConkie did in the 1970s. Clearly, there are some fundamentalist polygamists who still believe in it, maybe even practice it. The penalty oaths were in the temple ceremony until 1990. Nobody talks about it now, but I don't think that's because nobody thinks about it. I think there are still some people who believe some sins are beyond the atonement of Jesus Christ."

At the bottom of page, Abbie saw "D&C 42: 25–26, Rasmos Anderson" neatly printed in her dad's handwriting. Abbie's old copy of the Book of Mormon was precariously perched on top of a stack of her dad's notebooks. She opened it and looked up 42:25–26.

> 25 But he that has committed adultery and repents with all his heart, and forsaketh it, and doeth it no more, thou shalt forgive;
> 26 But if he doeth it again, he shall not be forgiven, but shall be cast out.

Abbie searched through her dad's notes on blood atonement, looking for Rasmos Anderson. Nothing. Then she Googled the name. There he was. A Danish Mormon who had slept with his stepdaughter during Brigham Young's reign. Not exactly the stuff that made you think the guy was a prince, but still. A bishop's council had supposedly found him guilty on the charge of adultery and voted in favor of death for violating his covenants. He was to die by having his throat cut, so that the running of his blood would atone for his sins. According to the references, the bishop's council ordered Anderson's wife to prepare clean clothes for him to be buried in and to tell anyone who asked about her husband that he had gone to California.

Had someone ordered Melinda to tell anyone who asked about her husband that he had gone to Costa Rica? Abbie didn't think that seemed quite right, but there was something here. Her brain kept teasing her. Abbie finished

THIRTY-FIVE

By the time Abbie got back to Flynn's, it was dark. She entered the security code quickly and headed upstairs to the bedroom to change into pajamas. Margene must have come by during the day, because there were fresh towels in the bathroom and the bed was made. It had been a while since Abbie had felt someone was looking out for her and, she had to admit, it was nice.

She took her dad's notes downstairs, poured a glass of the Rosé, and curled up on a love seat in the living room. She wasn't even remotely hungry after her enormous sandwich at Rainbow Gardens. She took a sip of the wine and her body relaxed a little. She was relieved to have the Bowen thing out in the open with Clarke.

She flipped through one of her dad's books, *The Journal of Discourses.* It fell open to a sermon by Jedidiah Morgan Grant delivered in 1856. Abbie recognized the fire-and-brimstone speech as the source of the idea for "committees of blood." If Abbie's memory was correct, these committees were supposed to designate a place where covenant breakers could have their blood shed to atone for sins beyond forgiveness.

her wine and debated pouring another glass, but decided sleep was the better course. Maybe it would all come to her in a dream, or, she thought wryly, maybe it would come to her in a revelation.

THIRTY-SIX

Abbie had left for the station well before dawn. It was Wednesday morning. They didn't have anything to counter the murder-suicide theory. No divine revelation had come during the night. She knew that Jess wasn't a killer, but she had no way of making a case against anyone else.

Abbie must have been completely distracted, because she jumped when Clarke stepped into her office.

"Clarke!" Abbie nearly spilled her coffee.

"Sorry, didn't mean to startle you. It's just I've been thinking. Is it possible we ruled out Melinda because we felt sorry for her? You know, if she knew Jess was pregnant, that would change things. In the Celestial Kingdom, assuming Smith was worthy to be there because he had atoned for his adultery, he could have been sealed to both Jess and Melinda and their children. Jess being sealed to him would have meant this child would be, too. I don't know, but that seems like motive." Clarke closed the door and took a seat in front of her desk.

"Even without the whole afterlife slant, having an affair, especially if pregnancy is involved, is a solid motive,"

Abbie said, then asked Clarke, "Do you think Melinda Smith is capable of murder?"

"More than Jess is," Clarke said. "Melinda's the only person who knew the exact time her husband was leaving. Her alibis for both her husband's and Jess's murders are her own children. She has plenty of personal and financial reasons for being angry with Smith and Jess. Jess wouldn't think twice about letting Melinda into her house, probably not even worry about letting her into her bedroom. It's not a stretch to think Melinda would've known Jessica liked to use that pale-pink paper for everything she printed. It was all over her desk."

"True," Abbie agreed, "but that's all circumstantial."

"Yeah, I know. I don't really want to believe Melinda Smith could do this, but there's no denying it's our most plausible theory."

"What about her response when we told her about Jess? That seemed real," Abbie said.

"I've been thinking about that," Clarke said, "I heard her throwing up just like you did. That wasn't fake. The fact that all the blood drained from her face when we told her about Jess wasn't fake either. We thought she was distressed because she was finding out for the first time that her husband was cheating on her. Maybe that wasn't it. Maybe she was distressed because we had found out her motive for killing her husband."

Clarke was right about all the pieces fitting. "Then why wait a week to go after Jessica?"

"Melinda found out about the pregnancy. I think something inside her just snapped. She couldn't take it. She didn't want someone else to be a mother to Smith's children, but she had to wait until there was an easy way to do it," Clarke answered.

"Okay, let's say you're right so far. What about the blood atonement angle?"

"That's actually what got me thinking about Melinda in the first place. Do you remember that time in the kitchen when we were talking to her? When she mentioned how her husband always went to the temple? I thought she was just bragging about what an active Latter-day Saint he was, but I think all that church stuff came out subconsciously. Melinda went through the temple back when the penalty oaths were part of the ceremony. She came from a really strict family. She's the only person who has an interest in Steve Smith atoning for his adultery. She wants her family to be together forever. If he'd had affairs before, she had no reason to believe that was going to stop. If she wanted her whole family to be worthy of the Celestial Kingdom, she was going to have to take matters into her own hands."

Abbie sipped her coffee as she mulled over Clarke's theory. There was a certain elegance to it. Clarke was right about how often Melinda mentioned what a good man—a good Mormon—her husband had been.

"Okay, let's say you're right, we've got to have more than a theory," Abbie said.

"I know." Clarke slumped in his chair, making his tall lanky frame look crumpled. "I think we need to talk to Meghan again. I bet she knew about Jess being pregnant. Even if no one else knew who the father was, Melinda would have suspected her husband. Smith had already spent an entire spring gallivanting in Costa Rica with Jess. We know they met at Meghan's. Melinda could easily have seen that. They live just a few houses away. We just need someone to remember something they saw but didn't think was important. Melinda seeing her husband talking to Meghan. Someone saw something. I know we don't have much time, but we can't let Jess be blamed for something she didn't do."

Clarke's phone buzzed. He looked down to read the text.

"You're not going to believe this. That was Meghan. They're having Jess's funeral this morning. It starts in half an hour. Meghan was worried I wouldn't hear about it."

"I didn't know Jess's body had been released, did you?" Abbie asked.

Clarke shook his head. "I've been checking the obituaries in *The Standard*, *The Trib*, and the *Deseret News*. There hasn't been any mention of the funeral. There hasn't even been an obituary." That obituary the brothers had been working so hard on when Abbie and Clarke had talked to them about Jess.

"Jim," Abbie heard someone whisper while standing with Clarke in the lobby waiting to enter the chapel. She turned around and saw Meghan. "I'm so glad you made it. I just found out about it this morning. Nobody's here. I texted as many people as I could think of, but everyone's at work or at school. I think some people don't even know what happened." Meghan took Clarke's hand. "Even my mom can't make it. Will you sit with me?"

Clarke, holding Meghan's hand, looked at Abbie. She

smiled the kind of half smile that was appropriate for a funeral. It was enough for Clarke to know it was okay for him to stay with Meghan. The young couple moved toward the door on the left of the chapel.

The first two rows were reserved for the family. An older woman was playing "I Am a Child of God" on the organ. The chapel was almost completely empty. Melinda Smith was sitting near the front in the center row with a few of her kids. There were maybe two or three other families Abbie didn't recognize sitting near the Smith family. Bishop Norton stood at the podium.

"Let's begin with singing 'We're Not Ashamed to Own Our Lord.' "

Abbie opened the hymnbook. She wondered who had chosen this song. It wasn't a common one. The choice about robes of righteousness struck her as poorly suited for a young woman's funeral.

Bishop Norton then asked Sariah to give the opening prayer. It could have been a prayer at any Sacrament Meeting; she made no mention of Jess at all, only that she was grateful for the gospel and Heavenly Father's plan. After the invocation, Bishop Norton welcomed everyone and introduced Jess's oldest brother.

"As Elder Dallin Oaks has advised, the passing of life is not a trivial thing. A funeral service is a time to speak of important ideas," Jess's brother said. "Jess, who had one of the strongest testimonies of the Church of anyone I know, would agree." The oldest brother went on, "I wish I could speak as eloquently as our Apostles, but I can't, so I will paraphrase Elder Oaks: one of the most powerful ideas we have as members of the one true Church of Jesus Christ is that mortal life has a purpose and that mortal death is not the end but only a transition. Brigham Young taught us that the sole purpose of our existence here is for exaltation and restoration to the presence of our Heavenly Father. Not all problems are overcome in mortality. The work of salvation goes on beyond the veil of death, and we should not worry about incompleteness within the limits of mortality." Jess's brother paused for a moment and bowed his head. "I say these things in the name of Jesus Christ. Amen."

No one else spoke. Bishop Norton stood up to instruct the congregation to sing "Ye Simple Souls Who Stray." Then Bishop Norton asked Jessica's dad to give the closing prayer; and the funeral was over.

Something seemed off to Abbie, but she knew she wasn't a good judge of these things. She'd always felt Mormon funerals were a little off. She wanted to talk to Clarke. He'd have a better sense of whether Jessica's funeral seemed normal, or as normal as it could under the circumstances. Abbie made her way across the nearly empty chapel to Meghan and Clarke.

"Meghan wants to go to the cemetery with the family," Clarke said.

Abbie wondered how Jessica's family would feel if they knew that the chief of the Pleasant View City Police Department believed she was a killer. Unless Clarke and Abbie found something to prove Jess wasn't Smith's murderer, by tomorrow at this time the official story would be that Jessica Grant had killed Smith and then killed herself.

Abbie felt tension spread from her stomach to her chest.

She needed air. She walked outside and watched as the small group of people who loved Jess drove to the cemetery to say their final good-byes. Abbie tried to take deep breaths from her belly, hoping she could loosen the tightness in her body. As she focused on her breathing, she gained a little space to think. Was the person who had actually killed both Smith and Jess right there in front of her? Was that person angry about their relationship or with how that relationship affected the Church? Or was it something else entirely? Abbie inhaled fully, letting her stomach and then her chest expand. What had Bowen been looking for at her cabin? How did he fit in?

Abbie walked back into the church. The lunch was set up: a few bowls of Jell-O salad, funeral potatoes, ham, and some soft store-bought rolls occupied a long table draped with a white tablecloth. On a smaller table were trays of brownies, a plate of oatmeal-raisin cookies, and a large platter of chocolate-chip muffins.

The words at the cemetery must have been as perfunctory as the words in the chapel, because it wasn't long before Clarke and Meghan were back. The three of them sat down at a table next to Melinda Smith, who was already eating from her plate heaped almost as high as Jim's with potatoes.

"Such a beautiful day," Meghan said to no one in particular as she picked at her food.

Melinda, who was sitting across the round table from Meghan, looked up from her plate, "Were you a friend of Jessica's?"

"Yes, since forever . . . we were . . ." Before Meghan finished her sentence, Sariah sat down in the empty seat next to Melinda.

Melinda put down her fork, took Sariah's hands in her own, and said, "I know you miss her now, but we're so lucky to know we'll all be together again with our Heavenly Father."

Sariah looked into her friend's eyes. "I know. I'm so grateful for the gospel and for a friend like you—"

Jessica's father approached the table and interrupted the two women. "Your mom wants you."

After Sariah left, it was just a matter of minutes before Melinda finished her plate and said good-bye. The room emptied quickly. Clarke offered to walk Meghan to her car before heading back to the station. Abbie watched the young couple walk out, then got up herself. She glanced at the table where they had been sitting. There was a small stack of programs on it. Abbie turned to pick up her own program when something caught her eye. There was a piece of folded pale-pink paper among the stack. Abbie's heart skipped a beat. She grabbed the programs, pulled out the pink paper, and read:

> The time has been in Israel under the law of God, the celestial law, or that which pertains to the celestial law, for it is one of the laws of that kingdom where our Father dwells, that if a man was found guilty of adultery, he must have his blood shed, and that is near at hand.
>
> —Prophet Brigham Young, *Journal of Discourses*, v. 4, p. 219

THIRTY-SEVEN

Abbie dashed out of the church looking for Clarke. The parking lot was almost empty. Clarke's squad car was gone. Abbie panicked when she couldn't see her green Rover, but then her mind clicked into gear when she saw the navy Karmann Ghia parked in the back corner. She pulled out Flynn's keys and headed to the car.

Driving on autopilot, Abbie's mind flashed with images. They still had only circumstantial evidence, but if they were lucky, there would be some prints on this pink piece of paper. Pink? Where was the missing pink diamond ring? Why hadn't she thought of it before? The likelihood that Smith had paid cash for such an extravagance was unlikely. If the ring existed, there had to be a credit card receipt. Did he and Melinda share credit card accounts? They probably had been sitting on Smith's credit card statements since the day Abbie got the thumb drive from Zion Commerce, but they hadn't thought to look through them to see what Smith had bought.

Clarke's car was already at the station when Abbie parked Flynn's car in her space. She sprinted inside.

"Find the receipt for the ring," Abbie said. "There has to be a receipt for the pink diamond engagement ring."

Clarke understood a receipt would be evidence. Not great evidence, but evidence that the ring existed. It would at least give them reason to ask more questions. It might lead them somewhere away from Jess being a killer. He started typing on his keyboard and then peered at his computer screen.

Abbie took the pink sheet of paper to the evidence room. Luckily, the officer who was in charge was actually at his desk.

"Check this for prints. You can rule mine out. See if there are any matches from any of the prints we took at the Smith and Grant scenes. I know we got prints for the family members." Abbie expected the officer to balk, but instead he said, "Right away." *Be grateful for small blessings*, she told herself.

Abbie closed the door to her office. She sat at her desk and took a few deep breaths, counting three on each inhalation and five on the exhalation. She was getting close, but she wasn't there yet. She closed her eyes and breathed. Before she got to her eighth cycle of breaths, Clarke knocked on her door. He didn't wait for an answer.

"Smith and Melinda had a quite a few joint credit cards. Smith had four personal ones but didn't seem to bother to hide anything from Melinda. There are expensive purchases from Neiman Marcus from last year, around the time they were in Costa Rica. Could've been for Melinda, but I bet if we check with Neiman Marcus, we'll find out the sizes were zero or extra small."

"Okay, that's good, but not good enough," Abbie responded.

"I know; I saved the best for last. There's a charge for a 'custom pink diamond ring' from OC Tanner for $65,000 a few months ago on one of the joint cards. If Melinda checked their statements, she could have seen it."

"Do you know how he paid off the balances?" Abbie asked.

"That's where it gets even more interesting," Clarke said, "The month with the ring was paid electronically from the bank account in Costa Rica. The Celestial Time Shares account."

"Did he do that for other months?" Abbie asked.

"A few times," Clarke said. "It's not like I've had time to do an exhaustive search of the records, though. I have to say, it makes me wonder about Bowen." Clarke lowered his voice when he said the General Authority's name.

As if on cue, the officer who ran the prints walked into Abbie's office and handed her the pink paper with the unnerving quote.

"Only two sets of prints on this: yours and Melinda Smith's."

"Thank you. Thank you very much," Abbie said.

"What's that?" Clarke asked. Abbie handed him the paper, now sealed in an evidence bag. He read it.

"It was folded among the programs on our table at lunch," Abbie said.

"Is this quote legit? I've never heard anything like it. I mean, they didn't teach us this stuff in missionary training."

Abbie didn't say anything. She opened her laptop to a

website dedicated to *The Journal of Discourses* and turned the screen so Clarke could read it.

He said nothing for a few moments. "You know, it drives the guys here crazy that you know your scriptures and Mormon history better than they do. Nobody will take you on anymore."

Abbie didn't smile. She didn't even feel any satisfaction. She actually would have liked it if the Church lived up to the hype, but she couldn't pretend it did. She couldn't pretend the dark parts weren't there.

★★★

Clarke and Abbie spent the rest of the afternoon combing through evidence to find enough to prove to Henderson they were not dealing with a murder-suicide.

"We can't rule out Bowen," Clarke said. "Smith paid off well over three hundred thousand in credit card bills using that Celestial Time Shares account. Plus, there's the beachfront villa. If we had more time and went through more of his financial records, I bet the number would be higher."

Clarke was right. There was plenty of evidence Smith had been stealing from the Church. It didn't take much of a leap to make a case that Smith had planned to pocket all the money he raised for Celestial Time Shares. There wasn't any hint that Jessica had played any role in that. Having met her, Abbie didn't think they would ever find any evidence that she had. Jessica had thought Smith was doing Heavenly Father's work.

"Why would Bowen kill Jessica?" Abbie asked.

"Because she was in on the scheme? Her affair with Smith was an embarrassment to the Church? I don't know. She knew who killed Smith?" Clarke said.

Abbie arched an eyebrow as she looked at Clarke.

"Okay, if you didn't know Jess, any one of those things could be true, but knowing her, well, they're pretty implausible theories. Although more plausible than the theory that she killed Smith and then herself," Clarke said. "The receipt and the adultery quote are pieces of real evidence and they point to one person."

As the light faded from the sky, Abbie knew they were out of time. You could set your clock by Henderson's hours. He would be on his way home any minute.

"It's now or never," Abbie said.

Abbie and Clarke walked toward Henderson's office as he was turning off his light.

"Is that my report?" He did not look happy.

"No," Clarke said. "I think we have something better: what really happened."

Henderson scowled but waved them into his office. Abbie shut the door behind her. Most of their colleagues had already left, but the evening shift officer was wandering somewhere around the station. Abbie didn't want to give Henderson any more reason to be angry after he'd been so clear about discretion and the deadline for closing the case. Abbie let Clarke explain the fingerprints on the pink sheet of paper and the diamond ring on the joint credit card. Henderson pointed out that they didn't have the report from the ME about Jessica being pregnant with Smith's child, but acknowledged that they had enough for an arrest even without it.

"What about the fact that Smith used his Celestial Time Shares account for personal reasons?" Henderson couldn't hide the tension in his voice as he asked the question.

"We don't think the Celestial Time Shares angle explains why anyone would want to harm Jess . . . Jessica Grant. It doesn't make sense," Clarke said.

Henderson exhaled. "Okay. I'll give you another day. Go ahead and do whatever you need to do, so long as this is all over by tomorrow afternoon." Then he added, "Make the arrest in the morning. Nobody wants to be processing this tonight. It's not like there's a flight risk."

THIRTY-EIGHT

It was after midnight and Abbie couldn't keep her eyes closed. Every time she was on the verge of sleep, something woke her up. It was like having a mosquito with you in a dark room. When the buzzing faded, you would think you could fall asleep. Then the infernal noise would be right at your ear and you'd be wide awake again. Abbie had been repeating this cycle of wavering between almost-sleep and wakefulness for hours. She couldn't figure out what the mosquito was. Everything seemed to fit. Henderson was on board. He'd given them an extra half-day. Melinda's fingerprints were on a piece of paper stating that a man guilty of adultery must die. The quote itself was incriminating enough, but the fact that Melinda had used Jessica's signature pink paper also demonstrated that she knew Jessica well. She could have written the suicide note.

Abbie tossed and turned until her alarm went off. She was glad they weren't closing this case with Jessica as Smith's killer, but as much as she wanted to believe the evidence pointed only to Melinda Smith, she didn't. She should be anxious to get into the station this morning, but she found herself dawdling. She wasn't really hungry, but she walked downstairs to Flynn's perfect kitchen anyway. Margene had left a half-dozen freshly baked muffins on a cake plate beneath a clear glass dome. She looked at them but wasn't even remotely tempted. That was when she realized what the mistake was. The assumption they had all made.

Abbie ran back upstairs. She hurried to pull on trousers, a T-shirt, and a blazer. She slipped her bare feet into a pair of loafers. She was about to wrap her husband's old Patek Philippe watch around her wrist when she paused. She took a moment and looked at the watch; then she placed it back inside her jewelry case. Instead, she put on her own old stainless-steel Cartier Tank watch.

Abbie climbed into the Karmann Ghia and drove to the station at just over the speed limit.

Clarke was waiting outside by the squad car when Abbie pulled in.

"Do you mind if I drive?" she asked.

Clarke tossed her keys to the squad car.

Abbie didn't need to rely on her GPS system or Clarke to get around Pleasant View anymore. She knew her way. She drove up a hill, passing several empty school buses returning from dropping off their young riders at the local schools. Traffic was already thinning after the morning rush. It was a beautiful spring morning. Lawns were green and flowers were in full bloom. The sky served as a clear blue backdrop for the white puffy clouds drifting across it.

"Taylor, I think you took a wrong turn. Take this next left and—"

"No, I know where I'm going."

"This isn't the way to Melinda's."

"No, it's not. We got it wrong about Melinda. We got it all wrong."

★★★

Abbie rang the doorbell. Sariah Morris answered. She looked as if she was in the middle of a workout: black yoga pants, formfitting top, and a healthy flush to her cheeks.

"Sister Morris, we're here on official business," Abbie began. "Are any of your children home?"

"Nope," Sariah answered matter-of-factly. "I've got the entire place to myself. I pick up my youngest at three fifteen."

"May we come in?" Abbie asked.

"Of course." Sariah stepped back to let Abbie and Clarke inside. They walked into the sitting room.

"Can I get you some water? Diet Coke?" Sariah asked.

"No, thank you," Abbie responded. "I think you know why we're here."

Sariah nodded. "Because of Steve . . . and Jess."

"Yes. We can get a warrant to search your house, but perhaps you'd rather just tell us what happened," Abbie said, then added, "You have the right to remain silent. Anything you say can and will be used against you in a court of law. You have the right to speak to an attorney. If you cannot afford an attorney, one will be appointed for you. Do you understand these rights?"

"I understand," Sariah said. "I don't need an attorney. I knew you'd be here sooner or later." Abbie had expected

Sariah to be calm, but even so, the woman's serenity was disconcerting. Sariah walked over to a small wooden box sitting on a side table and opened it. "You probably want these." She dropped two rings into Abbie's hand: one was a thick man's wedding band and the other was a woman's engagement ring with an enormous princess-cut pink diamond surrounded by smaller white diamonds.

Sariah sat down on the couch. "Steve had been a good man once, but he had fallen. He needed to return to his Father in Heaven. I was the only one who understood what needed to be done." Sariah's voice was soft and kind, almost like a favorite kindergarten teacher's.

"Steve had started down the wrong path the way most who fall away do, with small things. Sins that can seem so trivial they're either forgotten or easily justified. Then he began to break more important covenants. Temple covenants, the Law of Chastity. He had taken my sister down that path with him more than once. But there were consequences. I couldn't let him bring one of our Heavenly Father's children into this world that way. That soul can wait for another mother and father who are properly sealed in the temple. I had to help them atone for what they'd done before it was too late."

"Like your great-great-grandfather Jedidiah Grant?" Abbie asked.

"Yes."

"Did Steve understand?"

Sariah smiled, "Yes, he did. I knew Steve was leaving for Costa Rica, and he wasn't planning to return. He'd stolen money from the Church. He'd stolen my darling Jess's chastity. He needed to be punished. He needed to atone for what he'd done."

"You gave him a special muffin, didn't you, one with some Xanax in it?" Abbie asked. Abbie's brain had taunted her about the detail she had overlooked. The ME had assumed, as they all had, that Smith had eaten chocolate-chip cookies, but it wasn't cookies in his system; it was a chocolate-chip muffin. The same muffins Sariah had brought to her grieving friend Melinda, the same muffins she'd brought to her own sister's funeral.

"Yes. Yes, I did. I'm famous for my chocolate-chip muffins. I baked a special one for Steve. I've had a Xanax prescription for years. Everyone does. It was easy to put a few aside. I run early in the morning, so my family and the neighbors are used to seeing me at that hour. It was so simple to accidentally run into Steve on his way to the airport. He ate the whole muffin in three bites."

"What happened after he ate the muffin?" Abbie asked.

"He let me help him into his hideous yellow Hummer. He always thought I was pretty. He'd made inappropriate comments more times than I can count. I guess that's why he liked Jess so much. We're sisters and we do look a bit alike. He was happy to go to the empty house on Lake View. I think he was having unclean thoughts about why we were going there. He seemed very satisfied with himself; he kept mumbling about having both sisters."

"You drove his Hummer to the back entrance of the house. You knew he had his temple clothes in his garment bag, didn't you?"

Sariah nodded. "I carried his garment bag and helped

him out of the car. He took my hand. The door to the basement was open. I took him to the closet. I told him that he was going to have to take off his sinful clothes of this earth and become clean. He was happy to. He undressed so fast. At first he was angry when I told him to put on his temple clothes, but by then he was getting very slow. It took me some time to get him dressed because he was so heavy, but I was able to prepare him. He kept nodding off. When I asked him if he wanted to atone for breaking his covenants with our Heavenly Father, he said yes. I took his hand and helped him. His blood was spilt. I could see him smile. He knew he could now return to the presence of our Father in Heaven."

"What happened then?" Sariah must have driven the car to the airport, but Abbie wasn't sure how she had managed to pull it off without anyone else knowing.

"I folded Steve's clothes. I closed the closet door and left. I drove to the airport because I knew Melinda was going to pick up the car that afternoon. I threw Steve's bags in a big trash can near a construction site in Ogden on the way to the airport. I didn't want Melinda to know. She might know eventually, but she didn't need to know now. I didn't know the house had been sold. I thought it would be months before anyone found Smith's body," Sariah explained.

"How did you get home?" Abbie asked.

"I took the free bus from the airport to Temple Square and then a cab back home. I'm training for the marathon and do a lot of long runs. Nobody thought anything about me being gone for the morning. I was at church a little late, but no one noticed."

"And what about Jessica?" Abbie asked.

"I wish there'd been another way." Abbie watched Sariah's expression change. For a brief moment the older sister looked sad, but then she regained her countenance of certainty. "She forced me into this position. I didn't have much time. I couldn't let an innocent soul be brought forth from such a sinful union. She was going to start showing soon."

"She didn't know what was happening, did she?" Abbie asked.

"No. Jess never was the smartest girl in the room—the prettiest, maybe—but not the smartest. It was easy for me to stop by my parents' house after Jake left. Don't worry. She wasn't in any pain. I made sure of that. I dressed her in white for meeting our Savior. She needed her blood to spill to the earth, but no prophet has ever said she had to be awake for that. Now she is waiting for me on the other side of the veil. I will miss her until I see her again, but if she hadn't atoned, she'd never have had a chance to be with us all in the Celestial Kingdom. A few years of missing her in this life is nothing compared to eternity."

"You wrote the suicide note and left it the day after we found her?" Abbie added.

"Yes, I thought it would be nice if everything could be dealt with together. I guess I didn't think that through very well."

"Sariah Morris. You're under arrest for the murder of Steve Smith and your sister Jessica Grant," Abbie said.

Sariah smiled. "May I ask a favor? I need to get out of these workout clothes. May I have a minute to change?"

Abbie debated the idea of letting her murder suspect change her clothes. It was something she never would have considered in New York, but here in Pleasant View there didn't seem to be any harm. Abbie didn't think Sariah was going to try to escape. If she did, she wouldn't get very far.

Before Abbie could say anything, Sariah then asked, "Also, would you please let my husband know he'll need to pick up the little ones from school? I'm assuming I won't be able to make it."

"Sure, go ahead and change," Abbie said. "We'll make sure the kids get picked up from school."

Sariah wrote her husband's telephone number on the back of an old envelope and handed it to Abbie; then she walked upstairs.

Clarke broke his silence. "I can't believe it. It's so, so . . . I don't know what it is. She seems so at peace with it. She thinks what she did was good, that it was the right thing to do."

"Yes," Abbie agreed, "she did think it was the right thing to do. She still does."

"How did you know?" Clarke asked.

"When I saw the fourth volume of *The Journal of Discourses* the first time we were here, I wondered about Sariah's obvious pride in her genealogy. The Reformation period is a harsh time in LDS history. Jedidiah Grant was not a forgiving man. There are plenty of his descendants who would never dream of crossing this line, but Sariah found comfort in her version of atonement and forgiveness. It's not that hard to step over the line when you have no doubts about your own version of the truth."

Abbie looked at her watch. It had been more than a few minutes since Sariah had gone up to change. In a flash, Abbie was on her feet. She had miscalculated. She ran up the stairs before Clarke could even stand up. Abbie opened the door to the master bedroom. There, lying on a king-sized bed under a framed picture of the Salt Lake Temple, was Sariah Morris. She was dressed in her temple clothes with a veil over her face and a green satin apron across her lap. There was a bowie knife in her right hand.

The deep red gash under her chin looked like a smile.

THIRTY-NINE

Abbie stood outside the Morris house looking at the outline of Ben Lomond Mountain against the bright blue sky. Henderson and a few other officers had come to process the scene. Clarke gave Henderson all the details. Abbie overheard him say, "Detective Taylor was brilliant. I mean, we all should have seen it, but we didn't." Abbie didn't wait to hear Henderson's response to the praise, if indeed he responded at all. She had the sense that as long as Celestial Time Shares and Steve Smith's role in that enterprise weren't front and center, Henderson didn't much care how the case got resolved.

"We got the right person. That feels good, even if the whole thing is really twisted," Clarke said when he joined Abbie. She didn't say anything, but she smiled.

"If you'll give me back the keys," Clarke said. "I'll drive us to the station. The other guys can finish up here."

Clarke and Abbie were both exhausted. Henderson had begrudgingly told Clarke they could file all the paperwork the next day. He'd told them to go home and get some rest.

"I finished up your security system last night," Clarke

said as he drove them both back to the station. "I couldn't sleep. No system is perfect, but this one comes close."

"Thank you," Abbie said.

"Do you want to follow up on Bowen?" Clarke asked. "I'll talk to Henderson if you want."

"No," Abbie said. "We have a full confession, and we have the rings. We can write up the report tomorrow. Whatever Bowen was doing at my place isn't relevant to closing this case."

Clarke looked doubtful. "If you change your mind, you'll let me know. I think we should look into it."

"I'll let you know if I change my mind." Abbie appreciated Clarke's support, but whatever Bowen and his friend were checking on wasn't an incident they needed to include in their report. Abbie hoped it wasn't something she'd ever have to think about again.

Clarke dropped her in the parking lot at the police station and immediately headed home. Abbie sat alone in the Karmann Ghia for a few moments. She took her phone out of her bag and pressed a name from her contacts list.

"Dad, good morning. I thought you'd like to know it's over." Abbie explained what had happened and why.

"Darling, Abish. I'm happy for you. I have to give you credit where credit is due. I've been told there's been absolutely no media coverage—social or otherwise. It's like nothing ever happened."

"Yeah, Dad, it's like nothing ever happened." Abbie didn't take the same comfort her father did in the fact that someone had managed to keep two grisly murders in the quiet hamlet of Pleasant View entirely off the news cycle in

Utah. Her father found solace in secrecy. Abbie didn't. She preferred the discomfort of transparency.

"You know, this means you have a professional future here," her dad added. Abbie thought he sounded hopeful.

"I guess it does, Dad."

She turned the key and started the drive back toward Flynn's place. She stopped at the State Liquor Store first and bought the most expensive bottle of Scotch she could find. Next door at a craft shop, she picked up a pair of scissors and a roll of thick satin ribbon and the closest thing to good writing paper she could find. She wrote: *Flynn, thank you for being such a generous host. I'll never be able to repay you. ~Abs.*

With her bread-and-butter note in hand along with a token of her appreciation, she turned onto the private driveway off Ritter Drive. As she pulled in front of the garage, she saw a classic 1960s gunmetal-gray Porsche. Margene didn't drive a Porsche, did she?

Abbie climbed out of the car with the bottle of eighteen-year-old Macallan Single Malt. As she pulled her keys out of her pocket, the door opened. It wasn't Margene. It was Flynn.

"You thought you could stay here and just sneak away before I got back?" He raised his left eyebrow. "I see your bags are packed and ready to go."

Abbie hoped she wasn't blushing. Flynn was barefoot, wearing a pair of well-worn jeans that fit him better than they should. The gray Henley he was wearing made it clear he spent some time at the gym, or was extraordinarily genetically gifted.

"I don't want to overstay my welcome. You know what they say about houseguests and fish."

"You're not a fish." Flynn's eye caught sight of the Scotch with the satin ribbon wrapped around the neck of the bottle and tied in a bow. "That for me?"

"Here you go, kind sir." Abbie handed him the bottle and the note. He read the card.

"If you join me for a glass, I'll consider it partial repayment."

"You know I don't like to be in debt."

Abbie followed Flynn into the library. He walked over to an antique silver butler tray in the corner of the room. Abbie was quite certain the heavy crystal bottles on top contained brown liquid far more precious than what she'd managed to find at the liquor store on Pacific Avenue in Ogden. Flynn, ever the gentleman, gave no hint if that was the case. He poured two fingers into heavy cut-crystal old-fashioned glasses. He handed one to Abbie and raised his own.

"To debt."

Abbie touched her glass to Flynn's. "To debt."

Acknowledgments

I grew up to have faith. I do: in serendipity and kindness. This book wouldn't exist without both.

Thank you to Matt Martz, Crooked Lane publisher extraordinaire, who took a chance on a rough manuscript forwarded to him by a friend of a friend. Thank you to Derek Hansen, who was one of those friends. Thank you to my amazing agent, Paula Munier, who possesses the special magic of knowing exactly what to do and when to do it. I'm eternally grateful to my fabulous editor, Sarah Poppe, whose fresh eyes and meticulous attention to detail turned an unpolished story into a bona fide murder mystery. Thank you to Jenny Chen and the entire Crooked Lane team, who went above and beyond the call, checking long-forgotten LDS doctrines and little-known hamlets up the canyons of northern Utah.

Thank you to Stephanie Healey, Iván Morales, Antonia Sherman, Heidi Schmid, Marianne Wilson, and Archie Nagraj, whose friendship, support, and concrete advice kept me going. Thank you to my dear friends and author mentors, Melissa Roske and Evie Manieri, without whom

I never could have figured out what I needed to know but didn't.

Thank you to my dad, my sister/cousin Elizabeth Jones-Harris, and my dear friend Charlotte Triefus Zuckerberg. You believed in me when I didn't believe in myself. I'll never know why you did, but I'm grateful.

There aren't words to describe how grateful I am to my brother Mark Justin Bartley, who really is the best in the universe. I don't know how I got so lucky to be his sister.

Thank you to my daughter Kirsten, whose enthusiasm, brilliance, and loyalty inspire me every day, and to my son Tycho, whose intelligence, dry wit, and good-natured patience make our family work.

Thank you most of all to my husband—for everything.